VICTORIA BYLIN

Steeple
Hill®

Published by Steeple Hill Books™

STEEPLE HILL BOOKS

Steeple
Hill®

ISBN-13: 978-0-373-82788-6
ISBN-10:   0-373-82788-1

THE BOUNTY HUNTER'S BRIDE

www.SteepleHill.com

Printed in U.S.A.

"Maybe Beau will catch the man he's after tonight," the minister's wife said hopefully.

"I hope so." Dani shivered as she remembered the pistols she'd seen in his room. "But he's been looking for revenge for so long, I wonder if he can stop."

"A man can change."

"If he wants to."

"God has a way of making that happen."

Dani stared out at the rain. "But right now, Beau's out in the storm."

"It's what men do," the minister's wife reminded her gently. "They fight for the people they love. There's just one thing for you to decide—whether *you* love *him* enough to fight for him."

Dani's chest swelled with longing. "I do," she said, and realized it was true. She wanted Beau, and she wanted the children. *And she was ready to fight for them.*

Books by Victoria Bylin

Love Inspired Historical

The Bounty Hunter's Bride #8

VICTORIA BYLIN

fell in love with God and her husband at the same time. It started with a ride on a big red motorcycle and a date to see a *Star Trek* movie. A recent graduate from UC Berkeley, Victoria had been seeking that elusive "something more" when Michael rode into her life. Neither knew it, but they were each reading the Bible.

Five months later, they got married and the blessings began. They have two sons and have lived in California and Virginia. Michael's career allowed Victoria to be both a stay-at-home mom and a writer. She's living a dream that started when she read her first book and thought, "I want to tell stories." For that gift, she will be forever grateful.

Feel free to drop Victoria an e-mail at VictoriaBylin@aol.com or visit her Web site at www.victoriabylin.com.

Even the sparrow has found a home,
and the swallow a nest for herself,
where she may have her young—
a place near your altar,
O Lord Almighty, my King and my God.
—*Psalms* 84:3

For my brother John Bylin…
Dad would be proud of you. I know I am.

Chapter One

Castle Rock, Colorado
June 1882

"You know the story of Cain and Abel?"

"I do."

"Patrick was Abel. I'm Cain."

Daniela Baxter gaped at the man in the doorway. Unshaven and bleary eyed, he looked enough like Patrick to be his brother. Except Patrick would never have answered the door in dirty trousers and a wrinkled shirt.

Patrick and she were engaged to be married. Tomorrow. At the church she'd spotted outside of town. When he'd failed to meet her at the train depot, Dani had hired a buggy and driven the five miles to his dairy farm. She'd expected her fiancé to greet her with a smile and an apology for missing her train. Instead, a stranger had answered the door. She'd asked for Patrick by name and been assaulted by his sneering question about Cain and Abel.

Her insides knotted. "I don't understand."

"Patrick's dead."

Dani blinked. "I must be at the wrong house."

The road had forked a mile west of town. She'd guessed and taken the straighter of the two trails.

The man with Patrick's eyes studied her more closely. "Who are you?"

"Daniela Baxter. I'm his fiancée."

She and Patrick had been introduced through letters by Kirstin Janss, his cousin and Dani's best friend. They had corresponded for six months. He'd written often about the town of Castle Rock, his growing dairy business and his three young daughters.

The man's gaze stayed hard, but his voice softened like hot caramel, sweet but still sticky. "I'm sorry, miss. Patrick died five days ago."

Gasping, Dani clutched her reticule. It held her only picture of the man she loved, the one he'd taken just for her. He'd combed his thick hair with pomade and dressed in his Sunday best, a black suit with a crisp shirt. She knew his dreams. He knew hers. She loved him. She loved his daughters and yearned to be a mother, both to his girls and the babies to come.

The porch started to spin. Dani grabbed the rocking chair for support, but it tipped, throwing her to her knees. As she hit the threshold, pain shot through the marrow of her bones.

A strong hand gripped her elbow and hauled her to her feet. "Don't faint on me, lady."

"I won't."

As tears filled her eyes, he dragged her to a chair in the front room where she collapsed on the cushioned seat, taking in the horsehair divan and a scattering of flower petals. She smelled lilies and realized a coffin had sat in this room. Patrick...her love. An anguished cry exploded in her throat.

The man shouted into the kitchen. "Emma! Get some water."

Dani pushed to her feet. She'd come to be a mother to the girls, not a burden. "I'll be fine."

The man glared at her. "You don't look fine."

"Who are you?" she demanded.

Before he could answer, Patrick's oldest daughter came into the room with the glass of water. Judging by the tight pull of Emma's brows, she disliked this man. "Here," she said, shoving the glass in his direction.

He put his hands on his hips. "It's not for me." He indicated Dani with his chin.

The instant the child turned, her oval face brightened with hope. "Dani?"

"Yes, sweetie. It's me." Dani crossed the gap between herself and the child and offered a hug.

Emma clung to her like moss on a tree. Long letters had made them friends over a span of months. Grief made them family in an instant. Water from the tipped glass sloshed down the back of Dani's dress, but she didn't care. Holding Emma brought Patrick to life. He'd written proudly of his girls. Emma, Ellie and little Esther, who'd been born on Easter Sunday. *We'll have more, Dani. I want a son.* She'd written back about Edward, Ethan and Elijah. He'd countered with Earl and Ebenezer. Laughing to herself, she'd cried uncle in the next letter.

Dani released her grip on Emma, took the glass and set it on the table. "Where are your sisters?"

"Upstairs," Emma said. "Esther's taking a nap."

Emma, barely ten years old, had the tired eyes of a young mother. Who would take care of the girls now? Not this man with tattered clothes and bristled cheeks. As Dani turned in his direction, he paced to the front window. Standing with his feet apart, he peered through the glass, studying the sky like a man expecting a storm. Dani tried to imagine Patrick striking such a belligerent pose but couldn't.

The picture in her reticule showed a man with gentle eyes. He had described himself as wiry and slight, a man with the rounded shoulders of a dairy farmer. The stranger at the window stood six feet tall and ramrod straight. Judging by his stance, he bent his knee to no one.

Dani knew better than to judge by appearances, but the stranger had declared himself to be Cain, the brother who'd surrendered to sin rather than fight for his righteousness. Cain had murdered Abel and been doomed to restless wandering. Even so, God hadn't left Cain. Cain had abandoned God.

Dani put her arm around Emma's shoulders, then spoke to the man's back. "Perhaps the three of us could sit down."

He faced her but stayed at the window. "I'll stand."

In that case, so would Dani. "We haven't been introduced."

"I'm Beau Morgan. Patrick's brother."

Emma clutched a fistful of Dani's dress. Dani took the reaction as a confirmation of a warning in Patrick's letters. He'd mentioned his brother just once. *He's not someone you should know, Dani. Not a man I'd trust with my girls.* Patrick had been vague about his brother's shortcomings but clear about his intent. *I made a will years ago, before Beau went crazy. As soon as we're married, I'll change it. I want you to adopt the girls.*

Dani's throat tightened. Why had God taken Patrick now? Why not a year from now, after they were married and settled? Why not fifty years when they were old and gray? The questions rose like a vapor but vanished as quickly as morning mist on a hot day. God's ways were higher than hers; His knowledge greater. At her mother's funeral, Pastor Schmidt had preached from Isaiah, paraphrasing the ancient prophet. "Who among you walks in darkness and has no light? Let him trust in the name of the Lord…" Dani had leaned on those words every day since her mother's death. Isaiah had seen the future and persevered. Dani didn't have his foresight, only her faith that God was good, but she knew how to persevere.

She touched Emma's cheek. "Your pa's listening in Heaven, so I'm talking to him as well as you. No matter what happens, I won't leave you and your sisters."

Did you hear that, Patrick? Rest easy, my love.

Emma nodded in short bursts that made her eyes flicker with desperation. Dani lifted her gaze to the man at the window. What had he said to these children? Had he offered the slightest bit of reassurance? More than ever, they needed the comfort of familiar things, the promise they'd be together and that God Himself shared their grief.

Staring back at Dani, Beau Morgan sealed his lips in a hard line, then turned back to the window. Framed by lace curtains and panes of glass, he stood with his arms crossed and his feet spread wide. If he'd been wearing boots, Dani might have been intimidated. Instead she saw a hole in the heel of his sock. A tug on the yarn would unravel the entire garment. She suspected the man's life was in the same sorry shape and prayed he'd be eager to leave Patrick's daughters in her care.

Thoughts of the girls mixed with the scent of the lilies. Looking down, she squeezed Emma's shoulders. "Can you tell me what happened?"

Emma opened her mouth but sealed it without making a sound.

Dani looked to the man by the window. Hate glinted in his eyes. "It was ugly. Emma doesn't need to relive it."

The child shook her head. "I *want* to remember. He said he loved us. He said—"

"Emma, don't." Beau Morgan glared at Dani. "Patrick was struck by lightning. Emma found him."

Dani gasped, then closed her eyes. "Dear Lord in Heaven, be with Patrick. Be will all of us."

The man snorted. "I wouldn't call the Almighty 'dear.'"

Dani stiffened at the lack of respect. "Patrick had faith. He believed—"

"That's fine for him," the man replied. "But the Almighty and I don't see eye to eye, not anymore."

Emma choked on a sob. "It was my fault. I knew a storm was coming, but I didn't tell him."

The man scowled. "It's not your fault, kid. You didn't make it rain."

"But I knew!" Her voice rose to a wail. "He went to see Pastor Josh about the wedding. I asked him to buy some ribbon for Esther's dress. If he hadn't gone to the store, he'd have been home before the storm."

Dani trembled with regrets of her own. Patrick had wanted a September wedding. She'd pushed for June. If she'd shown more patience, he'd be alive. She knew her thoughts were crazy. She didn't control the weather. A lightning strike… What were the odds? She thought of Patrick's last letter. *Storms are common, Dani. Life here is hard. Are you sure you want to marry me?*

She'd written back. *I love storms!*

Noah had built an ark. Christ had calmed a stormy sea. She'd seen blizzards in January, tasted the cold and watched tornadoes drop from summer clouds. She'd felt the fear and clung to her faith. Not once had God let her down. She refused to doubt Him now, yet how could she not wonder, just a little, if God had blinked and left Patrick to die?

Weak in the knees, she led Emma to the divan. "When did it happen?"

Mr. Morgan shot her a look of warning, then spoke to Emma. "Go upstairs. I'll tell her."

"No!" the child cried.

Did this man really think silence would spare Emma the memories? Dani had been the same age when her mother died. She'd brought home a cold from school. Leda Baxter had nursed her daughter and died of pneumonia. Silence had turned Dani's childhood home into an open grave, leaving her alone with the same twisted guilt plaguing Emma. No way would she leave the child to suffer as she had.

Dani took Emma's hand. "What happened, sweetie?"

"The storm turned the sky black." Her voice dropped to a murmur. "I sent Ellie and Esther to the cellar, then I came up here to watch for Pa. I stood right there."

She pointed to a spot in front of the side-by-side windows looking into the yard. Beau Morgan's back blocked the view, so Emma leaned to the side to see around him. Dani craned her neck, as well, but he put his hands on his hips, blocking the view with his bent elbows. When Emma walked to the edge of the window so she could see the yard, Dani joined her. Standing behind the child, she placed her hands on Emma's thin shoulders and followed her gaze down the road to a distant pine.

"Do you see that tree?" Emma asked.

"I do." Dani looked at the charred branches and blackened trunk of a ponderosa. She'd passed it on the way to the farm.

"I saw the lightning strike. The air buzzed, then everything went white and thunder shook the house. A minute later, Pa's horse galloped into the yard."

Riderless.

Against her will, Dani saw the pelting rain, the mud, the empty saddle.

Emma's voice cracked. "Lightning hit again. Everything turned as bright as day. That's when I saw that Buck had no tail. His rump had a burn on it. I could smell the hair."

Beau Morgan reached across the span of the window and

touched the child's back. His sleeve rode up his forearm, revealing tense muscles and a jagged scar above his wrist. "Don't do this to yourself."

As the child stared into the yard, Dani stroked her arms. The images in Emma's mind were sacred, hers to share or bury as her heart demanded. The clock ticked. Chickens pecked the dirt by the barn as Dani stared at the gouges left in the mud by Patrick's horse. Next time it rained, she'd stomp them flat.

Emma saw the marks, too. "I knew Pa was hurt, so I ran outside. Buck died right in front of me."

Dani held in a groan that would do no good. As a child she'd embroidered samplers with her favorite Bible verses. *For God so loved the world…* *Peace I give to you…* Staring into the empty yard, she felt the thinness of the thread shaping those words. She'd snapped it with her teeth or snipped it with scissors. Listening to Emma, Dani felt a new tension stretching her faith.

Emma's shoulders sagged. "I found Pa by that pine tree. His clothes were burned and he was lying in the mud, but he was still alive."

Why, Lord?

It wasn't like Dani to doubt God's ways, but she couldn't stop the anger welling in her middle. These children had already lost their mother. Why had God taken Patrick, too? She stared at the window where a pale reflection of Emma's face stared back. Tears trickled down the girl's cheeks, glistening like silver ribbons.

Emma squared her shoulders. "He looked me right in the eye, then he touched my nose like he did when I was little. He said he loved us, then he saw Mama. I know, because he called her name."

Dani refused to be jealous. Patrick had loved his first wife with a dedication she admired and wanted for herself. He'd called her Beth, short for Elizabeth. They'd been childhood friends. Two years ago, Beth had died of a ruptured appendix.

Dani gripped Emma's shoulders. "He's with your ma now. I know for a fact he's looking out for you right this minute."

"He loved you, too." Emma wiped her eyes, then faced Dani. "You said in your letters that you'd be our new mother. Pa's gone, but—"

"I'm keeping that promise."

Dani hugged the girl hard. They sobbed together until the river of tears turned to a trickle. Grief would rain on them again, filling the wells, but for now they were spent.

Beau Morgan cleared his throat. "You may not be aware, Miss Baxter. I'm the girls' legal guardian."

Dani straightened, then met his gaze. "I'm very aware, Mr. Morgan. Patrick named you as executor several years ago." Her next words would settle the issue for good or start a battle she couldn't lose. "I have a letter in my trunk. It clearly states his more recent intentions."

"And what were those?"

"He asked me to adopt the girls."

"Contingent on marriage?"

"Of course."

Mr. Morgan raised one thick brow. "And the farm? Would he want you to have that, too?"

Dani hadn't thought that far. "I suppose." She needed a way to support the children.

Beau Morgan rocked back on his heels. "Miss Baxter, you're either naive or a con artist."

Dani's mouth gaped. "How dare you!"

"No, how dare *you*." His voice stayed as flat as a coin. "I'm a blood relative with legal authority. You waltz in here and announce you want my nieces and a farm that's worth a good amount of money."

"I don't care about the money!"

"Of course, you don't." His lips curled with contempt. "Frankly, it doesn't matter what you want. I have an obligation to see to my nieces and I intend to meet it."

Staring into the man's eyes, a green that reminded her of dying grass, Dani saw good reason to trust Patrick's assessment of him as crazy. She judged him to be in his midthirties, a few years older than his brother, but far less settled. Judging by the ragged ends of his hair, he'd cut it himself with a knife. The dark blond strands brushed his collarless shirt like a worn-out broom. Dani's eyes skimmed across the denim that had once been green or blue. She couldn't tell which. The sun had bleached it to turquoise, a soft color that blended with the dust on his brown trousers and the unraveling yarn of his gray sock.

If he couldn't take care of himself, how could he manage three young girls? Maybe he didn't want to... Perhaps he was eager to turn over guardianship and needed assurance of her honorable intentions. A woman could beat a mule with a stick or coax it with a carrot. Dani opted for the carrot. "I appreciate your concern, Mr. Morgan. In fact, I admire it."

"Good."

"Once you see Patrick's letter, I'm sure you'll agree with me."

"Don't count on it, Miss Baxter. The world's full of liars. How do I know you're not one of them?"

Emma thrust herself between them. "Pa loved Dani!"

The man looked Dani up and down, assessing her appearance without really seeing her. Before leaving the train, she'd put on her prettiest outfit, a pink taffeta suit with a snug jacket and ruffled skirt, and a sweeping straw hat that dipped across her brow. The outfit made her feel pretty. She'd dressed for Patrick, not this rude man with holes in his socks.

His eyes darted back to her face. "Men are fools, Miss Baxter. Especially lonely ones. Patrick fit that mold."

Dani had never felt so insulted in her life, or so alone. Back home, her reputation had shone like gold. No one would have questioned her motives for taking in three orphaned girls. Then again, no one in Walker County, Wisconsin had Beau Morgan's suspicious nature. Dani couldn't help but wonder who'd kicked him in the shins.

His eyes focused on hers. "A train leaves for Denver in the morning. I want you on it."

"Absolutely not."

"I'll pay your fare home."

Dani had fifteen dollars in her reticule, enough for a week in a hotel but not much else. Her brother would send money if she asked, but she refused to consider it. She'd made a promise to Patrick and intended to keep it, but she'd also left Wisconsin for a reason. When their father died, her brother had inherited the family dairy. A year ago, he'd married. Ever since, he'd been pushing Dani to leave. *This isn't your house, Dani. It's mine and Marta is my wife. You need a home of your own.*

Dani thought so, too. Some time ago, she'd been engaged to a young man named Tommy Page. They'd been childhood friends, but Dani hadn't felt any of the excitement she'd expected. Tommy had wanted to kiss and hug, but she'd said no. He was a brother to her, nothing more, so she'd ended the engagement. Dani wanted the right husband, the man God had made just for her. She'd been willing to wait, but her brother had lost patience with her. Against her will, he'd encouraged Archie Weldon to court her. A widower with a bad back, Archie had wanted a housekeeper, not a wife. Lars Jenson, a man who spoke in grunts, had been next on her brother's list. And so on…until Dani had met every bachelor in Walker County.

Eventually she'd given in and agreed to marry Virgil Griggs. She'd liked Virgil, but she hadn't loved him. A week before the wedding, she'd broken their engagement, embarrassing Virgil and shaming herself. *That Dani Baxter is fickle...* She'd heard the talk and been embarrassed and angry. She didn't have a fickle bone in her body. She simply couldn't lie to herself or to Virgil, who deserved better than a wife who couldn't bear the thought of kissing him. Dani had been near despair when Kirstin had mentioned her cousin in Colorado, a widower who needed a wife and mother for his three daughters. Dani had given Patrick permission to write. After three letters, she'd fallen in love with him.

Now he was gone and his wayward brother had the girls and wanted Dani to leave. She simply couldn't do it, not with Patrick's letter in her trunk. But neither could she stay at the farm with this man. Her best hope lay in convincing him to leave. Dani wasn't wise in the ways of the world, but she knew a little about men and carrots.

"I have a suggestion, Mr. Morgan."

"What's that?"

"There's a nice hotel by the railroad station. I'm sure you'd enjoy a good night's sleep."

His eyes flickered. Either he enjoyed a fight or he was tempted by the comforts of a hotel room. Judging by the dark crescents under his eyes, he hadn't slept in days.

Dani sweetened the deal. "The hotel has a restaurant. I saw it when I rented the buggy. Today's special is roast beef with raspberry pie for dessert."

His mouth hardened. "No thanks, Miss Baxter. Emma's a good cook."

Dani doubted it. The child had written about her kitchen foibles. *Will you teach me to make biscuits? Mine are rock hard, but Pa eats them and smiles.*

A lump pressed into Dani's throat. She'd trusted Patrick with her life, her reputation. She had no such faith in the man standing in his place. She also had nowhere else to go. She didn't like what she was about to say, but she had to get Beau Morgan to leave. "There's a saloon, too."

His eyes twinkled with mischief. "You want a drink?"

"No!"

"Me, neither." The corners of his mouth tipped up. "I'm not a drinking man, Miss Baxter. Never have been."

Was that good news? Dani didn't know. She wanted this man to be so low that any judge in Douglas County would deny him custody. Instead he sounded like her Aunt Minnie.

He leaned against the wall, crossing his sock-covered feet. "I'm also good at hearing what isn't said. I'm guessing you have about ten dollars in your bag and don't know a soul."

She blushed.

"That's what I thought." He eyed her thoughtfully. "I'd be glad to pay your room and board in town, but I suspect you're too stubborn to accept."

"It's not a matter of stubbornness." She reached for Emma. "I promised Patrick—"

"I know what you promised." His voice turned gentle. "I also know what it's like to be grief-stricken. It leaves you numb, but only for a while. Once the shock passes, you wake up screaming. It'll eat you alive if you let it."

Peering into his eyes, she saw a kinship born of suffering. Dani had grieved her mother and still cried for the woman who'd given her blue eyes and wheat-blond hair. Who had Beau Morgan mourned? The connection, as brief as lightning and as bright, frightened her.

If he felt the spark, he didn't let it show. Standing straighter, he looked ready for business. "If you're willing to bend a bit, I'm prepared to offer a compromise."

"What do you have in mind?"

"I'll move to the barn while we sort things out. You get room and board in exchange for keeping house."

Emma looked up at Dani. "It's time to start the garden. We could do it together."

For a thousand miles, she'd dreamed of planting tomatoes in Patrick's side yard. She loved the feeling of loamy earth and the scent of herbs growing in a window box. She'd imagined flowers, too. Tulips in the spring, roses in June. She had learned from her mother that touches of beauty nourished a family as much as good food.

Her gaze drifted to the hole in Beau Morgan's sock. His big toe curled as if to hide, then stretched in defiance. "As you can see, my clothes could use some mending."

"And a good scrubbing," she added.

"That's a fact."

His voice held a yearning that put Dani on alert. Which was more dangerous? The snake that rattled as it slithered or the one sleeping in the sun?

Emma squeezed her hand. "Stay, Dani. Please."

She wanted to say yes, but she had to protect her reputation as well as the children. "I'd prefer the hotel," she said. "But only if the girls can stay with me."

"I can't allow it."

"Why not?" She tried to sound confident. "It would be a change for them."

"You're naive, Miss Baxter."

Dani bristled. "I've just traveled a thousand miles—"

"And I've traveled ten thousand." He raised his chin. "Have you ever seen a pack of wolves?"

She'd heard howling in the forest near her father's farm, but the wolves had stayed out of sight. "No, I haven't."

"I have," he said. "The kind with two legs."

"Castle Rock seems safe to me."

His eyes glittered like broken glass. "It was—before I got here."

Chapter Two

Looking at Daniela Baxter, Beau felt the cut of sudden change. The last time he'd seen Patrick had been five years ago. His brother had come to the funeral for Beau's wife, traveling alone because his own wife, Beth, had been close to delivering their third child. Beau and his brother hadn't been close, but he'd appreciated the kindness. Patrick had made him promise to write now and then. He'd even offered him a place to stay.

Beau had said he'd keep in touch, but he'd broken the promise so badly he hadn't known about Beth's passing. He hadn't known a lot of things when he'd arrived in Castle Rock two days ago. Hot on the trail of an outlaw named Clay Johnson, Beau had found himself within a few miles of his brother's farm. He'd decided to pay a visit and had arrived to find a fresh grave and an old man in the barn. The fellow and his wife were neighbors who'd come to care for the cows and the girls until other arrangements could be made.

The girls could have been farmed out to friends, but the cows needed their routine. A lightning strike...of all the foolish things. Even more surprising was the news from

Patrick's attorney. Seven years ago, Patrick had written a will. It named Beau as guardian of his children—a fact Beau vaguely remembered. He'd have made a good guardian in the past, but not anymore. An ex-lawman, he sold his gun to the highest bidder. Like most shootists, he lived in the canyons between good and evil. He enjoyed the freedom and the money, but mostly he burned with the need to bring Clay Johnson to justice.

Whether God or the devil had given him a thirst for Johnson's blood, Beau didn't know. He only knew that Clay Johnson had killed the most precious person in his life. Lucy, his young wife, had put on her prettiest dress, a pink thing with puffy sleeves, and brought him supper at the sheriff's office. What happened next was an abomination. Beau no longer dreamed about that day, but he remembered every detail. Looking at Miss Baxter in her pink dress, he swallowed a mouthful of bile. He hated that color and the memories it brought. He always would.

Sending her to the hotel tempted him as much as that roast beef dinner. He'd lied about Emma's cooking. The girl made a mean pancake, but a man needed more than starch in his belly to do a day's work. He also needed to sleep at night, something Beau hadn't done since he'd arrived. He couldn't. Since Lucy's murder, he and Johnson had been playing a game of cat and mouse. Sometimes the outlaw vanished for months, leaving Beau to search aimlessly for his prey. Other times Johnson went on the prowl, leaving threats for Beau at local saloons. Sometimes he wrote notes. Sometimes he left tokens that chilled Beau's blood.

Daniela Baxter's eyes drilled into his. "Who are you, Mr. Morgan?"

"I told you. I'm Patrick's brother."

"That's not what I meant."

Beau held back a smart remark about jabbering females. If Miss Baxter ended up at the hotel, she might blather to every busybody in town. She looked like the kind of woman who'd want to go to church on Sundays. Beau knew all about gossip cloaked in prayer. He'd been the focus of his share after Lucy's death. Wishing he'd been less of a blowhard, he tried to smile. "Forget the bluster. I'm no one."

"Somehow, I doubt that."

Beau said nothing. In truth, his reputation stretched from Bozeman to El Paso, across the plains and over mountains that dwarfed a man's pride but not his pain. If word spread he was in Castle Rock, anyone he touched would be a target for Johnson. That included Miss Baxter. He didn't need another female in his care, but honor required him to see to her safety. Like it or not, he'd have to keep an eye on her.

No hardship there…Daniela Baxter was just plain pretty. Slender but womanly, she filled out the dress in all the right places. Not that Beau cared. Being a man, he couldn't help but notice her looks, but he knew the rules. When he'd married Lucy, he'd promised to love, honor and cherish his wife until they were parted by death. Lucy was gone, but Beau took comfort in keeping his vows. His eyes locked on Miss Baxter, saying things with a look that acknowledged the deepest of truths. He was male. She wasn't. He had the power to harm her. She needed to know he never would. He made his voice solemn. "I'm an honorable man, Miss Baxter."

"You're the one who mentioned wolves," she replied. "I understand they come in sheep's clothing."

"I'm not one of them."

Before she could reply, footsteps padded on the landing at the top of the stairs. He turned and saw Ellie and Esther peeking around the corner. Esther, as always, had her thumb in her mouth. She was five and too old for the habit, but Beau hadn't tried to stop her. Human beings, no matter their age, took comfort where they could find it.

"Are you Dani?" Ellie asked.

"I am."

The girls hurried down the steps and threw themselves into her arms. More hugs, more tears. Beau was tired of the flood but knew the girls would pull on Miss Baxter's heart in a way common sense couldn't. With a throat as dry as sand, he watched the swirl of pink and ribbons and locks of golden hair. All four of them were blond, though the girls' hair would darken with time as Patrick's had. Beau's hair had lost its shine a long time ago, though it lightened up in the summer.

He watched as the woman kissed Ellie's forehead, then lifted Esther on to her hip. In a voice choked with tears, she rambled about God and Patrick looking down from Heaven.

They loved you, brother. I wish I'd known you better.

Even as he thought the words, Beau stifled his regrets. He'd learned to live one day at a time. To take what pleasure he found and be content with it. A can of beans for supper. A lantern on a moonless night. If a man didn't have a home, he couldn't lose it. If he didn't love, he couldn't get hurt. Beau had drawn that line the day Clay Johnson shot Lucy and not once had he crossed it. He hoped Daniela Baxter would be wise and draw a similar line for herself. She had no future in Castle Rock. Even if he'd wanted to hand her custody of the girls, he couldn't do it. Running a farm required both brains and muscle. The thought of leaving a woman and three children at the mercy of hired hands struck him as gutless.

Beau glanced at the mantel clock. In two hours, he had an appointment with Trevor Scott, the attorney handling Patrick's will. If things went as planned, the girls would leave for boarding school at the end of the month.

Ellie, a tomboy in coveralls, broke the hug and looked at Dani. "You're staying, aren't you?"

Miss Baxter tousled the child's hair, then looked at Beau. Her eyes soothed his soul and laid it bare at the same time. "Can I trust you, Mr. Morgan?"

"With your life."

"In that case, we have a deal. If you'll stay in the barn, I'll tend to the house."

When she held out her gloved hand, Beau noticed the cupped shape of her fingers. His own hand, loose and open, was just a clench away from the violence that defined his life, but he offered it in good faith. He expected to see trepidation in her eyes. Instead she squeezed back with surprising firmness. The grip, he realized, came from hard work. The grit came from her heart. Beau saw her pink dress, the shadow of roses in her cheeks, and pined a moment for Lucy. How did it feel to grow old with a woman? To see your daughters marry and your sons grow strong? To live without the thirst for Clay Johnson's blood? Beau would never know. Most of the time, he didn't want to know. He let go of Miss Baxter's hand. He'd had all the innocence he could stand for one day.

He'd seen a rented buggy out front. "Where's your trunk?"

"At the train station."

Beau thought of his appointment with Patrick's attorney. "I have to go to town this afternoon. I'll take you and the girls and we'll pick it up."

"Thank you," she said.

Beau looked down at his nieces. "Get going. We leave in ten minutes."

They scurried up the stairs like frightened mice, leaving Beau to wonder what he'd done to scare them. He wished he could be less stern, but he had a melancholy nature. Miss

Baxter had turned her head to watch the girls. Even with tears on her cheeks, she seemed like the cheerful sort. Beau hoped so. The girls needed a woman's tenderness.

Leaving Miss Baxter at the stairs, he strode into Patrick's bedroom where he changed into a clean shirt, then balled up his laundry and slung his saddlebag over his shoulder. As he came out of the dark room, he saw Miss Baxter sitting on the bottom step with her head bowed.

Beau feared God but didn't much like Him. Taking Patrick's life struck him as wrong. Leaving this young woman to cope alone counted as cruel. He stopped a few feet away. "Miss Baxter?"

She looked up with damp eyes. "Yes?"

"I'm truly sorry for your loss."

"Thank you."

Beau shifted his weight. Handing her his dirty clothes didn't seem right, so he headed for the door.

When she called his name, he turned but said nothing.

"Is that your laundry?" she asked.

"Yes, it is."

"I expect to keep my end of the bargain. Leave your clothes and I'll wash them tomorrow."

Beau stepped back to the staircase where she'd pushed to her feet. Judging by the twitch of her nostrils, the smell of the barn reached her before he did. He had three horses in his care, his roan and Patrick's two workhorses.

"You've been mucking out stalls," she said.

"Someone had to do it."

"And the milking?"

"Of course."

What did she think? That he dozed in a hammock all day? Patrick had ten Jersey cows. They might have been "ladies" for Patrick, lining up at the gate at milking time, but they hadn't taken to Beau. Each one had bawled and squalled while he looped a rope around her neck and led her to the barn for milking. He'd felt ridiculous on a little three-legged stool, and his clumsy hands annoyed the cows until Emma had given him pointers. She'd also informed him the cows had names and liked it when her pa sang hymns. Beau had grunted, then listened to the child crooning words to a song he'd made a point of forgetting.

Blessed assurance, Jesus divine!
Oh what a foretaste of glory is mine...

Beau hadn't set foot in a church in five years and he didn't intend to start now. He handed his clothes to Miss Baxter. They needed a good scrubbing. So did he, but a visit to the bathhouse was out of the question with four females in his care and Clay Johnson nearby. With the saddlebag dragging on his shoulder, Beau headed for the barn. Maybe Trevor Scott had found a school. Beau hoped so. He didn't know how much purity and light he could tolerate.

Dani carried Beau Morgan's laundry through the kitchen and out to the back porch. Where did Patrick keep the washtub? In the barn? In the shed by the door? She'd have to ask Emma.

Why, Lord? I don't understand.

Hardly breathing, she dropped the garments in a heap and went back into the kitchen. For a thousand miles she'd dreamed of seeing this house for the first time. She'd imagined cooking at the stove, a new model with a fancy baking chamber. Patrick had described it in his letters. He'd written to her about everything...the view from the window above the sink, the number of shelves in the pantry. He'd been excited to share his life. Almost believing she'd see him, Dani looked out the window and saw the cottonwood he'd described in his letters. Just as he'd said, the branches curved up to the sky like open arms. Beyond it she saw a hill crowned by a white picket fence encasing two white crosses. It marked Patrick's final resting place and Beth's, too.

Dani choked back tears. Tonight she'd weep and find comfort in the Psalms, but right now she had children in her care. Wiping her eyes, she prayed for peace. When her thoughts spiraled into a black abyss, she reached for verses she'd memorized as a child in Sunday School.

Blessed is the man whose strength is in Thee; in whose heart are the ways of them. The ways of God…

Who passing through the Valley of Baca… the valley of tears.

Make it a well. A source of blessing.

The rain also filleth the pools. God in heaven adds his grace.

They… those who walk with God.

Go from strength to strength. Amen.

Dani tried to breathe evenly, but the air in the kitchen felt as heavy as sand. Her chest ached with the effort of sucking it in. God had promised strength, yet she'd never felt weaker in her life.

"Dani?"

She opened her eyes and saw Emma in the doorway with her sisters. The girls had braided their hair and put on fresh pinafores, but grief had dulled their eyes to pewter. Dani thought of the gifts in her trunk. She'd brought gingham for new Sunday-best dresses, books for Emma and Ellie, and a doll for Esther. Seeing their tearstained cheeks, she decided to save the gifts for a happier time.

"Are you ready to go?" she asked.

Emma looked over her shoulder, then urged her sisters deeper into the kitchen. A wall hid them from the front window and she leaned closer to Dani. "We don't like him," she whispered.

Dani's skin prickled. If Beau Morgan had been unkind to these girls, she'd chase him away with a frying pan. "Has he mistreated you?"

"No, but he stays up all night."

On occasion, so did Dani. "What else?"

Ellie's eyes widened. "He said a bad word."

Dani wouldn't condemn a man for cussing. Her father had let loose on occasion and colorfully at that. "It's wrong, but men do it sometimes."

Emma's voice shook. "I don't care about cussing. It's the guns that scare me."

"Guns?"

"He has four of them. Two rifles and two pistols."

Guns themselves weren't evil, but the men who used them sometimes did evil things. Dani forced herself to stay calm. "What exactly does he do?"

"He sits alone and fires the pistol," Emma whispered.

"He *fires* it?"

"Not exactly," the girl explained. "The gun's empty but I can hear it click. He does it over and over, like he's aiming at someone he can't see."

That settled it. The man was crazy. He was either wanted by the law or protecting them from a danger he'd brought to Castle Rock himself.

The front door swung open. Heavy boots thudded on the wooden floor. "Ladies?"

Dani whispered into Emma's ear. "We'll talk later."

As she stood straight, Beau Morgan stepped into the kitchen and crossed his arms as though he meant business. A tan duster hung from his shoulders but gaped at the waist, revealing a wide leather belt and the front edge of a cross-draw holster. He pulled his mouth into a smile that bordered on a sneer. "Pray tell, ladies. My ears are burning. I don't suppose you were talking about me?"

"No, sir."

Emma had lied, but Dani didn't correct her. She wanted to hide the girls under her skirts. No way could they share their home with a man who armed himself for a trip to town. She'd spotted the church from the window of the train. She'd never met Pastor Blue and his wife, but Patrick had said they were kind. Surely the couple would take them in until Dani could find safer accommodations.

"Let's go," she said with false cheer.

Mr. Morgan led the way out the door, grabbing the hat he'd left on a peg in the entry hall. As he pulled it low, the girls followed him down the steps with Dani bringing up the rear. In the front yard she saw the livery buggy and the family wagon. He was standing by the buggy, watching them like a coyote spying a flock of chickens.

He pointed his chin at the wagon. "The girls can ride in the back."

Dani steered them to the buggy. "I think we can fit. Don't you, girls?" The rig had a single seat. It would be a squeeze.

Mr. Morgan shrugged. "Suit yourselves."

When she bent to lift Esther, he reached for the child at the same time. Their hands overlapped on the girl's waist with Dani losing the race.

His eyes narrowed. "Let me. She's heavy."

"I can manage."

Esther grabbed for Dani, but Mr. Morgan scooped her up and plopped her on the seat before she knew enough to cry. Scowling, he offered his gloved hand to Ellie, then Emma, and finally to her. Looking at the leather, Dani wondered what it hid. Some people thought a man's eyes revealed his soul. Dani looked at hands. Calluses testified to hard work. Soft skin hinted at laziness or vice. If Mr. Morgan removed the gloves, what would she see? The trim nails of a gambler? The knuckles of a brawler?

His eyes glinted. "I won't bite, Miss Baxter."

Satan had said the same thing to Eve. Ignoring his hand, she climbed into the buggy.

He went to the wagon. "Stay in front of me."

She took the reins and drove out of the yard with Ellie pressed against her ribs and Esther in Emma's lap. The top of the buggy shielded them from Mr. Morgan's stare, but the creak of the wagon kept him close.

Ellie squirmed closer to Dani. "He's nothing like Pa."

Emma stared straight ahead. "Pa's gone. We have to get used to it."

"I don't want to!" Ellie cried.

"There's no choice." Emma tightened her grip on Esther's waist. "I'm the oldest. That means I have to look out for you."

Dani's heart broke for the girl. She knew how it felt to grow up overnight. They rode in silence, listening to the rhythm of Esther sucking her thumb and the creak of the harness. Behind them, Beau Morgan clicked to the horses, crowding the buggy in spite of the empty road. Dani wondered if he'd watch them this closely in town. The closer he rode, the more determined she became to escape. But how? She needed a plan. "Do you know where Mr. Morgan's going?" she said to Emma.

"Probably to see Mr. Scott."

"Who's he?"

"Pa's attorney. He sent Mr. Morgan a message."

Ellie frowned. "He said to call him Uncle Beau."

"I don't care," Emma replied. "I want him to leave."

So did Dani. She considered barging into his meeting with the attorney, but getting the girls to Pastor Blue and his wife took priority. "Where's Mr. Scott's office?"

"On Fourth Street."

The church was on the west side of town. The livery was on First Street. If she could convince Mr. Morgan to allow her to watch the girls while he met with Mr. Scott, they could make a run for the church.

"What are we going to do?" Ellie asked.

The older girls would understand, but Esther wouldn't. She gave Emma and Ellie a conspiratorial glance. "When Mr. Morgan visits the attorney, we'll pay a visit to Pastor Blue and his wife."

Emma's eyes dimmed. "The church is far."

"About a half mile," Ellie added.

Dani's heart sank. Her new shoes had dainty heels. Pretty or not, they hurt her feet. Esther posed another problem. Unless Dani took the wagon, she'd have to carry the child a good part of the way. The more she thought about sneaking the wagon out from under Beau Morgan's nose, the more she liked the idea. By then, they'd have picked up her trunk and she'd have possession of Patrick's letters. Unless he changed his mind about custody, she'd need them in a court of law.

Aware of three pairs of blue eyes on her face, Dani nudged the horse into a faster walk. "We'll make it," she said to the girls.

"I don't see how." Emma sighed.

Dani put iron in her voice. "Do you know the story about Daniel in the lion's den?"

"It's scary," Esther said.

"That's true, but God kept Daniel safe." Dani let the words sink in. "If God can put lions to sleep, He can get us to the church."

"We can see Miss Adie," Ellie said.

"That's right."

Esther pulled her thumb out of her mouth. "She has kittens!"

A lump pushed into Dani's throat. Emma, sensing her sister's need, chatted about the cats. Ellie joined in, leaving Dani to ponder her plan as she navigated the stretch of road into Castle Rock. With a little luck, she and the girls would be spending the night at the parsonage and Beau Morgan would see the wisdom of leaving them alone.

With the wagon rattling in the buggy's wake, Dani took in the rippling grass and patches of pine dotting the horizon. In the distance stood the dome of granite that gave the town its name. Round and high, the fortresslike stone capped a mesa jutting up from a meadow. To the east, Dani saw rows of buildings. Most were made of wood, but a few showed off the pinkish rhyolite stone that had given the town its birth. Twenty years ago, Castle Rock had been nothing more than a cattle stop. Now it boasted a school, two churches and dozens of businesses. Patrick had described it in his letters, filling her with excitement at the prospect of being a part of something new.

As they neared the train station, Dani saw the tracks stretching as far south as she could see. The train that brought her had left hours ago. Nothing remained. Not a trace of steam, not the six people who had disembarked with her. The only sign of humanity was her trunk sitting on the platform. It looked the way she felt…alone, abandoned and packed for a trip it would never take.

Dani reined in the livery mare. Beau Morgan halted the wagon next to her, climbed down and opened the tailgate. As he strode to the platform, she leaped down from the buggy and followed him.

"That's my trunk," she said.

"I figured."

"It's heavy. You'll need help."

Ignoring her, he hoisted it as if it held feathers instead of her life and lugged it down the three steps. Dani hurried to the back of the wagon where she saw a pile of quilts. Had Patrick kept them there for the girls? Or had Beau Morgan thought to bring them for the bumpy ride? Dani didn't know, but she doubted Patrick kept blankets in his work wagon. She knew from his letters that he owned a two-seat surrey the family took to church, yet kindness didn't fit her impression of Beau Morgan.

Now, Dani... The voice belonged to her father. Walter Baxter had been quick to love and slow to judge. She could imagine his words. *For all you know, Beau Morgan's an up-standing citizen. Judge not, daughter.*

Dani tried to keep an open mind, but she couldn't erase the picture of this man dry firing a pistol into the dark. As he latched the tailgate, she went back to the buggy. He took the reins of the wagon and led the way to the livery stable. The wagon rattled as they passed a feed store, then a mining office where men stood in a line. People on the street noticed them. Some smiled and a few waved to the girls, but Dani had no way to signal for help.

When they reached the livery, Mr. Morgan stopped the wagon. Without a word, he went into the barn and disappeared into the shadows.

"Let's go!" Dani cried.

She leaped out of the buggy and turned. Emma shoved Esther into her arms, then jumped out the other side with Ellie behind her. As the older girls piled into the wagon, Dani boosted Esther over the tailgate, then hurried to the front seat. Before she could hoist herself up, Beau Morgan strode through the doorway.

Faking a smile, Dani put a ring in her voice. "We're ready to go."

"I see." He handed her a silver dollar. "Here."

"What's this?"

"Miller's refunding the rental."

It wasn't much, but every dollar would help. As she took the money, her fingers brushed his glove. He stepped back as if she had the pox, then glanced across the street to a row of shops that included an emporium. Looking befuddled, he cleared his throat. "You've had a long trip. Is there anything you need while we're in town?"

Yesterday Dani had imagined browsing the shops with Patrick's daughters. That dream had died. "No, thank you."

"I'd pay."

"I'm fine, Mr. Morgan." She wanted to run, not shop.

"Suit yourself," he said with a grunt.

Intending to ride with the girls, she headed for the back of the wagon. As she turned, strong fingers caught the bottom of her forearm and turned her back to the seat. His touch was light, nothing more than a brush, but it felt like a shackle. His voice went low, barely a whisper. "You'll ride up front with me."

"I'd rather sit with the girls."

"I'm not asking what you want," he replied. "I'm telling you what's best."

"I don't see why—"

"That's right. You don't."

Dani pulled out of his grip but didn't move. His eyes tensed with the same worry she'd seen on her father's face just before the worst storm of her life had swept across their farm. As he'd ordered her to the cellar, a tornado had funneled down behind the barn. She'd learned that day to trust her father's instincts.

Beau Morgan's expression shifted to the mix of a smile and a scowl she'd seen in the kitchen. Her father had known best. Did Beau Morgan?

"Is there a reason?" she asked.

"None I care to give."

Dani opened her mouth to argue, then sealed her lips. It didn't matter where she sat in the wagon as long as he took them to a place where they could make a run for the church. When he offered his hand, she accepted his help onto the seat. He walked to the other side, climbed up and steered the wagon into the street. Anyone on the boardwalk would think they were a family.

And that, Dani realized, explained why he'd insisted she sit at his side. She and the girls were part of a disguise. They turned Beau Morgan into a family man. Who was after him and why? Dani's stomach clenched. With each block, they traveled farther from the church. Staring straight ahead, she risked a question. "Where are we going?"

"To see Patrick's attorney."

Dani thought of Emma's guess. The child had a good mind. "It must concern the girls."

The man glanced over his shoulder. Dani did the same and saw them huddled as far from the seat as they could get.

Looking straight ahead, he lowered his voice. "I haven't told them yet, but you might as well know. I'm selling the farm and sending them to school."

"You can't!" The whisper scraped her throat.

"It's for the best."

Dani knotted her hands in her lap. Was it wiser to make a break for the parsonage or insist on seeing Trevor Scott herself? Patrick had never mentioned Mr. Scott. On the other hand, he'd spoken well of Pastor Blue. She was weighing the choice when they stopped in front of an ice-cream parlor. Mr.

Morgan hooked his thumb toward the office building across the street. "Scott's office is on the second floor. I thought you and the girls might enjoy some ice cream while I take care of business."

Dani saw the answer to her prayer. "I'm sure they would."

"Can I trust you to watch them, Miss Baxter?"

"Of course." She'd told the truth. She wouldn't let the girls out of her sight until they reached the church.

He reached into his pocket, extracted a few coins and handed them to her. With her heart pounding, she put the money in her reticule and climbed down from the wagon.

As the girls scrambled to her side, Mr. Morgan stood in front of them with his hands on his hips. "I'll be keeping an eye on you."

If Patrick had spoken those words, they'd have promised protection. Coming from his brother, they made her skin prickle. Forcing a smile, Dani looked at the girls. "Mr. Morgan is treating us to ice cream."

Emma and Ellie murmured a polite "thank you." Esther squealed with delight and ran to the door.

"Don't leave the store," he said to Dani. "I'll meet you inside."

Feeling his eyes on her back, she led the girls into the ice creamery, then watched through the window as Mr. Morgan neared the attorney's office. He had to climb a flight of stairs, knock on a door and wait in a lobby. Dani grabbed Esther's hand. "Let's go."

Emma and Ellie headed for the door, but Esther dug in her heels. "I want ice cream!"

"Later, sweetie."

"Now!"

"Esther, we have to go."

Her bottom lip trembled. "But you said!"

The child wasn't being stubborn. She was a frightened little girl whose daddy hadn't come home for five days. Ice cream promised a bit of happiness. Dani searched her mind for something more appealing, found it and dropped to a crouch, putting herself at eye level with Esther. "Remember Miss Adie and the kittens?"

The child nodded.

"That's where we're going."

Esther tipped her head to the left, then to the right. The choices seesawed in the child's mind, then hit the ground with a thud. "I want ice cream!"

The woman behind the counter looked over the jars of penny candy with an arched brow. Dani thought of scooping Esther into her arms and running, but she couldn't risk creating a scene. Besides, they'd lost two valuable minutes. By now, Beau Morgan would be with Trevor Scott.

Straightening, she gave the clerk a wry smile. "I guess we're having ice cream."

As the girls placed their orders, Dani turned and peered at the window marking the attorney's office. Beau Morgan loomed behind the glass with crossed arms and an expression that gave her chills.

Chapter Three

"Have a seat, Mr. Morgan."

"I'll stand, thanks."

Beau was tired enough to sleep on his feet, but he planted himself at the window and focused on the ice-cream parlor. The odds of Clay Johnson walking down the street were slim to none, but Beau refused to let down his guard.

He also had doubts about Miss Baxter. Ever since he'd walked into the kitchen, she'd been giving him the evil eye. Her judgment of his character irked him. Time had tarnished his manners, but he'd tried to be considerate. He'd tossed blankets in the wagon for the girls, and he'd bargained with the livery owner for Miss Baxter's refund. A long time ago, simple courtesy had come naturally to him. So had conversation. He'd gone to church socials and asked pretty girls to dance. That's where he'd met Lucy. Miss Baxter reminded him of that happy time…and the hard time that had followed. She'd grieve for Patrick as he'd grieved for Lucy. Staring through the glass, Beau watched as she and the girls circled a small table.

Trevor Scott cleared his throat. "I have good news, Mr. Morgan."

"You've found a school?"

"Not exactly. I've located another relative, a Miss Harriet Lange."

"Who is she?"

"A great-aunt on Elizabeth's side of the family."

Beau frowned. She sounded old. "Where does she live?"

"Minnesota."

"It's cold there."

"There's another problem," Scott said.

"What's that?"

"She'll take Emma but not the younger girls."

The offer rubbed Beau the wrong way. He could see his nieces now, licking ice cream from glass bowls. Each one had impressed him. This week had been the worst of Emma's life, but she'd stepped up like a grown woman. He'd seen Ellie carrying a bucket of water to her daddy's grave. He didn't know what kind of flowers she'd planted, but she'd come to the house with muddy knees. And Esther...she'd never stop sucking her thumb without her sisters.

"Why Emma?" he asked.

Scott leaned back in his squeaky chair. "Miss Lange is an elderly spinster. I assume she wants companionship."

Or a servant, Beau thought. It made sense, but he knew he'd become cynical. He had a talent for spotting weeds but rarely noticed flowers, even when they filled a meadow. Maybe the woman had a kind heart but couldn't feed two more children. "Does she have an income?"

"She clerks at a bank."

A job that paid little money. Beau hooked his thumbs in his belt. He earned top dollar and saved most of it. "If money's the problem, I can solve it."

"With the sale of the farm?"

"No, that's going in the bank." He wanted the girls to

have a nest egg for later in life. "I'll pay for what they need."

"It's generous of you."

Maybe, but Beau felt no pride. What the girls needed most, money couldn't buy. They needed a home, parents who'd love them and tuck them in at night. He couldn't do those things.

Scott shifted in his chair. "If you'd like, I can present an offer to Miss Lange."

"Do it," Beau said. "Tell her it's all three or nothing. If she agrees, we'll discuss a monthly allowance."

"And if she says no?"

"We'll look for a school."

"I don't envy you, Mr. Morgan. The situation calls for the wisdom of Solomon."

Beau knew the story. Two women claiming the same child went to the Biblical king to resolve their differences. When he'd threatened to cut the baby in half, the real mother had given up the fight to save her child's life. Beau felt the same pressure. He'd do anything to keep the girls together. Anything except stay in Castle Rock. Peering through the window, he saw Miss Baxter wiping Esther's face with a white hankie. Someday she'd make a good mother. He hoped Harriet Lange would be as kind.

The attorney cleared his throat. "If you'll excuse my boldness, Mr. Morgan, there's another solution."

"What's that?"

"You could raise the girls yourself."

Beau laughed out loud. "Not in a million years."

"Why not?"

The duster covered his Colt .45, but the weapon weighed heavy on his hip. Even if he'd felt inclined to settle down, he couldn't do it until Clay Johnson had taken his last breath. Beau turned from the window and glared at the attorney. The balding man had spectacles, but that didn't mean he could see. One look at Beau's worn gun belt should have answered his question.

After staring for a bit, Beau stated the obvious. "I'm not inclined to settle down, Mr. Scott."

"Why not?"

"It's none of your business."

"You can't blame me for asking," the man said. "I knew Patrick well. We served together as elders at the church. He'd want his girls to be raised in Castle Rock."

"That's not possible."

Beau thought of Daniela Baxter but dismissed the idea of allowing her to adopt his nieces. Someday she'd marry and have babies of her own. Besides, what did she know about running a dairy farm? Since he'd been doing Patrick's work, Beau had come to respect farmers in a new way. The cows had no mercy when it came to being milked on time. Exhausted or not, Beau pulled himself out of bed at dawn, headed to the meadow to fetch the first cow, then milked them one at a time until he'd finished all ten. At night, the cows came to the gate bellowing precisely at five o'clock.

The milking started the day and ended it. In between, the driver from the local cheese factory picked up the milk cans and replaced them with empty ones. Beau had buckets to scrub and horse stalls to muck out. He also had a new field of alfalfa to plant. Patrick's first field, the one he'd planted seven years ago, would die out in a few years and no longer meet the needs of his growing herd. The cows had all given birth in March. Patrick had kept four heifer calves and sold the rest. The herd needed more forage, so he'd made plans for a second alfalfa crop. Beau had seen the half-plowed field and the seed bags in the barn. After just two days of work, he'd taken his hat off to his brother's dedication.

Hardworking or not, Patrick had died, leaving the work unfinished. In a blink the Almighty had cut him down. Beau turned back to the window. Instead of four blond heads, he saw four bowls of melting ice cream.

"What the—"

He scanned the boardwalk and saw Miss Baxter shepherding the girls to the wagon. When she glanced at the window, Beau saw the fear of a fugitive and bolted for the door.

"We're not done!" Scott called.

"Write to Miss Lange," Beau shouted from the stairwell. "Do it today!"

He raced through the door to the street where the wagon sat empty. He looked to the left but saw nothing. He snapped his eyes to the right and saw a pink skirt whipping around a corner.

He broke into a run, but the females had a two-block lead. When he reached the alley where they'd turned, he saw nothing but empty stairs, trash and piles of wood. Muttering an oath, he strode between the buildings, swiveling his head to look down each street and alley for another flash of pink.

He spotted them on Cantril Street. Miss Baxter and his nieces had slowed to a fast walk, a pace that would look hurried to bystanders but not panicked. Beau didn't know what to make of their flight. He didn't know much about little girls, but he'd tried to be pleasant. He hadn't raised his voice, and he'd cussed only once when a cow had stepped on his foot.

With Miss Baxter and the girls in plain sight, he followed at a distance, staying close to the buildings and ducking into doorways whenever the woman looked over her shoulder. He had to admire her instincts. She took numerous turns, blended with strangers and kept the girls at her side. Beau had no idea where she was headed. They'd passed the Garnet Hotel, the sheriff's office and the courthouse. He figured the girls had friends, but the houses in Castle Rock lay mostly to the east. Tired of the chase, he lengthened his stride. With his coat flapping and his boots thudding, he didn't have to maneuver around folks on the boardwalk. They jumped out of his way.

At the corner of Lewis and Sixth Streets, Miss Baxter glanced over her shoulder. Instead of taking cover, Beau stayed in plain sight. "Wait up!"

Her eyes rounded with fear. Breathless, she lifted Esther and ran with Emma and Ellie flanking her sides.

Beau broke into a run but stopped. He couldn't stand the thought of Miss Baxter catching a heel in the boardwalk. If she fell, she'd twist an ankle or worse. He'd also figured out her destination. The fool woman could have saved herself a lot worry if she'd stayed and finished her ice cream. Beau, too, had business with Josh and Adelaide Blue. With his hat low, he followed the females to the parsonage.

"Keep going!" Dani said between breaths. "We're almost there."

She didn't dare look over her shoulder. She'd spotted Beau Morgan near the bank but hoped they'd lost him by zigzagging through the grid of streets. The church rose in the distance, a wood frame building painted white with a bell and a tin steeple. The sun struck the metal, reminding her of the swords in the Bible. The Lord had told his people to turn some into ploughshares. Others were used for battle. As the steeple glinted in the sun, she thought of the sword of truth, a two-edged blade sharp enough to separate flesh from bone, truth from lies. Mr. Morgan hadn't been overtly dishonest, but neither had he been forthcoming. With three girls in her care, Dani couldn't take chances. If Pastor Blue and his wife would watch the girls, she'd go in search of the town judge. She'd show him the letters and—

"Oh, no," she mumbled.

"What is it?" Emma asked.

"Your pa's letters are in my trunk."

The girl whimpered. "That's the proof he wanted you to adopt us."

"That's right."

"Can we get them?" Emma asked.

"Not easily." Dani's plan to take the wagon had changed the instant she'd locked eyes with Beau Morgan through the window. She'd told him about Patrick's letter with good intentions, but now she wished she'd been more reserved. If he wanted to play dirty, he could destroy the letters. A custody battle would turn into a war of words.

Please, Lord. I need your help.

With mud sticking to her shoes, Dani focused on the house across from the church. Red curtains hung in the windows and flowerpots lined the railing on the wide porch. Behind the slats, she saw a hodgepodge of chairs. A large wooden spool, probably used for telegraph wire, served as a table, and a lantern sat on a barrel. The house called out a welcome.

Come and sit. Share your burdens.

Patrick had considered Reverend Blue a good friend and he'd spoken well of the man's wife. *They'll help you get settled, Dani. Pastor Josh tells stories that make the Bible come alive, and no one's kinder than Adie.* Looking at the chairs, Dani imagined pouring out her heart to a serene man of the cloth and his gentle wife.

"There she is!" Ellie said.

A red-haired woman in a green print dress and white apron stood in the doorway. At the sight of Dani and the girls, her eyes sparked with recognition, then clouded as she spied the man following in their steps. Leaving the door ajar, Adelaide Blue slipped out of sight. Clinging to Esther, Dani ran faster, praying she wouldn't stumble. Emma stayed at her side. Unburdened, Ellie outdistanced them. They had a hundred feet to go, then seventy, fifty…Dani could see the lilacs by the front door, the checks on the gingham curtains.

When they reached the yard, Adie waved them inside. The girls sped past her and collapsed on the floor. Dani spun around and saw the minister's wife facing the yard with a shotgun pressed against her shoulder. Dani went to the window, peeked through the curtains and saw Beau Morgan striding down the dirt trail parting the grass. With his hat pulled low and his duster flapping, he stirred the blades like gusting wind.

"Hold up, stranger!" Adie called.

He stopped and raised his hands over his head. Dani pressed her temple against the wall so she could see the front of the doorway. The shotgun barrel pointed steady and true.

Adie's finger rested on the trigger. "Who are you, mister?"

Laughter rumbled from Beau Morgan's chest. It struck Dani as sinister, but Adie lowered the gun.

"I don't believe my eyes," the woman said.

"Hello, Adie."

"Beau Morgan? Is that really you?"

"It sure is." Beneath the brim of his hat, his mouth widened into a roguish grin. "Are you gonna shoot me or ask me to supper?"

"What do *you* think?"

Gripping the curtain, Dani watched in shock as Adelaide Blue ran to Beau Morgan and hugged him like a long-lost brother.

Beau had thought of Josh and Adie Blue as family ever since he'd stumbled into the church Josh had started in a

Denver saloon. The Blues had taught him a simple truth. Even the mangiest of dogs liked good cooking and a clean bed. A few kind words and the meanest cur lost his growl. Add a little love—a good scratch, a woman's laughter—and that dog turned worthless. That's why Beau avoided good cooking and clean sheets. Until he brought Clay Johnson to justice, he had to keep his edge.

He stepped back from Adie. "You're as pretty as ever."

She smiled. "And you're just as ornery."

"Where's Josh?"

"Looking for Miss Baxter." Adie put her hands on her hips. "Would you care to tell me why that girl's running from you like a scared rabbit?"

"I don't know."

"Then you're blind." She looked him up and down. "You need a bath and that's the least of it."

"I·haven't had a chance."

"It's more than your looks that frightened her," Adie said. "What's got you in a twist?"

Beau lost his smile. "I got word that Clay Johnson's in the area. I'm still hunting for him."

"Oh, Beau."

"I was closing in when I stopped to see Patrick." Beau shook his head. "I ended up with a farm and a bunch of cows."

"And three little girls."

Adie's voice held a lilt. Beau appreciated her kindness but feared the glint in her eyes. Orphaned at the age of twelve, she'd suffered frightful abuses before settling with Josh and their adopted son. She treasured her family and wanted everyone to have the same joy. Until Lucy's death, Beau had felt the same way.

Adie cut into his thoughts. "Those girls need a home. What are you going to do about it?"

"I'm not sure yet."

"You could stay here and raise them."

"Forget it. I've got a call on my life and I'm following it."

Adie's face hardened. "You're talking about Johnson."

"Of course."

"Oh, Beau."

"What?"

Her eyes misted. "You've got to set that burden down."

How could she say such a thing? She'd laid out Lucy's body in the house he'd rented because his wife had liked the porch swing. That morning, Lucy had tossed up her breakfast and had gone to the doctor. Later Beau learned she'd been carrying their child. She'd put on the pink dress—his favorite—to tell him the news. Behind Adie, he saw Miss Baxter in her pink dress peeking through the red curtains. The colors turned his stomach.

Adie wrinkled her nose, then playfully fanned the air. "Go take a bath. You smell like a bear in April."

Beau grinned. "That good?"

"Worse!"

He appreciated the change in tone. "I've got business in town. I'll be back in an hour."

"Keep an eye out for Josh," she added.

Beau wanted to see his old friend but feared what the Reverend would say. The man dug deep, pulling up weeds by the roots and laying them bare for a man to see for himself. Adie had a different way. She planted seeds and expected flowers. If a man was thirsty, she gave him sweet tea. If he was hungry, she filled his belly. Beau had never known a more generous woman…or a more dangerous one. Watching Adie love the whole wretched world made him want a garden of his own.

Beau tipped his hat to her, saw that Miss Baxter had left

her post at the window, turned and headed to town. As he trudged along the path, he thought of his early years in Denver. He'd been a deputy sheriff when Joshua Blue had ridden into town with a Bible and an attitude. Before he knew it, Beau had been sitting in a saloon that doubled for a church on Sunday mornings. A year later, he'd met Lucy and married her. After her passing, Adie had fed him meals until he couldn't stand another bite and had lit out of town.

He wanted to leave now but couldn't. Patrick's girls needed him and so did Miss Baxter. What drove a woman to travel a thousand miles to marry a stranger? Beau didn't know, but he knew how it felt to hurt.

As he stepped onto the boardwalk, he caught a whiff of himself. Adie was right about that bath, but first he had to visit the Silver River Saloon. With a little luck, he'd pick up news about Clay Johnson. Beau disliked visiting saloons, but it had to be done. Men like Johnson didn't hang out at the general store, nor did they go to church on Sundays, or to socials where men and women rubbed elbows and made friends. Neither did Beau.

With his duster flapping, he strode to Scott's office to fetch the wagon, then drove back down the street, crossed the railroad tracks and found the saloon between a second mining office and a gunsmith. He stepped inside and surveyed the dimly lit room. Empty stools lined the bar. A poker table sat in the corner with a battered deck of cards but no players. He had the place to himself, so he stepped to the bar where a man with graying hair was wiping the counter.

"What'll it be?" the barkeep asked.

"Coffee."

The man set down a mug. Numb to the bitterness, Beau took a long drag of the overcooked brew. It splashed in his belly but didn't give him the usual jolt, a sign he was more tired than he knew. Grimacing, he set down the half-empty cup.

"You're a stranger here," the barkeep said.

"Sure enough."

"In town on business?"

"Just passing through." Lonely men liked to talk. Beau hoped this man was one of them.

The barkeep lifted a shot glass out of a tub and dried it with his apron. "If you need work, the mines are hiring."

"I'm looking for someone."

"Oh, yeah?"

"His name's Clay Johnson. He's about six feet with dark hair and a crooked nose." Beau wished he'd been the one to break it.

When the man raised a brow, Beau slid a coin across the counter. The barkeep slipped it into his pocket. "I've seen that fellow."

"In town?"

"About two weeks ago."

Before Patrick's death. "Any idea where he was headed?"

"None. He bought five bottles of whiskey, opened one here and walked out with the rest. I haven't seen him since."

"Anyone with him?"

"Two men."

"What did they look like?"

"I didn't pay much attention. I noticed Johnson because of his nose." The barkeep set down the glass and held out his hand. "I'm Wallace O'Day. I run a clean business."

Beau shook the man's hand. "Beau Morgan."

"Bounty hunter?"

"I'm not in it for the money."

Wallace picked up another glass. "This Johnson fellow. Is he wanted?"

"Yes." By Beau for Lucy's murder and the U.S. government for stealing horses. Of the two, the government would be kinder.

The barkeep glanced at the dregs in Beau's cup. "Want some more?"

"No, thanks." Beau slapped down a sawbuck. "If you hear anything about Johnson, remember it."

Wallace folded the money. "How do I find you?"

"I'll be back."

Beau left the saloon with thoughts of Johnson rattling like broken glass. He saw Lucy again, felt the wetness of her bodice and smelled the blood. He blinked the picture away, but the rage stayed in his blood, swimming like a thousand fish. Needing to get rid of the slithering, he walked two blocks to an emporium where he bought fresh clothes, then headed back to the bathhouse across from the Silver River.

As he neared the splintery building, one of the oldest in Castle Rock, he smelled steam, soap and dirt. The mix reminded him of a simple truth. He could get clean on the outside, but the inside was another matter. Until Clay Johnson met his end, Beau's hate would grow with every breath he took.

Weary to the bone, he stepped into a drafty building with a high ceiling. He paid a Chinese man to fill a tub, then undressed and slipped into the hot water. As he dunked his head, Beau thought about Clay Johnson. They'd been playing this game for a long time now. At first, Clay had run hard and far. Beau had nearly trapped him in Durango, but he'd fled to the Colorado Plateau and into the desert. Beau had picked up the man's trail later in Raton but had lost him near Cimarron. A year had passed before he'd gotten word of an outlaw gang raiding ranches in Wyoming.

Beau had taken a train to Laramie. He'd arrived in time

for a trial that didn't include Johnson. In exchange for prison in place of the gallows, one of Clay's cohorts had told the authorities where to find him. Beau had ridden out that day, but Clay had already vanished into the mountains.

With the memory haunting him, Beau raised his head out of the water and wiped his face. He'd been so close. A day sooner and his search would have ended. Instead, Clay had gotten word of Beau's presence and left him a message at the local saloon.

It should have been you, Sheriff. You know it. Leave me alone.

Beau had that note in his saddlebag. He had other things, too. A bullet etched with an *M* for Morgan, presumably from Johnson's gun belt. Other notes. Other tokens. Every time Beau got close, the outlaw taunted him but didn't stand and fight.

Beau wondered why.

What stopped Johnson from setting up an ambush? For five years, Beau had slept with one eye open and for good reason. In a game of cat and mouse, no man liked being the mouse. Someday Johnson would be sick of the chase and become the cat. The man would show himself and Beau would be ready. Dunking back into the scalding water, he hoped that day would come soon.

Chapter Four

"How do you know our uncle?" Ellie asked.

Dani and the girls were sitting in Adie Blue's kitchen. After insisting Dani call her by her given name, the pastor's wife had given the girls snickerdoodles and made Dani a cup of hot tea, lacing it with enough sugar to stop her hands from shaking.

With the girls staring at her, Adie sat down with a cup of her own. "Pastor Josh and I know your uncle from Denver. He used to be a sheriff."

"Where's his badge?" Ellie asked.

Adie paused. "I don't know. Maybe he left it in Denver."

"Why?" Emma hadn't touched her cookie. Of the three girls, she was most aware of their uncertain future and needed reassurance for herself and her sisters.

Dani wanted answers, too. And not just from Adie. Why had God filled her heart with love for Patrick and snatched him away? Even more troublesome, why had He left three little girls in the care of a dangerous man? Dani watched as Adie stirred her tea in slow circles, as if this were an ordinary day. But it wasn't ordinary. Each plink of the spoon sent tremors down Dani's spine.

Adie finally set her spoon in the saucer and looked at Emma. "Your Uncle Beau was married to a woman named Lucy. Something bad happened and he didn't want to be a sheriff anymore."

A wife... Dani didn't know what to think. Beau Morgan had loved a woman and been loved in return. She didn't want to feel his pain but she did.

Ellie's eyes filled with concern. "What happened?"

"It's hard to talk about, sweetie."

Emma glared at the pastor's wife. "As hard as losing Pa?"

"I'm afraid so."

Adie's eyes had the fragility of etched glass. Whatever Beau Morgan had suffered, it had been tragic, maybe violent. The girls needed to feel safe, so Dani stepped in. "I hear you have kittens," she said to Adie.

"I sure do."

Esther jumped up. Cookie crumbs bounced on the table. "I want to see them!"

Ellie caught the excitement. "Is Stephen home?"

Adie glanced at Dani to explain. "Stephen's our son. He and Ellie are the same age."

"We're best friends," Ellie added.

Dani almost smiled. It figured Ellie the tomboy would be friends with the pastor's son.

Adie looked at Ellie. "Stephen's staying at Jake Roddy's house until Sunday."

"Oh."

"But you can still play with the kittens," Adie said. "They're in the stable."

Esther ran for the door.

Adie looked at Emma. "I need to speak to Miss Dani. Would you take your sisters to the stable?"

Emma scowled. "But—"

"I know, sweetie." Adie motioned for Emma to lean closer. "You're old enough to know the facts, but Esther isn't. We need your help."

"Will you tell me later?" Emma asked.

Dani nodded. "I promise."

The girls left through the back door. Adie went to the stove where she lifted an enamel kettle and refilled their cups. "I wish Josh were here."

"Where is he?" Dani asked.

"Looking for you. He must have missed your train."

Dani squared her shoulders. "I'm glad he did. It gave me a chance to meet Mr. Morgan."

"That's not the real Beau." Adie put down the kettle. "Let's sit on the porch. I'll tell you his story, but I need to see the sky when I do."

"Why?"

"To remember that Lucy's in Heaven. Considering how she died, it's the only comfort we have." With her cup and saucer in hand, Adie led the way to the porch and indicated the hodgepodge of chairs. "Take the rocker. It's soothing."

Balancing her teacup, Dani dropped onto the chair and instantly felt the cradlelike rocking. It matched the beat of her heart, calming her thoughts as the hot tea had settled her nerves. Adie said nothing as a man in a black preacher's coat rode into the yard on a dapple gray.

"That's Josh." She set her cup on the table, then went down the stairs to meet him.

At the sight of his wife, Reverend Blue's face turned from stone to living flesh. He slid out of the saddle, slipped his arm around her waist and pulled her into a gentle hug. After lowering his chin, he whispered something in her ear. Dani ached with envy. A husband… A partner and friend. Marriage meant starting a family. It meant belonging to a person and making a home. Dani had lived in Walker County her entire life, but she'd never fitted in. She'd felt that oneness with Patrick and now he was gone.

Why, Lord?

It was a question for Reverend Blue, but the man looked nothing like the minister Dani had expected. When she dreamed of the wedding, she'd pictured him as a twin of her pastor in Wisconsin, an elderly man with kind eyes. Pastor Schmidt had called Jesus the Lamb of God. He'd taught his flock to turn the other cheek.

Reverend Blue had a mane of dark hair, hawkish eyes and a chin that looked as if it could take a punch. For a good cause, Dani suspected he'd welcome it. Would he find her cause worthy? The Blues considered Beau a friend, but they didn't know about the pistols on the porch or the secrecy in town. Dani had to convince them to help her keep the girls.

Reverend Blue guided his wife up the stairs. As Adie sat, he took off his hat and faced Dani. "I'm sorry about Patrick, Miss Baxter. It had to be a shock."

"Yes." Her throat closed.

He dropped into the chair on her right and turned it so they were seated at an angle. "Whatever you need, Adie and I will help. Train fare—"

"I'm not leaving." Dani had to make her case and she had to do it now. "I want to adopt the girls."

The Reverend's eyes stayed kind, but he lowered his chin. "I don't think—"

"I *have* to!" Dani's voice trembled. "I promised Patrick."

The Reverend traded a look with his wife. They had an entire conversation without saying a word. Jealousy raged in Dani's middle. She was mad at everyone right now—the Reverend, Adie, Beau Morgan, Patrick for leaving her, and especially God.

Adie spoke to her husband in a murmur. "I saw Beau."

"How is he?" The Reverend sounded grim.

"He looks terrible," Adie replied.

Dani jumped in. "The girls are terrified of him. Frankly, so am I."

"Of Beau?" The Reverend sounded incredulous.

"Yes." Dani pressed her point. "I don't know what he was like in Denver, but he's not fit to raise three girls. I don't care what Patrick's will says. I have letters. He'd want me to raise his daughters."

"Miss Baxter—"

"I can prove it."

Reverend Blue held her gaze. "Maybe so, but does it matter?"

"Of course, it matters!"

"Why?"

"They prove what Patrick intended."

The Reverend's eyes filled with sympathy. "God might have other plans. Patrick left a will, but—"

Her throat hurt. "The letter is more recent."

Reverend Blue sealed his lips. Dani didn't like his expression at all. He looked like a man keeping a secret. Had Beau already spoken to the Blues? Did they know about sending the girls to school?

She had to make her case. "You can't let him do it."

"Do what?" Adie asked.

"Send the girls away."

The Blues traded another look. Adie turned up her palms in confusion. "I spoke to Beau for less than a minute. I don't know what he's planning."

"I do," Dani said. "He wants to send the girls away to school. I can't let him do it. They need to be in their own home."

Adie's mouth tensed. "They certainly do."

"That's why I want to adopt them," Dani continued. "I grew up on the biggest dairy farm in Walker County. I know the business. I can run the farm and the girls can stay together. It's what Patrick would have wanted."

The Reverend said nothing. Why the silence? If he wouldn't speak, how could she convince him to support the adoption? She didn't know what to think of this hard, silent man, but she liked Adie. She turned to the preacher's wife. "Will you help me?"

"Hold on, ladies." Reverend Blue sounded like Moses about to deliver the Ten Commandments. "Things aren't that simple."

Dani frowned. "Why not?"

"Patrick's will gives Beau authority. He's a blood relative."

"He's also dirty and dangerous!" Dani didn't like her tone, but she felt overwhelmed by emotions. Sadness. Fear. An anger that needed a target. She stared hard at Reverend Blue.

He stared back. "What has Beau done to offend you?"

Dani related Emma's story about the guns, then described the trip to town. Her skin crawled at the recollection of Beau Morgan behind the window, the way his eyes had narrowed to her face. The more she relived the escape, the more deeply she disliked the man who had made it necessary. She took a breath. "I know you and Mrs. Blue consider Mr. Morgan a friend, but people change. He's not the man you once knew."

The Reverend drummed his fingers on the armrest. "Has Beau harmed you in any way?"

"No."

"Has he been harsh with the girls?"

Dani thought of the blankets in the wagon and felt petty. She recalled his smelly clothes and knew he'd worked hard. He'd sounded threatening, but his actions had been courteous, even caring. "He's been a perfect gentleman."

"That's what I'd expect." The Reverend looked her in the eye. "Let me tell you about Beau Morgan, Miss Baxter. He was the bravest, most dedicated lawman Denver ever had. He sang in the church choir. He pounded half the nails in my first church and served as a deacon. He put Bibles in jail cells for men who spat on him."

Dani didn't want Beau Morgan to be human, someone with a conscience who'd fight her for the girls. "That was five years ago. It's a long time."

"So is five minutes," he said. "That's how long it took for Beau's life to change."

Adie touched Dani's arm. "This is a horrible story, but you need to understand."

Dani's insides spun. "What happened?"

The Reverend's gaze shifted to the mountains rising in the west. "It started with a gang of horse thieves. Randall Johnson was the leader. I knew him. I knew Clay, too. They were brothers with Randall being the elder."

"How did you meet them?" Dani couldn't see the connection between the outlaws and this man of the cloth.

The Reverend's lips quirked upward. "Same way I met a lot of outlaws back then. I rode into their camp and introduced the Father, Son and Holy Ghost. That was a few months before the horse thieving started."

Dani sighed. "I guess the message didn't take."

"We don't know," the Reverend said. "But I *do* know what happened that day in October. The Johnson gang raided Cobbie Miller's place. They burned the outbuildings and made off with a dozen good horses. They also abused Cobbie's two daughters."

Dani felt both ill and furious.

The Reverend leaned back in his chair. "Cobbie stormed into town with the girls in the wagon, wrapped in blankets and looking pale. He went straight to the sheriff's office. Beau put together a posse. Three days later, he shot Randall Johnson in a fair fight. I know, because I saw it."

Dani let out her breath. "Justice was done."

"Not in Clay Johnson's mind. His brother was dead and he wanted revenge. He got it by murdering Beau's wife."

Dani gasped.

Reverend Blue stared into the distance, but his gaze lacked focus as he traveled to that bitter day in Denver. "It happened a week after Beau shot Randall. Clay sneaked into town and positioned himself on the building across from the sheriff's office. He must have been up there for hours, but Beau never made rounds that morning. Of all the stupid things, he'd busted his big toe chopping wood."

Dani blinked and saw Beau Morgan's sock with his toe poking through the hole. Five years ago, his wife would have darned it. She'd have knit him new ones. Dani didn't want to ache for him, but she did.

Adie touched her arm. "It's a hard story to hear."

"And hard to tell," said the Reverend.

"Go on," Dani urged. "I need to know."

Reverend Blue raised his chin in defiance of what he had to relive. "I know what happened because Beau told me. He's gone over that moment a thousand times. Maybe more."

Dani thought of Emma standing at the window, recalling Patrick's riderless horse and the smell of burned flesh. She heard Beau Morgan telling the child not to talk. He'd been trying to protect her from a heartache that rivaled his own. Dani had judged him as hard, yet he'd been acting with compassion.

Reverend Blue took a deep breath. "Beau was sitting at his desk with his foot on a stool when he saw Lucy pass by the window with a picnic basket. She'd been to the doctor that morning and had come to surprise him."

Her heart squeezed. A healthy young woman went to the doctor for just one reason. The picnic basket…a surprise for her husband. Tears welled in Dani's eyes.

Reverend Blue cleared his throat. "In spite of his bad toe, Beau got up to help her. When he opened the door, Johnson fired. Lucy died in Beau's arms."

In Wisconsin, Dani could look at a tulip and see God in the petals. She could catch a snowflake and see the divine beauty. Staring at the rippling grass, she saw nothing but Lucy Morgan's blood and Patrick's riderless horse. "Where was God?" she said in a whisper.

"Same place He is right now," said the Reverend.

"I don't feel Him."

"I think you do, Miss Baxter." She felt the Reverend's gaze on the side of her face. "I see tears in your eyes. Our Lord's weeping, too. For Beau. For you. For those three little girls. Bad things happen. It's a fact. But the Lord will see you through."

"I know that's true," Dani murmured. "It *has* to be true."

Yet she couldn't shake the niggling fear that she'd left God in Wisconsin. She looked to the Reverend for comfort but didn't find it. His eyes were on his wife, blazing with a protectiveness that tore Dani's heart in two. With Patrick's death, she could only dream of a man looking at her that way.

The Reverend's throat twitched with emotion.

Adie's eyes misted.

Dani's throat hurt. It tightened even more when the girls spilled out of the stable door. Emma had a blanket draped over her arm. Ellie had the box of kittens and Esther's little legs pumped as she tried to keep up with her sisters. Dani raised her chin. God had denied her a husband, but she could still be a mother.

The Reverend broke into her thoughts. "I spoke at Lucy's

funeral." He bit off the last word, as if he could barely say it. "I'm a man of God, Miss Baxter. I believe in Heaven and Hell and living well in between, but I could barely say a word that day."

Adie interrupted. "I'll tell the rest. I'm the one who cooked Beau his last meal."

"It was roast beef," the Reverend said.

"And raspberry pie. I'd given Lucy the recipe."

Dani bit her lip to fight the dread.

Adie laced her fingers together. "I'll never forget that last night on the porch. Lucy had been gone a month when Beau said he was leaving town. As cold as death, he said, 'I'm going to hunt down Clay Johnson and kill him.'"

"I believed him," said the Reverend.

"I still do," Adie replied.

Dani shivered. "That's why he's been so protective, isn't it? Clay Johnson…is he in the area?"

"Beau thinks so," Adie said.

Fear, danger and dirt. Beau Morgan had brought all three into the lives of three little girls. Dani's heart broke for his loss, but she feared for Patrick's daughters. She turned to Adie. "I have a favor to ask."

"Anything."

"Could the girls and I stay with you a few days?"

Adie tilted her head. "Are you still afraid of Beau?"

"No," Dani replied. "But I *am* afraid of Clay Johnson. What if he comes to the farm?"

Adie looked at Josh. "Dani has a point."

"I'll speak to Beau," said Reverend Blue. "He'll know best."

Dani thought of the ride through town. Surely Beau would want to keep them safe. "Thank you."

Adie touched her shoulder. "You must be exhausted. Would you like to rest a bit?"

Dani shook her head. "If I close my eyes, I'll see Patrick."

"A walk might be nice," Adie said kindly.

"I think I will. Is the church open?"

"Always," said the Reverend.

As she pushed to her feet, Dani looked at the tin steeple. The sun had dropped in the sky, turning it from silver to gray. The edges no longer seemed so sharp. Maybe she'd go inside. Maybe she wouldn't. Mostly she wanted to cry and she wanted to do it alone. She looked across the yard and saw the girls. They seemed content, but in the distance she saw the stirring of dust from a wagon and recognized Beau Morgan holding the reins. He had her future in his hands, as well. She had to convince him she could handle the girls and the farm. That would be hard to do if they stayed with the Blues, but neither did she like the idea of an outlaw stalking them.

Patrick? Are you watching? What should I do?

Silence.

With her heart aching, Dani headed for the cemetery.

Beau steered the wagon into the yard and stopped. The chairs on the porch sent him back in time to Denver, where Josh and Adie had lived in a Mansion named Swan's Nest. Beau and another deputy had taken to visiting on Wednesday nights. During the third visit, Josh had opened his Bible and read scriptures from Proverbs, the funny ones about fools and carping women. Their little group had turned into the Wednesday Ruckus, a men's Bible study that didn't mince words. That's how Beau got roped into church on Sunday... How he'd met Lucy.

As he climbed down from the seat, he saw Josh come out of the parsonage. The man looked harder than ever. Rail thin and tall, he resembled a chimney pipe. Beau wasn't in the mood for Josh's kind of fire, but he was glad to see his old friend.

"Hello, Reverend."

"Reverend?" The preacher faked a scowl. "You used to call me Josh."

Beau offered his hand to shake, but Josh pulled him into a bear hug and thumped him hard between the shoulder blades. Beau pounded back. In Denver he'd enjoyed having friends, men who'd told jokes when times were bright and stayed quiet when they weren't. He missed them. He missed a lot of things. He stepped back. "It's been a long time."

"Five years, friend." Josh's eyes burned like coal. "Where in the world have you been?"

"I think you know."

"Only what you told Adie." Josh put his hands on his hips, pulling back the flaps of his coat. "You and I need to talk."

"No, we don't." Beau's voice dropped to a growl. He didn't want to hear about forgiving his enemies. He wanted an eye for an eye. He wanted Clay Johnson to swing from a rope.

Josh aimed his chin at the girls. "You have three children in your care."

"I know that."

"And Miss Baxter, too."

"Only because she's too stubborn to go home." Beau looked at the red curtains in the window. He half expected to see Miss Baxter spying on him, but the gingham hung straight. "Where is she?"

"Taking a walk. I'm sorry about Patrick."

"Me, too," Beau said. "Those girls are suffering."

"So's Miss Baxter."

Beau didn't need to be reminded of the woman's tears. He'd been the one to deliver the bad news. He'd felt the same pain when Lucy died. "I know all about it."

"Yes, you do."

Beau appreciated Josh's plain tone. He hated pity, but he hated Clay Johnson even more. A bitter rage burned in Beau's soul. "Johnson's close, Josh. I can smell him."

"Is he a threat?"

"I don't know."

Beau told Josh about the trinkets Johnson had left him, the taunting letters. "I don't know what he'll do next. He could run, or he could turn the tables and come after me."

Josh folded his arms again. "You know what I'm going to say."

"I don't want to hear it." Beau thought back to Lucy's funeral. To Josh's credit, he hadn't said a word about forgiveness. He'd saved that speech for the day Beau rode out of Denver.

Bitterness will eat you alive, my friend. Vengeance belongs to the Lord.

Fine, but Beau wanted to be the man to put the noose around Johnson's neck. As soon as he took care of his nieces, he'd get back to the business of revenge. As for the bothersome Baxter woman, she'd be better off in Wisconsin with her family.

Josh's expression stayed hard. "Adie tells me you scared the daylights out of Miss Baxter. That was a fool thing to do."

Beau grunted. "She's as green as grass."

"Not from what I can see."

"Then you haven't seen much."

"I've seen plenty." Josh looked Beau up and down. "Looks like you found time for a bath."

Beau wished he'd worn his duster over his new clothes. The blue shirt made him feel like a dandy, and so did the brown leather vest. The gun belt still hugged his hip, but he'd slicked back his hair and his jaw had a shine. Beau scowled. "Adie shamed me into it."

"Adie's wise."

She was also a good cook. Beau smelled supper on the stove. His mouth watered, but he refused to be hungry.

Josh eyed him thoughtfully. "Thanks to your bad manners, Miss Baxter wants to stay here with the girls."

Beau toyed with the idea but rejected it. "The woman can do whatever she wants, but I want the girls on the farm."

"Is it safe?" Josh asked.

"As safe as I can make it." His nieces shared his name. Beau wanted them where he could see them. He didn't expect Johnson to ride into town, but the outlaw had a sick mind.

"Can I give you some advice?" Josh asked.

"Can I stop you?"

"No, so here it is. The girls think of Miss Baxter as their new mother. They think of you as an intruder. They trust her. No matter what you decide, things will be easier if she's on your side."

"That won't happen."

"Why not?"

"She made a promise to Patrick. She wants to adopt the girls."

"I know." Josh lowered his voice. "I know something else."

"What?"

"I can't share it with you."

Beau thought of Emma standing at the farmhouse window. *He went to see Pastor Josh. He was in a hurry.* Had Patrick gotten cold feet? Beau remembered the day before he'd married Lucy. He'd been crazy about her, but his knees had turned to jelly before the wedding. If Patrick had changed his mind, Miss Baxter's promise to adopt the girls meant nothing. She'd be free to go home to Wisconsin.

Beau hated secrets, but he trusted Josh. "You know best."

"I hope so."

No matter what troubled the minister, Beau knew he'd wield the sword of truth with discretion. Before coming to Colorado, Joshua Blue had been a high-and-mighty preacher in Boston. He'd suffered for his misplaced words and knew the power of a loose tongue.

So did Beau. He'd spoken too quickly when he'd asked Daniela Baxter to stay at the farm. His belly had been growling and he hadn't given the situation enough thought. The girls were already too attached to her. With each day, that tie would grow stronger and they'd all end up heartbroken. With Harriet Lange in the picture, Beau hoped the situation would be resolved in a matter of days, a few weeks at the most. He could live on pancakes until then.

As for Daniela Baxter, she'd be better off with the Blues. Once the shock of Patrick's death wore off, Beau felt sure she'd head home to Wisconsin.

"Where is she?" he asked. "I need to speak with her."

"Look in the church."

His stomach lurched. No way would he go inside that building. He turned to ask Josh to fetch her, but the minister had already slipped into the house. Beau turned back to the building and scowled at it. He'd gone to church twice after Lucy's death. With a groaning deeper than words, he'd hit his knees. "The Lord is my shepherd, I shall not want…"

That day, Beau had wanted Lucy so bad he couldn't catch his breath. He no longer felt the freshness of the first cut of loss, but he remembered those days bitterly…and the nights, too. He'd slept with his face buried in Lucy's nightgown, breathing in her lilac scent. He'd pressed her pillow to his belly and curled around it.

Surely goodness and mercy… What goodness? Mercy for whom?

Yea, though I walk through the Valley of the Shadow of

Death... A valley so long it never ended. A shadow so dark it mocked the night.

I shall fear no evil...

At least that much of the Psalm was true. Nothing scared Beau, least of all death. For five years, he'd been living in a fog of misery so thick it blinded him worse than night. Standing in the yard, he took in the church. The front steps numbered four and were as wide as the double doors. Brass knobs, lit by the sun, waited to be turned. The building, Beau realized, was a twin of the one Josh had built in Denver. Tall windows would line the sides, and the pulpit would be adorned with a soaring eagle.

Annoyed, he climbed the stairs and gripped the doorknob. The brass warmed his palm, but his blood ran cold. Where was God when Lucy died? Where was God now? Beau couldn't stand the thought of going inside the church. As he turned away, he heard someone weeping in the garden. It had to be the Baxter woman. When Lucy died, Beau had been embraced by friends. She had no one. He considered leaving, but he had to speak with her. He also knew exactly how she felt. With his throat tight, he headed for the garden. At the gate, he plucked a lily.

Too late, he realized the flowers marked a cemetery. In the far corner he saw the woman sitting on a bench. He took in her pink dress, the pink roses climbing on the rock wall, the pinkish hue of the grave markers. He couldn't stand all that rosiness, but neither could he walk away. With the lily in hand, Beau went to offer the comfort he'd yet to find for himself.

Chapter Five

The markers in the cemetery were unlike anything Dani had ever seen. They were made from rhyolite, a pinkish-gray stone that made her think of blood mixed with ash. In particular she noticed the stone cross in front of the bench. The crossbars ended in scallops that resembled open hands. The grass had been trampled and someone had left a single rose, now shriveled, at the foot of the marker. Tears welled in Dani's eyes. She'd miss Patrick forever, but God willing, she'd find comfort in raising his daughters and offer it in return. It all depended on Beau Morgan.

Dani bowed her head. *Are You there, Lord?*

Silence.

I need Your help and so do the girls. With her stomach quivering, Dani poured out her heart to the cross. Surely God had a plan for her life, a purpose. She *had* to believe that. She couldn't bear the thought of going back to Wisconsin and intruding on her brother. Apart from her tattered pride, she had no hope of a future in Walker County.

Please, Lord, make my path straight. Show me Your will.

"Amen," she said out loud.

A man cleared his throat.

She opened her eyes and saw a shadow across the grave. Expecting to see Reverend Blue, she looked up. Instead of the minister, she saw Beau Morgan with his hat in one hand and a lily in the other. He'd bathed and bought new clothes. The blue shirt turned his eyes a truer green, and his brown trousers still had a crease. He'd been to the barber, too. Dani took in his clean-shaven jaw and the dip in his upper lip. Without the grit and the dust, Beau Morgan was a handsome man. Even more handsome than Patrick. Dani felt disloyal, but she had to tell the truth. She also had to convince him she could care for the girls and run the farm.

He offered her the lily. "This is in honor of Patrick."

"Thank you."

She held the white trumpet by the stem. Missing Patrick's funeral had denied her a line in the sand, a place that marked before and after. She'd found it today in the cemetery.

Beau glanced at the lily, then stared into her eyes. "It's hard saying goodbye, even harder with things unsaid."

Dani's heart ached. "You understand."

"I do."

She didn't want any deception between them. "Adie told me about your wife. I'm sorry for your loss."

He gave a curt nod. "It was a long time ago."

"But you still miss her."

"Of course."

Dani didn't want to bring up painful memories, but she had to put the girls first. "I don't mean to pry, Mr. Morgan. But the Blues told me about Clay Johnson."

"What about him?"

"Are the girls in danger?"

"That's my concern." He put his Stetson back on his head and pulled it low. The sun lit up half his face, leaving the other side in the shadow of the brim. In a cemetery, the gesture smacked of disrespect.

Dani stood up from the bench and faced him. "The girls are my concern, too. The Blues are willing to take us in. I think that would be wise."

"You're free to accept," he said. "But the girls are staying with me."

"If there's danger—"

"There's *always* danger."

Bitterness spilled from his skin. Dani couldn't stand the thought of leaving the girls in his care. She looked him hard in the eye. "I have to know, Mr. Morgan. Is it safe to be around you?"

As soon as Dani said the words, she regretted them. His wife had taken a bullet meant for him. Being around Beau Morgan wasn't safe at all.

He sneered at her. "Let's put it this way. It's as safe to be around me as it is to be on a horse in a thunderstorm."

Dani blinked and recalled the charred pine. This morning she'd expected Patrick to greet her train. Now she was at the mercy of this bitter man. If he wouldn't let the girls stay with the Blues, Dani would have to stay with them. "You have a point," she said mildly. "We'll be fine on the farm."

The man rocked back on his heels. "I won't be needing your help after all. The situation's changed."

Dani stiffened. "How so?"

"Scott's located another relative, a great-aunt in Minnesota."

He told her about Harriet Lange's offer to take Emma, his concern about the woman's finances and his offer to provide a monthly allowance if she'd take all three girls. Dani searched her memory, but Patrick had written nothing about the girls' grandparents or cousins. She had asked about Elizabeth's family, but he'd ignored her question. She'd figured his first marriage was too personal to share in writing and hadn't pushed.

Beau Morgan shifted his weight. His gun belt creaked. "If things go as I expect, the girls will be leaving for Minnesota in a week or two."

"You can't do that!" Dani cried.

"Yes, I can."

"But this is their home!"

He said nothing.

She gestured to the town. "The girls have friends here, people who know them."

"It's for the best."

"Who says?"

"I do." He sounded kind. The tone threw Dani off balance, so did the regret in his eyes. "If I could, I'd bring Patrick back to life. I'd do a lot of things, Miss Baxter. But I don't have that power. If Harriet Lange's willing to raise my nieces, I'm going to let her."

Dani felt close to panic. "Let me do it."

"No."

"Why not?"

His brow furrowed with impatience. "Where would you live?"

"On the farm, of course."

"I mean no disrespect, Miss Baxter. But do you have any idea how much work it is to run a dairy?"

If a man could be judged by his hands, so could a woman. Dani tugged off her gloves a finger at a time. She put them in her pocket, then held out her hands palm up. "What do you see, Mr. Morgan?"

His eyes softened. "Calluses."

"What else?"

"You've got long fingers."

"Would you care to guess how many times I've milked a cow?"

"Quite a few."

Dani lowered her hands. "My father owned the biggest dairy in Walker County. He grew it from five cows to fifty. I know the business and I'm not afraid of hard work. We'd have to hire help for the busy times, but—"

"No."

Her words came faster. "Did you see the lumber by the barn?"

"What about it?"

"It's for a silo. My father built one six years ago. It'll hold enough feed for the entire winter. I sent Patrick the plans before I left."

He spread his boots in the dirt and crossed his arms. "That's all well and good, but—"

"The cows should have been bred a few weeks ago. Did you check his records?"

He stared in disbelief.

Dani had no time to be shy about nature's ways. "If a bull didn't visit, we're in trouble. Without calves, the cows won't have milk."

Mr. Morgan looked amused. "Is that a fact?"

"Of course." Dani didn't see the humor. "A second cheese factory is opening. Have you gotten prices?"

He said nothing.

"Denver's booming. With a daily train, we can sell twice as much dairy as we do now." Dani saw boundless opportunity, but Beau Morgan looked like a man with a headache.

He put his hands on his hips. "You're obviously knowledgeable, Miss Baxter. But my answer is still no."

"Why?"

"Who's going to do the heavy lifting?"

"I'll do what has to be done."

"That's foolish."

She wanted to quote Proverbs, the verses about the woman who bought land and sold it, fed her family and worked tirelessly into the night, but Beau Morgan had made it clear that he didn't feel close to God. Quoting scripture would serve no purpose, but neither would she apologize for telling the truth. After years in the dairy business, she knew how to bargain. "I'll make you a deal, Mr. Morgan."

"What's that?"

"The way I see it, you have a problem. You have three little girls in your care, and you don't know the first thing about children."

"That's true."

"You're an honorable man. You want to provide for their future."

"Right again."

Dani's heart pounded. "The problem is your demeanor. You showed up looking like a grizzly bear, then you scared the daylights out of them by sitting on the porch with your guns. They don't like you, but they like me."

"What's your point?"

"I *know* I can run a dairy farm. Give me two weeks. If you're not convinced that it's best for the girls to stay with me in Castle Rock, I'll take them to Minnesota myself."

Beau Morgan shook his head. "I can't allow it."

"Why not?"

"Like I said, the girls will get attached to you."

"They already are."

He rubbed the back of his neck, a sign of frustration.

Dani decided to press. "I know my way around a kitchen, Mr. Morgan. Just think…fried chicken and biscuits as light as air."

He glared at her. "That's not fair."

"I thought you said Emma was a good cook." Dani knew from the child's letters that her biscuits were rock hard. Even Patrick had complained. *Emma tries, but she doesn't have a knack for cooking.*

Beau's grimace showed he held the same opinion, but his eyes twinkled. "I lied and you know it."

She smiled. "There's a peach tree on the side of the house. Do you like cobbler, Mr. Morgan?"

He looked ravenous but said nothing.

"How about peach jam?"

Laughing out loud, he pushed back his hat. The shadow dividing his face disappeared, leaving only light. "You win. But on one condition."

"What's that?"

"I like raspberry pie."

Dani thought of Adie's story about Beau's last meal in Denver. "I'd be glad to make it for you."

"In that case, we have a deal. You have two weeks to prove yourself and my word that I'll be fair."

"I never doubted that you would be."

Dani held out her hand. Beau glanced down, then gripped her fingers, engulfing them in his. The handshake sealed the deal, but the future was far from certain. She didn't doubt Beau's integrity or her ability to run the farm, but today had taught Dani a lesson. Anything could happen to anyone at any time.

She looked into Beau's eyes and saw the same uncertainty. Earlier Dani had prayed for God to make her path straight. For reasons she didn't understand, that path now involved this hard, troubled man. She didn't understand why. She only knew she liked him. He cared about his nieces. He worked hard. A long time ago, he'd loved his wife with the devotion commanded by God. As for Clay Johnson and Beau's search for justice, Dani prayed he'd find peace.

He broke off the handshake and stepped back. "It's time to go, Miss Baxter."

"Please, call me Dani."

His eyes darkened. "We're not friends. We're business partners."

"Whatever you'd like," she replied gently. "I was thinking of the girls. They might like you better if you seem less…distant."

"I like distance." He jerked his chin toward the gate. "Let's go."

With the lily in hand, Dani brushed by him. She caught a whiff of shaving soap and thought about the odd way of appearances. Beau Morgan had cleaned up on the outside, but his soul was still full of grit. She didn't care for his bad manners, but she could tolerate them. As long as he gave her a chance to prove herself, she'd could put up with just about anything.

As they left the cemetery, Beau called himself a fool. Raspberry pie? What had he been thinking? No good could come from letting Dani Baxter stay at the farm. He didn't believe for a minute she could handle the cows and the crops alone, but he couldn't back out now. When they reached the parsonage, he caught a whiff of pot roast, thought about fried chicken and scolded himself for thinking with his belly instead of his brain.

Adie met them on the steps. "You're staying for supper, aren't you?"

"Yes, thank you," Dani answered.

Almost drooling, Beau followed the women like a hungry puppy and took a seat at the maple table he remembered from Denver. His nieces filled the chairs at his sides, Josh sat at the head, and Dani sat across from him and near Adie and the kitchen. It was the most company he'd had in a long time. To his embarrassment, he became the guest of honor.

Your Uncle Beau caught a bank robber.

Your Uncle Beau helped us build our church.

The chatter lasted through supper and into dessert. With his plate clean and his coffee cup empty, Beau felt both satisfied and empty. Esther slid out of her chair and climbed on Dani's lap. Ellie smiled at him. Even Emma seemed at ease. If it hadn't been for Clay Johnson, this would have been his life. He and Lucy would have raised a family.

Beau drained the last of his coffee, a brew far better than the muck at the saloon, then set down the cup. His gaze landed on Dani with Esther wiggling in her lap. Like himself, she looked wistful. Clay Johnson had robbed Beau of a family. A lightning bolt had robbed Dani of the same pleasure. God, it seemed, had turned His back on them both.

Seething inside, Beau pushed to his feet. "It's time to go. The cows won't wait."

"Of course," Dani said.

Esther jumped down from her lap. "We have to say goodbye to the kittens."

Beau opened his mouth to say no, but Adie took the child's hand. "Let's go, girls. I have something special for you."

Dani stood. "I'll start the dishes."

"No, you won't." Josh had used his preaching voice, the one that boomed. "You've got enough to do with those girls. I'll give Adie a hand."

Beau grinned. He couldn't help it. He remembered Josh and Adie teasing each other in the kitchen during a church potluck. Every bachelor had been envious. That night, Beau had decided to marry Lucy. Before his gaze could slide to

Dani, he turned his back and walked into the front room where he saw a stone hearth. Tonight Josh would build a fire. Adie would sew and he'd read his Bible.

Beau had spent a thousand nights under open sky, sitting by fires he'd built for himself and no one else. He craved that solitude now, but he had four females in his care and a pasture full of cows who'd be bawling up a storm if they didn't get home soon. Dani had passed him and was putting on her hat. He turned to tell her to hurry up but stopped without saying a word.

She'd bent her neck and raised her arms to stick in a pin. Tendrils of blond hair fell across her nape, brushing the collar of her pink dress. Beau couldn't stand the sight of her, but neither could he turn away. How long had it been since he'd seen a woman put on a hat? How long would it be before it happened again? Weeks, months, maybe years…whatever it took to bring Johnson to justice. Never mind the lonely ache in his chest. He owed it to Lucy to hunt down the man who'd robbed them of a future. God had blinked that day, but Beau had seen every drop of her blood. He wanted vengeance, no matter the cost.

Daniela Baxter was a distraction he couldn't afford. He made his voice hard. "Are you ready?"

"I am now," she replied.

Beau strode forward. Josh cut in front of him and opened the door, motioning her to pass as if she were a queen. When she smiled her thanks, Beau wanted to slug Josh. His reaction made no sense. Josh had been raised in Boston, the son of a shipping tycoon, and he had the manners to prove it. He was also a minister, a shepherd guiding a lost lamb.

Why hadn't God provided that protection for Lucy? Seeing Josh and Adie, sharing a meal, Dani and her hat… Beau couldn't take the reminders of what he'd lost. He wanted to get home, milk the blasted cows and sit alone in the dark. Pulling his hat low, he followed Dani to the wagon where Adie and the girls were huddled at the tailgate.

Beau smelled trouble. He'd have gone for his gun, but the suspects were three little girls and a preacher's wife. Striding forward, he tried to sound casual. "What are you ladies looking at?"

Emma hunched over something in her arms. Ellie gave him a pleading look. Esther was bouncing on her feet like a rabbit thumping its back leg. He looked to Dani for an explanation and saw a chin as hard as his own.

"Miss Adie gave the girls a kitten," she said. "Isn't that nice?"

Beau couldn't believe his ears. What was the woman thinking? As soon as he could make arrangements, the girls would be headed to Minnesota. What if Harriet Lange didn't like cats? What if she was allergic? If she didn't take the girls, he'd be sending them to school. They'd suffer another heartbreak, one that could have been avoided.

Beau glared at Adie. "You should have asked me."

"Maybe," she said. "But it's done now."

Emma straightened her shoulders, revealing a black-and-white kitten with blue eyes and a pink tongue. It yawned, then snuggled in the crook of her elbow. As hard as he'd become, even Beau couldn't tell the girls to give the cat back. Feeling like a fool, he worried about where the kitten would sleep. Tonight the little fellow would cry for his mama and brothers.

Dani scratched the kitten's neck. "A boy or a girl?"

"A boy," said Adie.

"He'll be a fine mouser," Josh added.

The kitten stretched, revealing three white paws and one black one. He looked as if he'd lost a shoe.

Beau gave up. "We best get going."

After hugs and promises for Sunday, the girls scrambled into the wagon. Beau closed the tailgate, then approached Dani and Adie who were jabbering like magpies. Beau felt an old stirring. In Denver, Lucy had taken forever to leave church because she'd had so many friends. Beau would stand at her side, grinning like a fool.

Josh shot him a look of male commiseration, but Beau wasn't grinning now. He cleared his throat. "Miss Baxter?"

Dani glanced at him. "I'm ready."

She hugged Adie, then turned to the wagon. Before Josh could step forward, Beau gave her a hand up to the seat. The minister wasn't the only man with manners. Beau's just needed a little polishing. He tipped his hat to Adie, shook Josh's hand and climbed onto the seat. After pulling on his gloves, he took the reins and headed home.

Home.

The word caught in his mind like barbed wire. He didn't have a home and he didn't want one. The giggles coming from the bed of the wagon gave him a headache. So did the sun setting over the blue cut of the mountains and the streak of pink in the sky. Dusk usually calmed him. It meant the end of a day, solitude and the peace of sleep. Today the fading sun pressed him to hurry. The cows needed milking. The girls needed their beds.

"Beau?"

Dani's voice matched the dusk. He hadn't invited her to use his given name, but it sounded natural.

"What is it?" he asked.

"Supper was nice. When we first met, I didn't know you were a lawman."

He grunted. "Josh talks too much."

From the corner of his eye, he saw Dani lace her fingers in her lap. "They like you."

Beau said nothing. The man they'd known in Denver had died with Lucy.

"I don't mean to pry." Her voice dipped low. "But you were good at your work. Do you miss it?"

"I never gave it up."

"You mean Clay Johnson."

"And others." Beau shifted his weight. "Johnson rides in and out of my life. Sometimes I get close and he runs. Sometimes he comes after me, makes a threat and runs again. It can take months to pick up his trail."

"What do you do in between?"

"I check Wanted posters."

"How do you choose?" Dani asked.

Mostly Beau got a feeling. "I pick the man with the deadest eyes."

He heard the soft rush of her breath. "You're a bounty hunter."

Beau frowned. "I don't do it for the money. I do it for—"

"Lucy."

He doubted his wife would approve. "I was going to say justice."

Dani stared straight ahead. "The Blues respect you. I want you to know. I do, too."

A woman's praise shouldn't have made Beau square his shoulders, but it did. Aside from earning a living, he found satisfaction in his work. He brought peace to widows and orphans. He helped people who couldn't help themselves. Most of the time, he felt content with his cause, but tonight he missed the things he'd given up.

With dusk settling, he wished he'd never set eyes on Daniela Baxter and her pink dress, his nieces with their blond hair, even the kitten. Parted from its mother and brothers, the poor thing was meowing its heart out. Beau knew how it felt.

If the girls weren't careful, it would bite and scratch out of frustration.

Emma's voice carried over the rattle of the wagon. "We have to decide on a name."

"I like Fluffy," said Esther.

Beau winced. No male deserved a handle like Fluffy. He felt offended on the cat's behalf but didn't say anything.

"He's a boy," Ellie said, sounding superior. "Let's call him Prince."

Beau clenched his teeth. Prince beat out Fluffy, but not by much. The kitten was destined to lose all dignity.

Dani turned to the girls. "How about Boots?"

It fit, but Beau didn't like it.

"It's kind of plain," Emma said.

The females batted around names, each one as unmanly as the last. After a mile, Beau had heard enough. "Name him Fred."

"Fred?" The females cried out in a horrified chorus.

"Or Hank or Sam," he said. "Anything but Fluffy."

He'd stunned the girls into silence. Beau reveled in the quiet until Esther spoke up. "Uncle Beau?"

Until now, no one had called him by that name. His belly flipped. "What is it?"

"What name do *you* like?" asked the child.

He thought for a minute. "I'd call him T.C. for Tom Cat."

"I like it," Emma said.

"Me, too," Ellie added.

Dani hummed her approval. "T.C.'s an excellent name."

Beau turned in her direction and saw a shine in her eyes, a longing that matched the pull in his gut. Children…laughter… hope. When she turned to the kitten and smiled, he saw it as an act of defiance. Dani Baxter would grab the rope of happiness, no matter how frayed, and hold on. His belly burned. If Harriet Lange took his offer, that rope would be yanked from her hands.

Beau knew how that felt. Her flesh would tear and bleed. He wanted to tell her to let go now, to forget the kitten and the little girls, but he knew she wouldn't do it.

She must have sensed his gaze, because she turned to him. When her lips tipped into a smile, a sad one but honest, Beau felt it like his own. He jerked his eyes back to the road. T.C. meowed hungrily. Dani stared straight ahead. "We'll give him milk as soon as we get home."

Fool that he was, Beau felt happy for the cat.

Clay Johnson lifted the rope from his saddle, made a noose and slipped it around his horse's neck. It pained him to put her down, but Ricochet had stepped in a prairie dog hole and busted her leg.

He'd ridden a thousand miles on the mare, maybe more. Unlike other females, she didn't recoil when he came near. She'd nuzzle his hand and look for apples. Sometimes he thought she liked him. Clay had nothing to give but a quick death, so he unholstered his pistol, pressed the barrel between the mare's eyes and pulled the trigger.

Clay would have said a prayer if he'd thought God was listening, but he had no such illusions. No one could forgive a man who'd done as much harm as Clay. He'd hated. He'd stolen. He'd cursed. He'd even murdered a woman.

He'd never forget shooting Lucy Morgan. He'd been aiming for her husband when she'd rushed into the man's arms. The bullet had hit her square in the back. Clay could still see Morgan's eyes, going wide and then searching the roof across the street. He'd seen the puff of smoke and spotted Clay lowering the rifle. Clay knew he'd signed his own death warrant. A wife trumped a brother in any man's book, including Clay's. He hadn't been ready to die, so he'd run.

He still wasn't ready, though at times like this, with

Ricochet gone and Morgan dogging him, he thought about eternity and wondered if the stories about Heaven were true. He remembered his ma's Bible and a picture of Noah's ark. Did animals go to Heaven? Clay hoped so. As he looked back at Ricochet's remains, he coughed to hide the lump in his throat. Holstering the weapon, he looked uphill for his partners. Before putting Ricochet down, he'd transferred his saddle to his packhorse. To keep the other animals from spooking, his partners, Goose and Andy, had led them up the trail.

Clay called out to them. "It's done. Bring my horse."

"Sure thing, boss," Andy shouted.

Clay watched as Andy led the gelding down the hill. With his red hair and freckles, he looked more like a kid than the con man he was. Goose, short for Augusto, watched him from the top of the trail. Mounted on a mustang, he took off his hat and wiped his brow, revealing white teeth and the blue-black hair brushing his shoulders. Goose liked guns and money, in that order.

Clay had met the pair in Laramie. Like himself, they were horse thieves by trade. For the past six months, the trio had been raiding ranches near the Rockies, staying a step ahead of Beau Morgan and the law. Clay didn't mind posses on his tail, but Morgan had gotten on his last nerve. The man wouldn't quit. Deep down, Clay didn't blame him. Was there a greater sin than killing a man's wife? Clay didn't think so.

Andy arrived with the gelding. "Too bad about Ricochet. She was a good animal."

"The best," Clay said.

Andy turned his pony, a quarter horse with a pretty face and big rump, and spurred it up the trail.

As Clay mounted the gelding, he missed Ricochet even more. The packhorse had a swayback and no spirit. When

Clay nudged it with his heels, the animal laid back its ears. He kicked it hard. The beast bucked forward, throwing him off balance.

Andy cackled.

"Shut up," Clay bellowed.

The kid hooted like a coyote.

Clay tasted venom. "I said *shut up*."

When Andy hooted again, Goose chuckled with him. "Face it, boss. That horse is a cut *below* a mule."

Clay pulled up next to his partners. Goose's mustang had sure feet. Andy's pony could outsprint anything with legs. Ricochet could have bested them both. Clay missed her so much he felt the press of tears. No animal could replace her, but he needed a better mount than the gelding. The problem was finding one. He couldn't go into Castle Rock and buy a horse. The last time Clay had gotten wind of Morgan, he'd been in Denver. The man was closing in.

Mounted on a nag, Clay wouldn't have a chance if Morgan caught up to him. He and his partners had been headed south to the San Juan Mountains. That course still seemed wise. They needed to move as quick as they could. As soon they reached a town, Clay would buy a horse or steal one.

As he neared his partners, Clay saw Andy's stupid grin and Goose's mocking eyes. "Let's get moving," he said.

Goose rested his hands on the saddle horn. "Hold up, boss. Andy and I have a plan."

"What?"

Goose's lips thinned to a sneer. "The Rocking J's twenty miles back."

Clay had heard of the place, but he'd never seen it. The Rocking J, owned by John Baylor, raised the finest quarter horses in Colorado.

"What's your point?" Clay asked, though he suspected he knew.

"I say we make a raid," Goose answered.

Andy rested his hands on the saddle horn. "So do I."

"Think about it," Goose said. "We take as many horses as we can manage and head for the mountains. We get money in our pockets, and you get a decent horse."

Clay saw the logic. If it weren't for Morgan, he'd have been eager. Sticking around Douglas County didn't appeal to him, but neither did getting caught on a swaybacked gelding.

He turned to Goose. "I'm listening. How's the place laid out?"

"Open. Unprotected. The man has three daughters—"

"Whoo-hooo!" shouted Andy.

Clay wished he'd left the fool in Wyoming. "Shut up. We're talking about horses, not women."

"That's right," Goose said.

"How many head?" Clay asked.

"Twenty, maybe more."

Clay liked the idea of making money and the lay of the land worked in their favor. The canyons twisted like gnarled fingers attached to a hand. A man could move south or hide, depending on his mood. Clay saw one drawback. "If we raid the Rocking J, Morgan'll come after us for sure."

"So what?" Goose said.

Clay stayed silent. Sometimes he felt compelled to draw Morgan out. He half hoped the man would catch up to him and end the misery. Other times, Clay felt so guilty for killing the man's wife he wanted to die himself. He hadn't meant to shoot Lucy, though he doubted God or Beau Morgan would believe him.

Andy read Clay's frown for cowardice and made chicken sounds.

Clay slapped him with the back of his hand, cursing him for more than a fool. "You don't know a blasted thing about me and Morgan."

Goose squared his shoulders. "I know you've been playing stupid games. Why not stand and fight?"

Clay had asked himself that same question. At first he'd run because he wanted to live. Then he'd run because he was afraid to die. The guilt would hit anew and he'd do something foolish, like leave Morgan a note or a trinket that would inflame his rage. The nights were the hardest. In his dreams he saw Lucy Morgan wearing a bloody pink dress, picking wildflowers in an endless meadow of rich grass. She'd turn and stare into his eyes. "Give up," she'd whisper. The dream would shift and he'd see his mother in her Sunday best, walking in the same meadow. He couldn't see her face and didn't want to. He felt sure she'd be weeping for what he'd become. Clay could barely live with himself these days. He didn't dare share his thoughts with Goose and Andy. If he lost their respect he'd be a laughingstock.

The gelding shifted under Clay's weight, reminding him of Ricochet lying dead in a patch of grass. Clay almost envied her the peace. No dreams. No guilt. Maybe Goose had a point. Maybe the time had come to stop running. If they raided a ranch, Morgan would get whiff of Clay's trail and resume the chase. One way or another, the men would come face-to-face.

Clay looked hard at Goose. "Let's do it."

Andy did his coyote hoot.

Goose merely smiled. "If Morgan follows us, I promise you, he'll die."

Chapter Six

Dani startled awake. She'd left the bedroom window open, so nothing stood between her and the shriek of an animal. Her stomach turned to acid when she thought of T.C.. A week had passed since they'd brought him home, and last night he'd been officially moved to the barn.

The shriek turned to silence. If the kitten had left the barn, he'd met his end. Dani had no illusions about saving him, but she had to know the facts before the girls woke up. She threw off the quilt and pushed to her feet. Fumbling in the dark, she grabbed her day dress from the hook on the door. When she'd arrived, the hook had held a shirt belonging to Patrick. She couldn't bear the thought of the girls suffering another loss.

Please, Lord. Protect T.C.

Even as she thought the words, Dani felt a surge of anger. So far, God had been slow to answer her prayers. In spite of her best effort, Beau hadn't changed his mind about sending the girls away. Every night Dani prayed for peace, but she mourned Patrick with every breath. The girls were just as raw. Esther sucked her thumb all the time. Ellie wouldn't wear anything but her coveralls, and Emma worried about everything. If something happened to T.C., Dani feared they'd slide beyond her reach.

She stepped into the slippers she'd brought from home and hurried to the barn. Moonlight shone on her path, warning her of ruts and throwing her shadow a step ahead of her. The silence held an eerie stillness. Dani thought every day about Clay Johnson. Beau no longer sat on the porch at night, but she knew he was on guard. Unable to sleep herself, twice she'd looked out the bedroom window and seen him sitting in a chair outside the barn. He'd had a rifle at his side and a hard gleam in his eyes. God pity the man who crossed his path.

Dani glanced at the bunk room door but didn't see Beau. Either he was asleep or he'd gone to investigate the shriek. Maybe he'd heard something else… Maybe Clay Johnson was lurking down the road. Or more likely, Dani thought, her imagination had taken flight. Telling herself to stay calm, she lifted the latch on the barn door, stepped inside and lit the lantern hanging on a post. It flared to life, revealing the hard eyes of a man just two feet away.

She shrieked, then burst out laughing. Beau had beaten her to the barn and had T.C. tucked against his chest. With his tousled hair and sleepy eyes, he looked boyish and relaxed. Dani's heart rose to her throat again, and not because she was afraid. When T.C. yawned and rolled tight against Beau's shirt, she felt as cozy as the kitten.

Startled by her peaceful thoughts, she looked at Beau's face. The man had the audacity to grin at her.

"You scared me," she said.

"I didn't mean to." He glanced at the door. "You must have heard that scream."

"It sounded like a rabbit, but I couldn't be sure."

"Me, neither."

Dani glanced at the kitten. The barn had been pitch-black when she'd entered. "How did you find him in the dark?"

"He found me." Beau told about hearing an animal scream. Like Dani, he'd worried about the cat for the sake of the girls. "I came to take a look. When I opened the door, T.C. ran up to my leg."

Beau absently stroked the cat. Dani's heart warmed with hope. Until now, he'd avoided T.C. at all costs. He'd avoided her, too. How could she convince him she could run the farm if he wouldn't speak to her? Dani saw an opportunity and decided to take it.

"I don't know about you," she said. "But I'm not going back to sleep. Would you like breakfast?"

"Don't mind if I do."

"Bring T.C. I bet he's hungry, too."

As Beau looked up from the kitten, Dani became aware of his eyes taking in her day dress, a blue calico she'd worn for years, and then her hair. She usually wore it in a braid coiled around her head. At night she let the braid fall down her back. Sleep had pulled the strands into wisps that framed her face. Self-conscious, she tucked a curl behind her ear. What did a woman say to a man in the middle of the night? She had no experience in such matters, but she knew what she wanted to say to Beau. She had plans for the farm and he needed to hear about them.

"Let's go inside," she said.

She paced across the yard with Beau in her wake. When they reached the porch, he passed her and opened the door. She led the way to the kitchen, lit the lamp and stove, then shook out the match. She turned and saw Beau sitting in a chair, angled so he could stretch his legs. He still had T.C. on his chest and was stroking the kitten with his large hand. Beau looked as relaxed as the cat.

Dani opened the icebox and filled a saucer from a pitcher. When she put it on the floor, the cat leaped off Beau and ran for the food.

As Beau straightened, Dani met his gaze. "I've got something to show you."

"What?"

"I'll be right back."

She hurried to Patrick's bedroom, her room now, and opened the desk drawer. She removed three drawings, walked back to the kitchen and handed them to Beau. "Take a look."

He held the first drawing a foot from his face, studying the lines as if they made no sense. "What is it?"

"It's the silo I told you about."

"For feed storage."

"That's right."

He looked at it dead-on. "Why is it round?"

"It's easier to clean." Dani pulled eggs and ham out of the icebox. She heard the drawings rustle, glanced back and saw Beau spreading the papers on the table.

"Patrick must have liked the idea. He bought the wood."

"I suppose." She'd mentioned the idea in a letter and sent the drawings, describing how to dig a hole and build the structure over it. She and Patrick had never talked about it. Looking back, there were a lot of things he hadn't said. Dani felt her throat tighten. She should have been cooking breakfast for her new husband.

Beau looked up. "How'd you come up with the plans?"

"My father built one of the first silos in Wisconsin." She told him how successful it had been.

Beau stacked the papers. "It's a good idea."

"I have others."

"Like what?"

Dani cut a slice of ham. Her future depended on convincing Beau she could run the farm, but she didn't want to step on his toes. She kept her voice mild. "I already told you about the second cheese factory."

"I recall."

Dani cracked an egg into the pan. "We could sell twice as much milk, maybe three times."

Beau frowned. "You'd need more cows."

"Patrick kept the four heifers. Next year we'll have more."

"More cows mean more work."

"*And* more profit." She tried to sound confident, but her body tensed. She'd caught Beau's skeptical tone. Needing time to think, she placed a ham steak in the fry pan, then spooned butter over Beau's eggs. He liked them over-easy. He also liked toast with jam. She put four slices on a rack in the oven and set the butter crock on the table.

"Coffee's ready," she said brightly.

"I'll pour my own."

Beau lifted two cups from a shelf, took a hot pad from the drawer, then lifted the pot from the back of the stove. The hot pad in his hand had come from her trunk. She'd made it during her engagement to Virgil. Dani's heart pounded. Going home to Wisconsin would mean years of loneliness. She had to convince Beau to let her adopt the girls.

As he filled the cups, she dished up their breakfast. She handed Beau his plate, then filled hers with half as much. They sat at the same time, staring at each other.

Dani folded her hands in her lap. "I'm serious, you know."

"Miss Baxter—"

"Call me Dani." As long as he considered her "Miss Baxter," he'd see her as the woman who'd arrived in a fancy dress, not a woman accustomed to work. She could feel the wall between them and had to break it down.

Beau took a bite of ham, chewed to avoid speaking, then shook his head. "I just can't see it."

"Why not?"

He shook his head. "Running this place is hard work."

"We have ten cows," she said. "My brother has fifty."

"And hired help, I'd guess."

"Three men," she countered. "I could run this place with one. Do you known Howie Dawes?"

Beau frowned. "I know Tom Dawes. He's the sheriff."

"Howie's his son. Patrick hired him to help now and then. I could do the same."

She watched as Beau slathered butter on a slice of toast. "Dairying's not for the lazy, that's for sure."

"I love it," Dani declared. "And I'm good at it."

She felt all the hope she'd had with Patrick. She missed him, but her dream of a new life could still come true. She just had to convince Beau she could do the job. But how? She could talk all day, but he needed to see her in action to believe. Nibbling her breakfast, she flashed back to mornings in Wisconsin, teasing her brother and racing him to the barn. He hadn't been able to resist a dare. If Beau had the same taste for a challenge, Dani had her answer. She set her napkin on the table. "I have an offer for you."

"What?"

"We have a contest for the farm."

His eyes twinkled. "You want to arm wrestle?"

"No. You'd win." She'd seen him haul fifty-pound sacks as if they held feathers. "I was thinking of something else."

He set his napkin on the table and sat back in the chair. He hadn't agreed but she'd earned his attention. "What do you have in mind?"

"You milk half the cows and I do the other. We'll see who gets the most milk the fastest."

"What's the prize?"

"If I win, you admit I can run this place."

"And if *I* win?"

She searched her mind for something that mattered, but he already had complete power over her future. She tried to sound brave. "I don't have anything you want."

He leaned back in his chair and looked at her with mirth in his eyes. "Yes, you do."

Dani had no idea. "What is it?"

"Raspberry pie."

She'd made one three days ago from Adie's recipe. Beau had eaten a third of it and gone to the barn, but not before Dani saw a wistfulness in his eyes. If he wanted more raspberry pie, she'd be glad to bake one.

She smiled at him. "Just to make things clear… If I win the milking contest, you'll admit I can run this place."

"That's right.

"And if you win, I make a raspberry pie?"

"Exactly."

"It doesn't seem fair." She wanted the contest to matter.

"It's not about pie," Beau said. "If I win, I expect you to take the girls to Minnesota, then go home to Wisconsin. The pie's just because I want one."

Dani raised her chin. "You're pretty confident."

"Very."

"So am I."

He looked her in the eye. She saw no malice, only the twinkle she'd seen earlier. "It's a deal."

Dani stood to clear the table. Her stomach lurched. She *had* to win this competition. After a last swig of coffee, Beau carried his plate to the counter, bent to pet T.C., then winked at her. "Get ready, Miss Baxter. We square off at dawn."

* * *

A half hour later, Beau had his backside planted on a milking stool and an empty bucket between his feet. Earlier, he and Dani had met at the pasture gate. Being a gentleman, he'd given her first pick of the cows. She'd looped a rope around the closest one, Buttercup, and led the animal to the barn where he'd cleaned a second spot for today's milking.

Beau's first cow, a stubborn thing named Sweetness, had run from him. She wasn't cooperating any better in the barn.

"Come on, old woman," he muttered.

Reminding himself to be gentle, he looped his thumb and index finger around the Jersey's teat, curled the rest of his fingers and pulled. He'd been milking the cows for more than a week. The first time had been tedious, but he'd taken Emma's advice and tried singing hymns while he worked. He wasn't about to do that with Dani working next to him.

She, on the other hand, had no such reluctance. He'd already heard three choruses of "Shall We Gather By The River," each verse accompanied by the hiss of milk hitting the bucket. They'd been working for five minutes, and she'd already emptied a pail into one of the metal cans by the door. Each one was numbered and waiting for Webb, the old man who picked up for the cheese factory.

Beau tugged again on the Jersey's teat. It didn't help his concentration to recall Dani hurrying across the yard with a determined look in her eyes. She'd put her hair up, but he'd recalled the tendrils loose around her face. She'd looked lovely, a fact that filled Beau with memories of Lucy and a deep regret for what he'd lost. After watching Dani with the girls and eating her cooking, having all the buttons on his shirts and his socks mended, he couldn't help but like her. She had a good heart. If ever a female needed a family to love, it was Daniela Baxter.

He even liked her name. Dani-ay-la. It felt nice on his tongue, sweet like the pie. Dani suited her, too. He could imagine her as a tomboy shoveling hay from the loft, riding horses and daring her brother to best her at contests like this one.

Sighing, Beau counted his reaction as another reason to win the milking contest. He was dead sure that stepping into the life she'd imagined would limit her future. It took a brave man to marry a woman with three children in her care. If Dani took on the farm and the girls, she might never find a husband. On her own, a pretty blonde in a town full of ranchers, she'd be married within a year. Beau had known the joy of marriage for only a short time, but he remembered the goodness, especially with Dani singing to the blasted cow who was giving more milk than it ever had for Beau. She was on her second bucket and nearly finished with the first cow.

Beau didn't want to listen to the hymns, but he couldn't cover his ears and milk at the same time. As Dani's soprano filled the barn with the words to "Blessed Assurance" and its promise of Heaven, Beau tasted bile.

Irked, he tugged too hard on the Jersey's teat. The bovine stomped her foot. He muttered an oath, then straightened his back and glared at Dani. "Do you have to sing?"

"The cows like it." The milk hissed into her bucket. "I'm not hearing anything from your side of the barn. You might try it."

He chuffed.

She stood and lifted the bucket, grinning as she turned to the milk can with a swing of her hip. "By the time you and Sweetness make peace, I'll be done."

Beau saw nothing "sweet" about Sweetness. All the cows had names. Sweetness and Light were sisters. Martha, Dolley and Mary Todd were named for former first ladies. The last five, known as the "flower girls" were Buttercup, Rose, Daisy, Lily and Daffodil. Beau watched as Dani neared the milk cans. She set down the bucket, used her long apron to get a better grip on the handle, then hoisted it and poured the milk into the can, not spilling a drop. Beau knew how much the bucket weighed. As slender as she was, Dani had strong arms and a strong back.

She covered the can with a clean towel, then went to fetch another cow. She came back with Lily. After getting the cow settled, she scratched its ears and even kissed its nose.

Sweetness swung her head around, stared at Beau, then bellowed.

Laughing, Dani sat on the stool. Five seconds later, Lily let down her milk. Dani looked over her shoulder. "Sweetness wants you to sing. There's no getting around it."

No way would Beau sing a hymn, but both his pride and his common sense told him he had to do something. He gave the old cow a pat on the leg, realigned the bucket and broke into "Camptown Races." By the second "doo-dah," Sweetness let down her milk. White streams hissed into the bucket in perfect time to the song.

Dani's laughter pealed through the air. Beau had never heard anything quite like the mix of the silly song, her laughter and the beat of the milk. The high ceiling caught the music and bounced it back and around, filling his ears with harmonies he'd never heard. He'd become accustomed to silence, men grunting in saloons, the rush of wind and rivers and the rustling of dried leaves. Today he heard unity, oneness, especially when Dani switched from laughing to singing the "Doo-dahs" in "Camp Town Races."

Before Beau knew it, his bucket was close to full. He stood, patted Sweetness and strode to the can assigned to him.

Dani hurried up behind him and added another bucket to her can.

He had some serious catching up to do. Lowering his chin, he eyed her. "I wouldn't get cocky if I were you. It's not over yet."

She smiled back. "We'll see about that."

She turned so fast her apron flapped. Beau went back to Sweetness, finished the milking and led her to the pasture. He came back with Light and saw Dani filling a new milk can.

He couldn't let her win. Being a man of his word, he'd have to give serious consideration to allowing her to stay with the girls. Beau found the idea both appealing and irksome. As long as Dani and the girls were in Castle Rock, he'd have something akin to a home. Pushing the thought aside, he positioned the bucket under Light and went back to work, singing whatever tune popped into his head.

Thirty minutes later, Dani had milked Rose, Lily and Daisy. Beau had finished with Sweetness and Light. Martha, the oldest of the cows and named for Mrs. Washington, didn't appreciate "Camp Town Races," so he switched to "Pop Goes the Weasel." Martha didn't care for it and neither did Beau.

An old favorite came into Beau's head. Without thinking, he sang the opening line of "The Battle Hymn of the Republic," the verse about a man's eyes seeing the glory of the coming of the Lord. It lifted Beau up. So did the next verse, the one about grapes of wrath. He'd sung the song in church in Denver. It called to his blood and his cause. Beau understood wrath. When he dreamed of finding Clay, the images weren't pretty. He'd shake off the pictures when he awoke, but the bitterness never left.

Except right now, he felt good. Martha liked the song and let down her milk with the ease that made her the best producer. In minutes she'd given all her milk and he'd caught up with Dani. After hauling the bucket to the milk can, he fetched his fourth cow, a sweet thing named Dolley. Dani's fourth cow was named Daffodil. Dolley had a sweet nature and gave generously. Daff was the most stubborn of the ladies, the cow who'd stepped on his foot and inspired his one use of profanity. Beau smelled victory.

As he pulled up the stool, he glanced at Dani who was coaxing Daff with clucking sounds as she worked the teats. Nothing happened. The lines tightened around her eyes.

"Come on, girl," she said. "What's bothering you?"

Beau had a feeling he knew. He and Daff didn't get along, but he knew she liked being scratched between her eyes. He'd gained on Dani and almost had the lead. If he said nothing, he'd win, but he felt like a heel. He sat straight on the stool. "Give her a scratch between the eyes. It works every time."

"Thanks." She pushed to her feet, gave Daff a long scratch that made Beau think of his own itchy back, then sat on the stool. Milk squirted into the pail.

Without breaking the rhythm, Dani turned her head. "That was nice of you."

"It beats hearing 'Camptown Races' again."

She smiled. "I enjoyed it. You have a fine voice."

He said nothing.

"Do you like to sing?"

His voice choked, but he answered. "Back in Denver, I sang in the church choir."

"That's nice."

He blew air through his nose. Lucy had sung alto. Choir practice had been on Thursday evenings. They'd eaten supper out, and… Beau groaned out loud.

Dani stopped milking. "Are you all right?"

"I'm fine."

But he'd wasn't. She'd used his given name before, but today he liked the sound of it. His chest swelled with breath, with life. The barn had a window high in the wall. It cast a beam of gold light to the floor between them, catching dust motes and making a gossamer wall between himself and Dani. If he wanted, he could pass through that dust and be her friend, maybe more. But to what end? He had a call on his life. She had a broken heart. She needed the kind of life he couldn't give.

Can't or won't?

Pushing aside the whisper of his conscience, Beau focused on the milk filling the bucket. A little scratching and some sweet talk and the cows gave generously. He thought of Dani's good cooking and the girls playing checkers on the porch. If he didn't watch himself, he'd react as generously as Martha. He'd give his all for this little family.

The barn door creaked open. Along with the hiss of the milk, Beau heard the pad of little-girl feet. He'd never heard that particular scuff until he'd arrived at the farm. Men took long, thumping steps. Boys ran. Little girls scampered, even when they were sad and missing their daddies.

"Who's there?" Dani called from the stall.

"It's me."

Beau recognized Ellie's voice and looked up. She'd reached Dolley and had stopped to scratch her. Dressed in coveralls as always, she reminded Beau of Patrick at that age. They'd grown up in Indiana on a farm similar to this one, half brothers with Beau the elder by three years. Patrick had been the baby of the family, their mother's favorite and his father's pride. Beau's own father, a man he didn't recall, had died in a wagon accident. Beau had toughened up early in life. Losing a father forced a boy to grow up.

Ellie rubbed the side of Martha's head. "I used to help Pa with the milking."

What did a man say to a hurting little girl? Did he talk about Heaven? Beau had rebelled every time some well-meaning fool told him Lucy was in a better place. What could have been better than sharing his bed, his home, meals at the table he'd built with children in mind.

His gaze slid to Dani. She had already straightened and was looking at him with the same sad expression he'd seen in the cemetery. Then and there, Beau lost the milking contest. Dani needed these children. She needed the farm, a home of her own, and he could give them to her.

He rose from the stool and called to Ellie. "Want to finish with Dolley?"

The child's eyes showed all the chaos in her heart. He wasn't her father, but he looked enough like Patrick to stir up memories. Just for now, he could fill the hole in her life.

"I don't know," Ellie said.

Beau kept his expression gentle. "Dolley misses your pa, too. She'd like it if you'd help."

Ellie's eyes widened and her lips parted as if she wanted to speak. Beau recognized the signs of knowledge dawning on her face. Her father was gone, but life would go on. He'd felt that way when he'd eaten Dani's raspberry pie.

Ellie stroked Martha's nose, then looked at Beau. "I can finish. My pa taught me everything."

As she took his place, Beau stepped into the aisle. He heard the hiss-hiss of Dani milking Daffodil. As he turned, she met his gaze with a question in her eyes. *What about the contest?*

Beau had no doubt about the outcome. Even if he'd edged Dani by a pound or two, she'd bested him in spirit. She knew about breeding, milk prices, feed crops, even confounded things called silos. Even more important, she loved the animals like children. Never again would he hear "Camptown Races" without thinking of this day.

Beau spoke softly. "You won, Dani." He'd used her given name. It tasted sweet, like the berries.

She blushed. "Does that mean…"

She was asking about adopting the girls. "I don't know yet, but you're closer."

He still had concerns. What would happen if Dani lost her heart to a man with his own ambitions? Grief-stricken women made foolish choices. They married too soon and lived with regrets. Before he handed her the responsibility of the farm, he had to be sure she knew the facts. That meant having a long, private talk. Maybe tonight… Beau bristled at the thought. He didn't want to see Dani in the moonlight. He'd have to find another time.

She'd filled a bucket, so he lifted it and carried it to the milk can. When he brought it back, he took Ellie's pail and did the same thing. When the last cow was milked, Dani carried the buckets to the well for scrubbing. Beau lifted a shovel and headed for the horse stalls. Ellie picked up a smaller shovel and followed him.

"Uncle Beau?"

"Yes?"

"Do you like to fish?"

"Sure."

A graybeard in Wyoming had taught him to fly-fish on the Snake River. Beau liked it quite a bit. If he kept his eyes on the water, the current caught his thoughts and carried them away.

Ellie dumped a load of dirty straw into the wheelbarrow. "I like it, too. Pa used to take me."

Beau felt the itch as if it were his own. "Where'd he take you?"

"To a stream that's near the mountains. It's pretty far, but I bet it's running fast."

"Trout?" Beau asked.

"Big ones."

Beau thought for a minute. Planting season was coming to a close. He had to get the alfalfa in the ground, and he wanted to build Dani's silo. Fishing sounded like pure pleasure, but he couldn't say yes. He looked at Ellie, intending to change the subject. Her blue eyes were alive with hope, a bit of sunshine that melted Beau's heart. He'd plant tomorrow. Today had needs of a different kind. Ellie needed new memories, plus he could speak to Dani in private while the girls caught tadpoles.

He braced the shovel on the floor and put his boot on the blade. "How'd you like to go fishing right now?"

"I'd like that."

"Me, too," Beau said.

Ellie smiled. "Can I tell my sisters?"

"Let's check with Miss Dani first."

They went back to shoveling, working even faster than before. When Dani brought the clean buckets into the barn, Ellie blurted the question about fishing.

Dani smiled. "That sounds like fun."

"We can have a picnic," Ellie added.

Dani looked at Beau, saying with her eyes that he'd made her proud. Peace washed over him. Just for today, he belonged on the banks of that stream, listening to the water, the wind, the chatter of three little girls and a pretty woman. As Dani turned to leave, he watched the sway of her skirt, a deep blue that matched her eyes. The light from the window caught in the crown of her braid and glinted gold.

Beau pitched another forkful of straw. Before he knew it, he was humming "Camptown Races."

Chapter Seven

Dani watched Beau's hands as he wielded his pocketknife against an apple, removing the red peel in a single strand. When she'd first laid eyes on him, she'd taken his measure by his hands and doubted his character. Today she saw a man capable of a gentle touch and great patience.

The picnic had been relaxing except for Emma's fussing. Back at the farm, she'd been uninterested in packing the food and had worried about the long wagon ride to Sparrow Creek. She'd also been rude to Beau, who'd endured the girl's sass without a single harsh word. While he and Ellie caught trout, Emma had followed Esther like a shadow, warning her about rocks and ruts and everything in between.

With the sun high in the sky, the five of them were seated on a blanket Dani had spread beneath a cottonwood. She'd passed out sandwiches and apples and was enjoying the sunshine. Beau sat across from her with his back against the tree, his legs bent and his forearms resting on his knees while he peeled the apple. Ellie had positioned herself at his elbow, and Esther had curled up in Dani's lap. Emma was seated between Dani and Ellie.

Beau held up the peeled apple. "Who's first?"

"Me!" Ellie took the fruit and bit into it.

A drop of juice shot in Emma's direction. The older girl jerked back as if Ellie had spit on her. "Cut it out!"

Dani didn't know what to do about Emma's foul mood. She was hurting, but hurting others wouldn't bring her father back. Dani touched her stiff shoulder. "It was an accident, sweetie."

Emma's mouth trembled. "I know."

Beau had a second apple in hand. He finished peeling it and offered it to Emma. "This one's for you."

She took the apple and heaved it as far as she could. "I don't want it."

Dani gasped. "Emma!"

Beau shot Dani a look, the one that belonged to the lawman who'd broken up fights in Denver. *I'll handle this.* Dani welcomed his help. She understood the cause of Emma's anger but didn't know how to handle it. When Dani felt melancholy, she wanted to be left alone. When she cried, she did it in private. She didn't understand Emma, but she suspected Beau did.

He handed Emma a third apple. "If it makes you feel better, throw this one, too."

Tears flooded the girl's eyes. "*Nothing* makes me feel better."

Beau worked his knife around the fruit. This time the peel broke. "It can't be fixed, but it's still an apple and it tastes good." He held the fruit out to Emma.

The child shot daggers with her eyes. "What's going to happen to us?"

Dani wanted to know, as well, but she'd hoped to discuss the matter with Beau in private. He'd conceded the milking contest, but did that mean he'd approve the adoption? Neither of them had told the girls about Harriet Lange. Until now, his nieces had been too afraid of Beau to ask about the future. When they approached Dani, she'd told the truth. Their Uncle Beau had legal authority and was still deciding.

Emma's outburst made the waiting seem cruel. Dani looked pointedly at Beau. "I'd like to know, too."

"I see three possibilities," he replied.

Esther paid no attention, but Ellie stopped chewing the bite of apple.

Emma tensed. "What are they?"

"You're not going to like the first one." Beau kept his gaze on Emma. "I asked Mr. Scott to find a boarding school."

"No!" she cried.

Beau held up one hand. "Hold on. That's not likely to happen."

"It better not." Emma raised her chin. "I won't leave my sisters."

"Fair enough," Beau said. "The second option concerns your Aunt Harriet."

Ellie turned to her big sister. "Who's she?"

"She's a witch!"

"Emma!" Dani cried.

"She's mean," the child declared. "We visited her when I was little. She's mama's great-aunt. She's old and ugly and she slapped my hand for touching one of her stupid little teacups."

Dani felt outraged but cautioned herself. *Judge not.* "That was a long time ago."

"I don't care," Emma said. "If she liked children, she'd have some of her own."

"Not necessarily." Dani's back stiffened. Maybe, like herself, Harriet Lange hadn't found the right man. Dani had jilted Virgil Griggs and ended up the town pariah. Perhaps Miss Lange had a similar story.

Beau's voice broke into Dani's thoughts. "We don't know what Miss Lange is like."

Emma frowned. "I know she doesn't like *me*."

Dani weighed Emma's comments and worried. Harriet Lange had asked for Emma only, not the younger girls. Beau, thinking money was a problem, had offered to pay an allowance for all three girls. If Harriet Lange took the offer, how would they know she'd done it out of love? Judging by Beau's frown, he'd gone down the same road.

Ellie had her half-eaten apple in her hand. "Uncle Beau?"

"Yes?"

"Why can't *you* stay with us?"

"I've got business elsewhere," he said simply.

Ellie hugged her knees. "If you stayed, you could marry Dani."

No one said a word, not even Emma.

Ellie's voice sped up. "She's pretty and she can cook. Emma and I can do most of the chores. Esther's too little, but she's fun. That counts for something, doesn't it?"

Dani's heart broke in two. Not for Ellie, who looked desperate. And not for Emma, who looked helpless. But for Beau, whose eyes had taken on the color of grass stirring helplessly in a breeze. Across the blanket, she saw the man who'd loved Lucy and married her, the sheriff who'd sung in the church choir in the tenor she'd heard bouncing in the cavernous barn.

Her heart raced with feelings she couldn't name. She loved Patrick. She always would, yet she'd come to know Beau in a way she'd never known his brother. She and Patrick had traded dozens of letters, but he'd never shared his secrets. Dani had his photograph in her box of keepsakes, but she'd never seen his eyes change with emotion the way Beau's were changing now. The dark glint had turned into a twinkle that matched the grass. He looked at Dani with a wry smile, silently sharing the humor of Ellie's naive remark.

She smiled back.

Beau's eyes lingered on hers, but then he blinked. The twinkle faded, leaving behind the man who'd called himself Cain. Looking away, he hurled the half-peeled apple into the stream. It bobbed once and raced away.

Beau kept his eyes on the apple. "It's not possible, Ellie."

"Why not?" the child asked.

Dani felt sorry for them all. "Your Uncle Beau and I are friends, but we don't love each other."

Esther wiggled in Dani's lap. She hadn't sucked her thumb since they'd left the house, but she had it in her mouth now.

"Why not?" she mumbled through her fingers. "You could be our mama and he could be like Pa."

Dani blushed. "It's not that simple."

Esther pressed even closer. "I want you to stay."

"Me, too." Emma glared at Beau. "My pa wrote to Dani every week. He said *you* disappeared."

Dani knew why, but Emma didn't. Someday the girls would learn more about their Aunt Lucy and Beau's loss but not this minute. "Emma, there are things you don't understand."

"Then tell me," the child demanded.

Beau's expression stayed blank. "My name's on the will. That's all that matters.

"But it's not right," Emma insisted. "Dani knows us. She knows about cows, too. A *lot* more than you do. *And* they like her!"

Beau shifted his gaze to Dani. His expression shot her back to her mother's kitchen and the times her parents traded looks she hadn't understood. Those moments usually involved her brother getting into trouble. Beau, she realized, wanted her to understand him in a way the girls couldn't. They were two adults—equals—addressing a problem.

He made his voice formal. "Birthing season's a tough time of year. Tell me, Miss Baxter. Can you handle it?"

"Yes." She'd helped her father.

His brows lifted with surprise. "Can you build that silo you're planning?"

"I'd hire someone."

"What about the alfalfa?" he asked. "Can you handle the planting, harvesting *and* the baling?

"If I have to." Dani held his gaze. "The seed should have been in the ground two weeks ago. If you can't finish it in the next day or two, we should hire help."

Emma chimed in. "Howie Dawes will do it. Pa hires him every harvest. We all help. We can help Dani, too."

Ellie sat straighter. "I can do a lot."

"Me, too," Esther said.

Beau drummed his fingers on his knee. "I'll be straight with you, girls. The third option is to leave Dani in charge and get back to my work, but I can't. I have to do what's best, not what's easy."

Emma frowned. "This *is* best."

"Hear me out." Beau held up his hand. "You girls have lost too much already. I know that. I want to see you safe and settled. *How* that happens is my decision."

The suck-suck of Esther's thumb beat with Dani's heart.

Beau looked at the child, then at Emma. "I'd like to speak to Dani in private. Can you watch out for your sisters?"

Emma stared at Beau with the haughtiness of a little girl playing dress-up. "Of course, I can."

"Good." Beau focused on Dani. "Let's take a walk."

When she nodded yes, he pushed to his feet. Dani slid Esther off her lap, tried to stand and wobbled. Her leg had fallen asleep. Before she could steady herself, Beau grasped her elbow. Blood rushed to her toes. They tingled, but not as much as her elbow. She thought of Beau milking cows and peeling the apples. He had strong hands, steady hands. She'd come to trust him...except where it came to the girls. Dani knew best about the adoption. She had to prove it to him.

As soon as she steadied herself, he let go of her elbow. "Let's go upstream."

With the grass twisting around her boots, she cut across the slope to the bank of the stream. She saw prints where Beau had cast his line and caught tonight's supper. Ellie's smaller feet marked the ground next to his. In the distance she spotted a cluster of boulders surrounded by lupines, poppies and tiny pink flowers she didn't recognize.

"That's a good spot," she said. They could see the girls, but the stream would cover their voices.

Beau nodded. "I want privacy."

When they reached the boulders, Dani smoothed her skirt and sat on a slab of granite. She expected Beau to sit at her side. Instead he stood in front of her with his hands behind his back. She felt like a witness in a court of law and didn't like it.

Before she could stand, Beau looked into her eyes. "I have just one question, Miss Baxter."

So she'd stopped being Dani. If he thought formality would give him an edge, he was wrong. "What is it?"

"You traveled a thousand miles to marry a man you'd never met. I want to know why."

She'd been expecting Beau to challenge her skills, not her motives. What could she say? That she'd been courted by every man in Walker County and was impressed by none? That she'd been engaged twice and had jilted Virgil Griggs a week before the wedding? Dani still cringed when she thought of Virgil trying to kiss her. She hadn't loved him, not even a little. He'd smelled like bad onions, and she'd turned her head in revulsion. When she'd broken the engagement, Dani had sealed her future as a spinster.

That Dani Baxter, she's as fickle as they come!

Dani didn't have a fickle bone in her body. She'd been lonely and had made a mistake when she'd said yes to Virgil, but the town had other ideas.

Beau crossed his arms over his chest. The longer she waited to reply, the darker his eyes became.

"Does it matter?" she finally asked.

"Yes, it does."

"Why?

His voice went low. "There's only one reason a woman leaves her home for a man she's never met."

Dani stiffened. "What's that?"

"She's running from something."

He'd struck dangerously close to home. She'd been running from loneliness but saw no reason to admit it. "You're wrong."

"Am I?"

"I wasn't running *from* anything," she insisted. "I was running *to* Patrick."

Beau dropped down next to her. Their knees brushed. They both pulled back, but he didn't seem to notice. "I don't believe you, Dani."

He'd used her given name. It made her feel soft inside, but she kept her back straight. "It's true."

"You didn't even know him."

"We wrote letters."

Beau shook his head. "It's been years since I've seen Patrick, but leopards don't change their spots."

Dani's heart pounded. "What do you mean?"

"When we were kids, Patrick had a way of avoiding the facts. He saw things as he wanted them to be, not as they were. He was the youngest. Our ma spoiled him."

Dani bristled. "That was a long time ago."

"Maybe, but I have to wonder… Why did Patrick write to *you?* Why not find a wife in Castle Rock?"

Dani had asked herself the same question. Sometimes it haunted her, especially since she had no one to ask. "I don't know."

"I don't, either." Regret salted his voice. "I *do* know one thing and it's this. If you adopt my nieces, you'll have a harder time finding a husband."

"I'm not looking for a husband. Not anymore."

"Why not?"

"I'm grieving Patrick."

"I know how that it is," Beau murmured. "I also know that the pain eases with time. One day you'll wake up and be ready to breathe again."

"Did that happen to you?"

"In a way." He stared across the meadow. "I miss Lucy, but I know she's gone. It's the hate for Johnson that keeps me on the road. I promised myself I'd bring him to justice. I'm going to keep my word."

Dani saw a link. "I made a promise, too."

"To Patrick?"

"Yes."

"He wouldn't expect you to keep it."

"But I want to." Without the girls, she had nothing. For all Beau's talk of husbands, Dani had no reason to believe things would be different for her in Castle Rock. Except for Patrick, she'd never been in love. She pushed to her feet and faced Beau. "I love the girls. I want to be their mother."

"You also want a husband."

Dani was tired of being pushed. "Not if he's as bossy as you are."

"Bossy?" Beau chuffed.

"Yes!" Dani glared at him. "You act like you know what I'm thinking, but you don't. You have no idea what happened in Wisconsin. If you did—" Too late, she sealed her lips.

Beau's eyes glinted. "So you *do* have a secret."

"If you must know, I was engaged twice. Both times, I called off the wedding. Once at the last minute." She blushed. "Virgil Griggs didn't appreciate my change of heart."

"Why'd you break it off?"

Dani's cheeks turned red. "He smelled like onions."

Beau burst out laughing.

"It wasn't funny at the time," she said. "I earned a reputation for being fickle. I'm not. It's just that…" She shrugged. "I can't explain it."

"You don't have to. I understand."

How could he? She didn't understand it herself. She was about to ask what he meant when he focused his gaze on her face. "I have a bit of wisdom for you."

"What's that?"

His eyes twinkled. "Not all men smell like onions."

Her father had smelled like leather. Her brother used bay rum when he shaved. Dani had no idea how Patrick would have struck her nose, but she knew the scent of Beau's shaving soap. As they'd walked to the rocks, she'd smelled apples.

The thought rocked Dani to her marrow. For all his bluster, she liked Beau and his bossy ways. Her feelings made no sense. She was grieving Patrick. She had no business noticing the mischief in Beau's eyes. He had a glint of male superiority, as if he knew something she didn't.

Dani bristled. "Are you going to let me adopt the girls or not?"

"I haven't decided yet."

"Why not?"

Silence.

Dani wanted to scream. "You *know* I can run the farm."

"There's no doubt about it."

"Then what's the problem?"

His eyes locked on to hers. "I like you, Dani. I want you to be happy."

"Then give me the girls."

His gaze hardened. "Under one condition."

"What is it?"

"Look me in the eye."

She did what he asked.

"Now tell me you don't want a husband."

If she rushed her words, he'd sense her desperation. But the longer she thought, the more her heart pounded with the truth. Of course she wanted a husband, someone to love and cherish. She wanted everything God intended for a husband and wife. She wanted her belly to swell with child. She wanted to laugh in the dark and snuggle at dawn. She'd also made a promise and believed God wanted her to keep it. Why else would he bring her to this moment? As painful as this week had been, she felt needed. She had a purpose. She didn't understand God's logic, but she felt His love.

She took a breath to steady herself, then faced Beau. "I can't say that."

He raised his chin. "That's honest."

"There's more," she said. "I've dreamed of children all my life. I expected to get married and have my own. Instead God sent me here."

Beau's jaw tensed. "Leave God out of it."

"I can't," she said. "I don't know why He took Patrick home, but I know what I promised. I want to adopt the girls."

"Dani—"

"Say yes," she pleaded. "You know it's right."

Barring a miracle, she'd never have a husband. As Beau had said, only an exceptional man would marry a woman with three children. Dani's courtship days were over. For whatever reason, God had made her a widow without ever being a wife. She raised her chin. Someday she'd come face-to-face with the King of Kings. She'd sit at His feet and feel His love. At that glorious moment, she wouldn't recall her earthly loneliness. The thought made her strong.

Beau stood up, putting them eye to eye. "It's a big decision. You don't have to decide now."

"Yes, I do."

"Why?"

"The girls need an answer." So did Dani. "I *know* what I want." She wanted to be a mother. She also wanted to weep for what she'd never have. A husband of her own, a child growing in her belly... She stared harder at Beau.

His expression softened. "If you're sure—"

"I'm positive." She took a breath. "When shall we tell the girls?"

"Now's fine. I'll go to town early in the morning to tell Scott to wire Harriet Lange. As of today, my offer to give her the girls is off the table. They're yours, Dani."

He pulled his hat low, hiding his eyes. Before she could thank him, he walked away.

Chapter Eight

Beau wasn't fond of cleaning fish, but today he welcomed the chore. Not even Ellie wanted to stick around. She'd gone inside with her sisters, leaving Beau to prepare the trout with T.C. meowing at the base of the worktable behind the barn. The racket didn't bother Beau at all. After listening to female chatter all the way back from the stream, he'd felt a lot like T.C. Beau could see the life he wanted, but it glittered like gold at the bottom of a deep pond.

When he and Dani had told the girls about his decision, they'd hugged her hard. She'd made a point of saying Beau cared about them and had made the decision out of love. She'd been right and the girls had sensed it. Esther and Ellie had hugged him. Emma had called him Uncle Beau and apologized for flinging the apple. He'd felt their blood ties in his marrow. If he'd been Emma, he'd have thrown things, too. He'd told her so and she'd smiled. Today had been the best day of his life since Lucy's murder, but it couldn't be repeated. As long as Johnson drew breath, Beau had a call on his life.

He also had three girls and a woman waiting for supper.

He lifted the fish from the bucket, slit it open and removed the bones. He didn't care for the sight of fish guts, but a man did what he had to do. Beau set the fish pieces on a plate, then wiped the mess into a bucket he'd dump in the garden later.

As he lifted the second fish, T.C. meowed in outrage.

"You'll get yours," Beau said to the cat.

As he worked the knife, he wondered if he could say the same for himself. After five years, he was no closer to Clay Johnson than he'd been the day he left Denver. The man had a knack for goading Beau and then disappearing. Why wouldn't Johnson stand and fight? Beau didn't understand. If the outlaw wanted to hide, he could have traveled east and lost himself in a big city. Instead he'd started a game of tag by leaving Beau messages. Why? Beau saw only one answer. Clay Johnson had the mind of a snake. The sooner he met his end, the sooner Beau could settle down.

For the first time since Denver, he liked the idea. He'd grown fond of sleeping in a bed and even fonder of Dani's cooking. When he finished cleaning the fish, he'd milk the cows. He'd clean up and go inside the cozy house. He'd sit at the head of the table, passing platters of food and listening to female prattle. As he filleted another fish, Beau muttered an oath. He had to track down Johnson and kill him. Why was he torturing himself with thoughts of Dani and the girls?

T.C. wove around his ankles, meowing with the desperation befitting an annoyed feline. Beau tossed him a bite of fish. "Now scat."

The cat swallowed the tidbit, sat and stared at Beau. He wanted more. He wanted it all.

So did Beau. Looking at the kitten, he faced a sad truth. Dani and his nieces would live in his heart forever. He'd never forget them. Maybe he'd visit once a year, at Christmas when snow made the days bright. He'd bring toys for the girls and something nice for Dani. Maybe cloth for a dress or a fancy hat. Maybe a necklace made of gold. She liked pretty things. Who knew what the future held? Maybe someday, after Clay Johnson had been caught, Beau would call the farm home.

The thought made his belly roll. Once he finished with Johnson, he'd be a free man. He could marry Dani… He liked the idea quite a bit, but he couldn't expect her to wait for him. In spite of adopting Patrick's girls, Beau figured she'd be married within a year. Only a fool would let her get away.

Sighing, he picked up another fish.

"Nice-looking trout."

Beau turned and saw Josh. "There's plenty. Can you stay for supper?"

"No, thanks. Dani already asked."

"You're missing out."

"This isn't a social call."

Josh rarely sounded grim. When he did, he had a reason. Beau lowered the knife. "What brings you out here?"

"The Rocking J had some trouble."

"What kind?"

"Horse thieves made off with some prize stock."

The local ranch had the finest quarter horses in Colorado. Clay Johnson had an eye for good horseflesh. Beau's nerves prickled. "Any witnesses?"

"Baylor's wife saw three men."

Beau forgot the fish. "Last I heard, Johnson had two partners. What else did she see?"

"Not much. They were wearing masks."

"What about their mounts?" Johnson had ridden the same horse, a buckskin mare with black stockings, for five years.

"One of them rides a pinto," Josh answered. "Another had a nag."

"Anyone on a buckskin?"

Josh shook his head.

The facts didn't point to Johnson, but neither did they point away. The outlaw had been riding with two other men. Beau had been closing in on them when he'd stopped to visit Patrick. Every instinct told him Johnson had raided the Rocking J. He stabbed the knife into the table. "It's Johnson. It has to be."

With the blade twanging, he looked at Josh in his black coat. The man kept a Bible in the front pocket and a pistol at his side. Truth and justice. Heaven and Hell. Josh would have added mercy and forgiveness. Beau didn't care. He wanted vengeance.

The Reverend kept his voice low. "Sheriff Dawes is riding out tomorrow with a couple of men. He wants you to join them."

Beau wanted to leave so badly his calves twitched. His weapons were clean and loaded. If he saddled his roan, he'd be ready to ride. Instead he muttered a curse. "I can't go."

"Why not?"

"Because I've got ten cows to milk, alfalfa to plant and a silo to build for a know-it-all woman!"

Josh raised an eyebrow. "Dani seems capable to me."

"She is."

"So why not go?"

If he didn't finish the planting, Dani would be left to wrestle with a mule and a plow. He couldn't stand the thought. "It's my job," he said. "If the alfalfa doesn't get planted, she won't have winter feed."

Josh arched a brow. "I thought you were selling the farm."

"Not anymore. Dani's staying."

"Are you?" Josh asked.

"Not a chance." Beau explained the adoption and why he'd made the choice. "I'll ask Scott to file papers next trip to town."

The Reverend didn't say a word.

Josh never lied, but neither did his silence ring true. Beau looked him in the eye. "What's wrong?"

"It doesn't concern you."

Beau hated secrets. "Does it concern Dani?"

"In a way."

"Then I have a right to know."

"No, you don't." Josh crossed his arms. "This is between me and God. If something needs to be said, I'll say it. As things stand, you're the girls' legal guardian and using your best judgment. From what I can see, Dani's promise to Patrick hasn't affected your decision."

"Not really," Beau said. "The woman knows cows and loves the girls. That's what made me change my mind."

That, and the fact he liked her. Josh didn't need that information.

The minister nodded. "That's all I need to know."

Beau wanted to know what had led to Josh's concern, but he knew his friend wouldn't break a confidence. He'd proven himself in Denver. Late at night, when Beau had spilled his guts, Josh had kept their talk private. Beau had a feeling he'd done the same for Patrick. If his brother had been having second thoughts about marriage, Beau didn't much care. Dani loved the girls. That was enough. He'd filleted five trout for supper. That was enough, too. So was five years of chasing Clay Johnson, but Beau couldn't rest until the man swung from a rope.

He snatched the last fish from the bucket and slit the belly. "Tell me about Dawes. Is he any good?"

"Average."

"Can he take Johnson?"

"Not alone."

Beau lowered the knife. "I've been after Clay Johnson for five years. He could be in shouting distance and I can't finish the job. It's not right."

"Maybe it's not your job to finish," Josh said. "'Vengeance is Mine—'"

"—saith the Lord.' I know." Beau jerked the bones from the trout's flesh and flung them into the bucket. He glared at Josh. "Where was God when Lucy bled to death?"

The Reverend's gaze stayed steady. "The same place He was when His son died on the cross."

Beau wiped the knife on a rag. The table stank of fish and death and blood. Clay Johnson was riding free and the Baylor family was left to struggle with loss and violation. For the second time, Beau stabbed the knife into the wood. "Don't give me that talk."

"What talk?"

"That God knows what I'm feeling. Johnson killed my *wife*."

"I know, I was there."

"I want him dead!"

"I know you do, Beau. It's just that—"

"Just *what*?"

Josh held Beau's gaze. "The bitterness is eating you alive. You know the cure. 'Father forgive them—'"

"Don't you *dare* say it."

They know not what they do. Clay Johnson had carried a loaded rifle to a rooftop. He'd known full well what he intended to do. At best, he'd been sniping for Beau. At worst, he'd shot an innocent woman in the back.

Beau lashed out at Josh. "Don't you *dare* tell me to forgive that piece of human filth!"

"I wasn't going to," Josh said. "That's between you and God."

"That's right."

"I'd say the same thing to Clay. He's going to Hell, my friend. Unless he squares things with the Almighty, he's going to suffer more than you can imagine."

"He has it coming."

Josh raised his chin. "We all do."

Beau felt the words like fire, mostly because Josh counted himself in the same camp as men like Clay Johnson. Fallen short. Weak-minded. A lost soul except for the blood of Christ. Beau knew Josh's story. A long time ago, he'd been a holier-than-thou preacher. He blamed himself for his sister's death and still carried the guilt.

Beau had no illusions of holiness. He sinned as much as any man and he knew it. He was sinning right now… "Love one another as I have loved you." No way could he bring himself to "love" Clay Johnson. Not now. Not ever. Right now, he didn't think much of Josh, either. He wanted the man to leave.

Beau picked up the plate of fish in one hand and the scrap bucket in the other. He looked pointedly at Josh. "Anything else?"

"Any advice for Dawes?"

"Shoot to kill."

Beau strode past Josh. The pastor followed him around the barn and into the yard where he'd left his horse tied to a post. Josh loosed the reins and climbed into the saddle. "See you Sunday."

"Not in church."

Like last Sunday, Beau would leave Dani and the girls at the foot of the steps, then head into town.

Josh looked down from the saddle. "I didn't expect so, but I'll see you in the afternoon."

"What for?"

"A church picnic."

Beau wanted to spit. "Did Adie plan it?"

"Of course."

Back in Denver, Adie had been every bachelor's hero. She'd organized picnics, dances and Saturday suppers that forced even the shyest men to rub elbows with the ladies in town. Beau had rubbed a lot of elbows before he'd clapped eyes on Lucy. He'd enjoyed those spirited times. He wanted Dani to have fun, too.

Or did he? The thought of her sharing a meal with another man—even one with marriage on his mind—made Beau grit his teeth. He didn't know which annoyed him more, not riding with Dawes or keeping his eye on Dani in a crowd of single men. All in pursuit...full of hope and dreams and things Beau couldn't have.

Josh tipped his hat. "See you Sunday."

The Reverend rode out of the yard, leaving Beau with a bellyache. As if to rub Beau's nose in his helplessness, Josh pushed his gray into a gallop, racing past the charred pine and fields of lush grass. With each stride, the horse and rider grew smaller until the minister was a black dot on a dusty road. Stinking of fish and hate, Beau tensed with frustration. He should have been leaving with Josh, not holding a reeking bucket while ten cows told him what to do.

Beau couldn't stand being in the dark. Had Johnson led the raid on the Rocking J as Beau suspected? Was he still in the area? Beau's nerves twanged like the knife. With horses to sell, the outlaw would head for the mountains, where a maze of canyons twisted through the foothills below the Rockies. Johnson could hide for days, raiding ranches until he'd bled the area dry. He had two partners, both unidentified. Either one could slip into town, catch the gossip and stay a step ahead of the law.

And a step ahead of Beau…

If Johnson stayed true to form, he'd want Beau to know he was close. He'd leave a message at the Silver River Saloon. A taunt. A threat. Did the outlaw have a bead on Beau? On Dani and the girls? Beau blinked and saw pink. If Johnson had left him a message, he had to know. Dani needed him to plant the alfalfa, but she could do without him for tonight. With the stolen horses in his care and the law on his tail, Johnson would stay hidden in the canyons. She'd be safe.

Beau strode to the garden, left the bucket and headed for the back door to the house. Emma saw him coming and opened it. He handed her the plate of fish.

She smiled at him. "Thank you, Uncle Beau." She meant for everything—the day, the meal, especially for Dani.

His belly rumbled with hunger. If he ate supper with the females, he'd sit at the head of the table. He'd share smiles with Dani and eat like a king. Longing stabbed through him, but he pushed it back. "Tell Dani I'm not eating supper."

"Why not?"

"It's none of your business."

Emma lost her smile.

Beau felt like dirt. He'd hurt the child's feelings, but he didn't dare apologize, not when he could smell biscuits and pie. Instead he barked an order. "I left the fish waste in the garden. Someone needs to bury it."

"I'll do it after supper."

"The milking—"

"I can do that, too."

"Good."

Emma raised her chin. "We don't need you to run this place. You can leave and never come back!"

Beau heard the defiance, but he didn't see it in her expression. Tears pooled in her eyes and he knew why. Emma wanted a father. He couldn't be that man, not until Clay Johnson lay dead in a ditch.

He pulled the door shut, then strode across the yard to the bunk room where he'd stowed his things under the cot. Some of them were practical. Some were sacred. Beau dropped to his knees, reached under the bed and pulled out a box that held Lucy's ring, their wedding picture and a ladies' handkerchief, one of two Lucy had embroidered with flowers.

The linen no longer held her scent, but he recognized the pink roses. Beau had carried a similar hankie in his pocket until he'd come across a young mother in a run-down café. She'd had a small child in her lap, a boy with a cough and a nose as red as fire. Knowing Lucy would approve, Beau had given her the hankie. He'd let go of his grief that day, but not the rage. Today, Beau realized, that rage had flickered and almost died. He'd had a good day. For a few hours, he'd forgotten about Clay Johnson.

Furious with himself, he slipped Lucy's handkerchief into his pocket and pushed to his feet. He strapped on his gun belt, cloaked it with his duster, then saddled his horse and led it into the yard. With dusk turning the sky to pewter, Beau swung into the saddle.

Dani hurried out the front door. Her eyes asked questions he didn't want to answer, so he dug his heels into the horse's side. Josh had left the yard at a gallop. Beau left at a dead run. He barely noticed the rise and fall of the road, the change in the sky from blue to orange, then purplish-black. His thoughts tumbled like rocks in a can, clattering against each other until he arrived in town.

Businesses had closed for the day, but upstairs apartments were alive with families having supper. As he rode toward the Silver River, he heard an argument about a boy eating his peas. Did the mother know how precious this moment could be?

Anything could happen. The child could catch a fever and die. A wagon accident could take his life. Tonight could be her last memory.

Beau thought of the handkerchief in his pocket. A week before Lucy died, he'd watched her working a crochet hook. The yarn had been baby blue. He'd wondered, but she'd only smiled and said it was too soon to be sure.

Fiddle music pulled Beau's attention to the saloon. He steered to the wailing notes, hitched his horse to the railing and went inside. Pausing at the door, he surveyed a small crowd of locals, mostly businessmen ending their day with the amber cure. Beau headed for the counter.

Wallace set down the glass he was wiping. "Coffee?"

"And information." Beau slapped down a greenback.

The barkeep put it in his pocket, sent a waitress to the kitchen for the coffee, then looked at Beau. "What can I do for you?"

"Anyone leave anything for me?"

Wallace shrugged. "Not a thing. That man I saw, he hasn't come back."

Beau was glad Johnson hadn't left a vile threat, but he didn't want to lose him, either. He turned his attention to the facts at hand. "What's the word on the Rocking J?"

Wallace summarized what Beau had heard from Josh, then leaned forward. "Rumor has it they did more than steal the horses."

Beau tensed. "What are you saying?"

"Baylor's daughter…"

Beau held in a curse. A tender girl had been brutalized. Where was God?

Wallace wiped another glass with his apron. "Her brother stopped the attack before too much happened, but she's pretty shook up."

Beau wouldn't bother the girl, but he wondered about the brother. "Did he see the man's face?"

"They all had masks."

The waitress brought Beau's coffee. He took a swig, weighing the evidence as the liquid scalded his tongue. His instincts told him Johnson was behind the raid, but he needed hard facts, something peculiar to Clay. If no one had seen the horse thieves, he'd have to find another way to tie Johnson to the theft.

"What else have you heard?" he said to Wallace.

The barkeep shrugged. "A geezer found a dead horse about ten miles south of here. It could be why someone raided the Rocking J."

Beau set down the cup. If the dead horse matched Clay's buckskin mare, Beau would have the clue he needed. "Tell me more."

The barkeep aimed his chin at the back of the room. "That's the fella who saw it. Ask him."

Beau pushed to his feet and turned. In the dim light, he saw an old man with a ragged white beard and the stooped shoulders of a prospector. He was seated at a round table in the corner, hunched over a bowl of chili. As Beau approached, the man looked up with rheumy eyes. He pointed at an empty chair with his spoon. "Have a seat."

Beau dropped down but stayed on guard. "I hear you came across a dead horse a while ago."

"That I did."

"I'm looking for someone. It could have been his mount. What color was it?"

The old man stopped with the spoon an inch from his mouth. "What's it worth to you?"

Beau slapped a silver dollar on the table.

The old man snickered. "That's not enough."

Beau didn't like being taken, but he'd have given every cent he had to find Clay Johnson. He opened his billfold, took out a five-dollar bill and laid it next to the silver.

The prospector snorted, then looked at Beau. "What else do you have?"

Beau slapped down a sawbuck.

The old man laughed out loud.

Beau added greenbacks to the pile one at a time, watching the man's eyes for signs of greed. When he hit twenty-five dollars, he stopped. "You're a thief."

"No, I'm not." The prospector nudged the money back at Beau. "I'll tell you about that horse for free. I just wanted to see how far you'd go."

Beau looked into the man's eyes and saw a sympathy he hadn't expected. It shook him to the core. "What for?"

"I sold my soul to greed," said the old man. "I had a wife, a family. I left them to search for gold and found nothing but mud. I had everything. Now I've got nothing."

"Thanks a lot," Beau drawled. "But I don't need a sermon."

"I think you do."

"I'm not after gold."

"No," he said. "But you're after something. What is it?"

Beau said nothing.

The old man raised a brow. "Only three things make a man crazy enough to throw away his life. Women, money and revenge. You don't need the money. As for the woman—"

Beau saw a flash of pink. "Mind your own business."

"That leaves vengeance."

"Shut up!"

The graybeard hunched forward. Beau saw madness gleaming in his eyes and smelled the heat of the chili. The man's beard twitched as he spoke. "Don't make the same mistake I did, young fella. Go home before it's too late."

"I don't have one." Except his mind flashed to Dani and the girls around the kitchen table.

The old man grinned, revealing a row of rotten teeth. Beau's stomach turned. He didn't want to end up alone and bent, an old man stinking of sweat and onions. He felt cursed. Trapped. He wanted to be free from that fate. That day would come when he brought Johnson to justice.

Beau gripped the old man's collar. "Tell me about the horse."

"You're lost, son."

His fist tightened. "What color was it?"

"A buckskin."

"What else?"

"It had four black stockings, the high kind."

The description matched Clay's horse to the letter. Beau loosened his grip. "Thanks, old man."

The prospector looked at him with stark pity. "You won't thank me when you're as old and rotten as me."

Beau's belly burned. So did his eyes from the stink of the onions. He looked down at the money on the table, then up at the prospector. With one finger, as if it were filthy, he nudged it toward the old man. "Keep it. Go see your wife."

"She went west."

"So find her."

The miner shook his head. "She married my best friend. Doesn't that beat all? I hear they have grandbabies...."

Beau turned his back and left the saloon. He had enough regrets of his own without listening to a bitter old man. He needed air and he needed it now.

Chapter Nine

Dani touched Daff's udder and winced. The hot spot she'd noticed before supper, when she'd done the milking because Beau had taken off, had changed from the size of a penny to a half-dollar. Concerned, she had left Daff in the barn for the night. Now she knew why the cow had been fussy. She had a condition called mastitis and it hurt. Left untreated, it could damage her udder for life.

"You poor thing," Dani crooned.

The cow sidestepped.

Although Daff had fidgeted during the milking, Dani hadn't been alarmed. Cows were sensitive creatures, and Beau's departure had left tension in the air. She didn't mind doing the evening chores. What she minded was worrying about Beau. She knew Pastor Josh had spoken to him behind the barn. She didn't know what the Reverend had said, but she doubted an invitation to a church picnic had sent Beau racing to town. When she'd glimpsed his face, she'd seen the man who'd called himself Cain.

Dani stood and scratched Daff's head. She whispered a prayer for Beau, then stepped out of the stall and surveyed the barn for a cabinet holding liniment and herbs. She hoped Patrick kept camphorated oil. Her father had used it in Wisconsin. She scanned the shelves by the door but saw only cans of nails and what-not. Looking deeper into the barn, she spotted a door. It led to the back room, a likely place for the oil and where Beau spent the night. Dani had no desire to invade his privacy, but she had to help Daff. She lifted the lantern from the wall, walked to door and opened it.

Cool air touched her face, bringing with it the scents of gunpowder and shaving soap. Raising the lantern, she saw shirts hanging from hooks, trousers draped over a chair and a pair of work boots. A set of saddlebags lay jumbled on the floor, open and unbuckled, as if Beau had rummaged for something. What she didn't see was his gun belt.

Her gaze strayed to a cot neatly made with a pillow and wool blanket. The tidiness surprised her. So did the wooden box lying open on the bed. Looking closer, she saw beveled corners and etched roses. It was the kind of thing a woman would own.

Dani had no business looking at the contents. She had a similar box of her own. It had belonged to her grandmother, then her mother. When she'd turned sixteen, her father had given it to her with his blessing and told her to fill it with wisdom before she passed it on to a daughter of her own. Dani's box held memories of her mother, Patrick's letters and keepsakes from home. She knew the meaning of such things. The contents of the box on Beau's cot would reveal his deepest feelings.

With trembling fingers, she lifted a photograph and saw a man and woman dressed for a wedding. Lucy Morgan had the serious expression befitting a formal occasion, but her eyes glowed with happiness. Beau looked ten years younger, not the five that had passed since his wife's death. In the photograph, Dani saw the man who peeled apples and sang to cows. Her pulse raced. She cared about Beau…deeply. How could she not? He'd given her the girls. He respected her abilities. He'd understood why she'd jilted Virgil Griggs. He understood *her*.

With trembling hands, she set the picture on the bed, then looked at the rest of Beau's treasures. She saw a woman's gold ring, a silver badge and a gray rock. A pink ribbon curled around a watch fob engraved with a date, presumably the day of his wedding to Lucy.

"And the two shall become one flesh…"

Beau had known that joy. Dani never would. Tears pushed into her eyes. She had no doubts about adopting the girls, but deep down she wanted more… She wanted a photograph like the one in Beau's box. She wanted a husband.

With her eyes on the photograph, Dani barely heard the slide of metal against leather. She whirled to the door and saw Beau. He holstered the Colt, then pinned her in place with his eyes.

"I'm sorry," she said. "I didn't mean to pry."

"What are you doing in here?"

"It's Daff."

"What about her?"

His gaze bordered on murderous. Dani didn't blame him for being angry. She'd overstepped, but she'd had a good reason. "She has a hot spot on her udder. I was looking for camphorated oil."

Beau stepped inside the room, opened a cabinet and handed her a brown bottle. "Here."

She wanted to flee, but he was blocking the door. In his duster and hat, he seemed huge. His shoulders spanned the doorway, and the shadow he cast into the barn made him even taller. Heat spilled from the canvas coat. The man she'd seen in the photograph was dead and buried. This one was very much alive. His gaze darted to the picture on the cot, lingered, then slid to Dani. "That's Lucy and me."

"I know."

"She was a good woman."

She swallowed a lump. "I didn't mean to look at your things. The box was open and I saw—"

"I know what you saw." His eyes burned even brighter. "Now you know why I have to kill Johnson."

"I do," she murmured. "But it's not right."

"Who are you to judge?"

"No one. I just know what I see. You're dead inside."

"Far from it." Hate burned in his eyes.

Beau tossed his duster on the chair. Next he unhooked the gun belt and draped it over the back. Without the coat and the gun, he looked like himself...almost.

"Go on," he said. "Get out of here."

Dani stepped to the door. "I'll be with Daff."

Beau blocked her way. "I'll take care of her. Give me the oil."

"No."

His eyes blazed. "I don't want you here. Go inside."

"I can't." She gave him her sternest look. "You're upset. If you go near Daff, she'll feel it. She needs kindness tonight."

"She's a cow!"

"She has feelings!"

So did Beau. He looked mad enough to pound the wall, but behind the rage Dani saw the ragged edges of his heart. Josh's visit had upset him. His trip to town had made him even angrier. She wanted to know what had happened, but she'd invaded his privacy enough for one day.

"Please," she murmured. "Let me by."

She could see Beau fighting with himself. He didn't want her in the barn, but he knew she was right.

Finally, he stepped back. "Suit yourself."

Dani left with the lantern, plunging the room into darkness. Every instinct told her to turn around with the light, but Daff needed her as much as Beau. She could see the cow fidgeting. As she drew close, Daff let out a bellow that shook the rafters.

"It's okay, girl. I'm here."

Dani pulled up a stool, poured oil into her cupped palm, then rubbed her hands together to warm it. Leaning forward, she rubbed the smelly mixture onto Daff's udder. Over and over, she massaged the cow as she'd done on her father's farm. Losing a few pounds of milk would cost money. Losing Daff altogether would be a disaster. The cow, just three years old, had a lot of good years ahead of her.

Prayer filled Dani's mind. She asked God to heal Daff, then thanked Him for giving her the farm and three daughters to raise. She'd never understand the lightning bolt that took Patrick, but she could see God's healing in the aftermath. She prayed for Beau, too. The words came in a rush. *Set him free, Lord. Heal his heart.* Tears pushed into her eyes. She felt his suffering as if it were her own and welcomed it. If her tears would save him a moment's grief, she'd gladly cry for him. This feeling, she realized, was a gift from God, a shadow of how deeply the Lord loved His children.

Love… Dani's hand went still on Daff's udder. With her heart pounding, she thought about apples and raspberry pie, "Camptown Races" and Beau's broad shoulders spanning the doorway. She thought of his hands, too. Strong. Sure. Gentle. Her heart jumped and her eyes opened wide. Had she fallen in love with him? She couldn't have. She loved Patrick…didn't she?

With her stomach churning, she kept on tending Daff. She felt as fickle as Virgil Griggs thought she was, but she couldn't stop the rush of feeling for Beau. He was everything she wanted in a husband, a man who commanded respect but knew when to bend. Beau could make her smile and feel proud. He also had a stubborn streak, cranky moods and a heart full of hate. Somehow those flaws made her love him even more. Dani turned the thought over in her mind. She loved lots of people…the girls, her family and friends in Wisconsin. Her feelings for Beau *had* to be in that vein.

So why was her heart pounding with hope? She wanted to offer him comfort but worried that he'd send her away. Her own feelings shouldn't have mattered, but they did. She'd never felt a pull so strong, a need to give of herself that went beyond friendship, beyond family. The desire to comfort Beau sprang from her very soul.

The door to his room creaked opened, filling the far side of the barn with a dull light. A moment later, his shadow stretched across the floor.

"Dani?"

She didn't dare look up. "The oil stinks, doesn't it?"

"I'm sorry."

He wasn't talking about Daff. He meant for his rudeness. Dani forgave him instantly, but she couldn't bear to look into his eyes. She'd see his suffering and want to hold him in her arms. She thought of reaching for his hand, but the gesture seemed like a confession.

"It's all right," she finally said. "You were upset."

"That's no excuse for my behavior." He let out a breath. "You saw Lucy's picture and the badge. The watch—"

"I figured it was a wedding gift."

"It still keeps time."

He seemed eager to talk, so Dani looked up. "What about the rock?"

"I picked it up the day I asked Lucy to marry me."

"That's very sweet." Dani's heart pinched. "You must have loved her very much."

"I did. I always will, but I know she's gone. God and I aren't close right now, but Lucy's watching from Heaven."

"There's comfort in that thought."

Saying nothing, Beau dropped to a crouch, putting them almost cheek to cheek. He laid his hand on Daff's udder. "Where's the hot spot?"

"Here." She pointed to it.

Beau slid his hand to the place she indicated, then looked into her eyes. "I'd have never found it."

They were so close she could feel his breath on her cheek. He smelled like coffee and leather, nothing like apples. She didn't want to notice his manly ways, but she couldn't help it. She focused on Daff. "She's calmer now."

"You have a way with animals," he said. "Including mules like me."

Dani stared at the glistening oil. "You're not a mule."

"I was tonight. I ran out of here without an explanation. Then I got mean-tempered when you went looking for the oil."

Her heart ached. Only a good man would humble himself. "You caught me being nosy. Anyone would have been angry."

"And anyone would have looked in the box." Beau pushed to his feet. "There's no harm done. In fact, seeing the picture might help you understand where I went tonight."

Dani kept rubbing Daff. "I was worried."

"With good reason." He told her about Josh's visit, the trouble at the Rocking J and his suspicion that Clay Johnson was in the area. "That's why I went to town. If anyone knows what's going on, it's Wallace at the Silver River Saloon."

"What did you find out?"

"A prospector found a dead horse. I'm convinced it belonged to Johnson."

Dani tensed. "So he's in the area."

"I'm sure of it."

"Do you think he'll come after you?"

"I don't know." He pushed a piece of straw with his boot. "Most of the time he runs, but sometimes he leaves messages."

"Like what?"

"Notes telling me I'm going to die. Once he left a pink ribbon."

"That's horrid."

Dani stopped rubbing Daff. The cow stomped her foot, then settled down. Dani looked up and saw Beau scratching the cow's ears. How could a man talk about his wife's murder and soothe a cow at the same time? Sensing her gaze, he looked down. His eyes blazed with the glow she'd seen when he'd looked at the photograph. Only instead of seeing Lucy, he saw her.

Her cheeks turned pink. "I worry about you, Beau."

"Don't."

"I can't help it."

"Johnson can't hurt me any more than he already has."

Not even death scared this man. She ached for him, but she also recalled the gun belt that lived on his hips. Dani quivered with fear. "Maybe he'll take the horses and run."

"That's my guess. Just the same, I want you and the girls to be careful."

"Of course."

She'd answered quickly. Too quickly to hide the shake in her voice. In Wisconsin, her biggest worry had been bad weather. Here the weather was deadly and so were strangers.

Beau pulled up a stool. "Let me take a turn."

Dani barely heard him. She blinked and imagined Clay Johnson lurking in the yard. "I won't sleep knowing that man's around."

"Think of me instead."

His voice had gone low. He'd meant to sound reassuring, but Dani heard a lilt. It matched the beat of her heart and she wondered if she'd ever sleep again. When Beau laid his palm against the small of her back, her breath quickened.

"I'll keep you safe," he said. "I promise."

He'd felt her fear but had misunderstood it. Clay Johnson made her nervous, but it was Beau's touch that scared her. His knee rested an inch from hers. She could feel strength in his forearm and gentleness in his fingers. She wanted to stay in this spot forever. Air rushed from her lungs. She covered the sudden quivering with a yawn.

"You're tired." Beau slid his hand from her back, clasped her fingers and took her hand off Daff's udder.

Dani turned her wrist and matched their palms. The oil made their fingers slide together. She looked into Beau's eyes where she saw a fierce light.

"I mean it, Dani. I won't let Johnson get near you."

She wanted to believe him, but Beau wasn't God. He was a man, one who had loved and suffered a loss. She'd loved and lost, too. Both afraid and unwilling to let go of the moment, she squeezed his fingers. "Did you eat supper?"

His eyes darkened. "I lost my appetite in town."

"I could make you a sandwich."

"No, thanks." He let go of her hand. "Go on inside."

Before she could tempt him with pie, Beau went to work on Daff. Feeling dismissed, Dani stood and left the barn.

As she walked through the yard, the night air cooled her face but not her blood. She wiped her oily fingers on her apron, but she still felt the imprint of Beau's hand on her back. She felt all sorts of things…all of them confusing. As soon as the adoption was complete, Beau would leave. Losing her heart to a bitter man, one who'd turned his back on God, was pure foolishness.

Dani hurried up the steps. As she opened the door, the mantel clock chimed twice. As tired as she felt, she knew she wouldn't sleep. She needed to chase Beau's face out of her thoughts, so she went upstairs to check on the girls. With her heart pounding, she looked first at Emma, sleeping alone in the smallest bedroom. The child's hair lay like scattered straw on her pillow. Dani saw a precious gift and thanked God with a silent prayer.

Brimming with love, she stepped across the hall where Ellie and Emma shared a double bed. The sight of the little girls, curled in opposite directions to make a heart, made her breath catch. If Patrick had lived, they'd be sharing this moment. He'd have held her hand and led her downstairs. They'd have talked about Ed, Ethan and Ebenezer and dreamed of the future.

Desperate to feel close to Patrick—and safe from Beau and his bitterness—Dani went downstairs to her bedroom. She lit the oil lamp, opened her trunk and lifted the stack of letters from Patrick. With her heart aching, she put on her nightgown and brushed out her braid, climbed into bed, and unfolded the first letter she'd received from a dairyman in Colorado.

His descriptions of the girls came alive. When he said he had ten cows, Dani pictured each one. She knew their names, their quirks and how many pounds of milk each one gave. She also knew about the singing, though Patrick didn't mention it. How many other things didn't she know about him? Did he have a deep voice or a high one? Could he sing as well as Beau? Scolding herself for silly comparisons, she skimmed the letters until she reached the one where Patrick had proposed.

I need a wife and you need a change. I believe we'd be a good match. Would you marry me, Daniela?

She'd taken the use of her formal name as a sign of his

respect. Tonight it sounded foreign. He'd added a few compliments about her good mind and warm heart. At the time, she'd blushed with his praise. Now it seemed impersonal. He could have been writing to a business partner, someone he was hiring to do chores and care for his children. He'd signed the letter, "With great hope."

Dani stared at the bottom of the page. Not once had Patrick written that he loved her. She'd figured he was saving that special moment for when they met in person, but now, looking at his letters one after another, she wondered if he would have said the words at all. She had to know. Blinking, she thought of Beau's box of memories. They told a love story. Dani needed that story from Patrick. What treasures had he set aside? She knew where to look.

When she'd moved into the bedroom, she'd spotted a cherrywood case on the top shelf of the wardrobe. Dani hadn't opened it, but tonight she needed to see what it held. She climbed out of bed, lifted it off the shelf and set it in the middle of the bed. As she raised the lid, the hinges creaked. Light spilled from the lamp, revealing a package of letters tied with a black ribbon.

Her letters… With her heart fluttering, she touched the paper and realized she'd made a mistake. She'd bought special stationery to write to Patrick, the finest she could find. She'd used a fountain pen because it fit sweetly in her hand. These letters were written on newsprint. Feeling ill, she untied the black ribbon, opened the top letter and saw Patrick's bold hand.

"Dear Beth…"

Her stomach lurched, but she calmed herself. Patrick had written to his wife. Any woman would have treasured such letters and kept them in a special place. With her heart pounding, Dani read on.

Chapter Ten

You've been gone a week, my love. Alone in our bedroom with the lamp trimmed low, I don't think I can survive. You were the best part of me, Beth. The part that could love, the part that knew happiness of the finest kind. Without you I'm a lost man. My soul is drifting on the wind, a spirit parted from the body but nowhere close to Heaven. This is purgatory. I'm among the living dead.

Struggling to make sense of the letter, Dani looked at the date and saw the month and year of Beth's death. Patrick, she realized, had written them at the pinnacle of his grief. He'd loved Beth deeply. Dani admired him for that commitment. The letters held the private feelings she'd expected him to share with her once they were married. Bolstered by that thought, she continued to read.

She finished the first letter, read three more and realized Patrick had written to Beth every Saturday night, each time pouring out his grief and wondering if he wanted to live. By the fourth letter, Dani felt ill.

"Stop reading," she said out loud.

But she couldn't. She needed to know what he'd written about *her*. She skimmed through the stack until she found the first mention of her name.

Do you remember my cousin Kirstin? She wrote to me about a friend of hers, a girl named Daniela who can't find a husband.

Dani bristled. She'd *found* a husband. She'd found two of them, but neither man had made her feel alive. She didn't like Patrick's comment, but she couldn't blame him for Kirstin's introduction.

Miss Baxter has invited me to write to her. I hate to do it, Beth. But our girls need a mother. I'm going to write back. If this woman is at all acceptable, I'll think about writing to her again.

Dani's heart plummeted. She wanted to be more than "acceptable." She wanted to be loved. She wanted to be understood. Until now, she'd thought Patrick had been courting her, not judging her usefulness. Had his feeling changed from resignation to hope? Dani had to know, so she read the next letter with her name in it.

She's educated and seems kind, though you can't know a person from letters alone. She sent a picture. I suppose she's pretty. Blond, not brunette like you. She's thin, too. Maybe that's why she hasn't found a husband.

Dani gasped with outrage. She'd made a trip to Madison with Kirstin to have that tintype made. She'd spent hours

picking her dress and fixing her hair. She'd even let the pho-
tographer apply rouge, something that felt foreign and
naughty. Now, reading Patrick's comments, she felt like a cow
on an auction block.

The letters went on and on. He questioned himself with
every stroke of the pen, criticizing Dani to Beth for faults both
real and imagined. By the time she opened the last letter, she
felt nauseous. She looked at the date, saw it was written the
day before Patrick died and knew this letter mattered the most
of all.

Dear Beth,

I give up. I can't live another minute with this lie of an
engagement. It's too late to tell Daniela to stay home.
I figure she's on the train outside of Chicago. Her arrival
will be my punishment. After months of letters, she
deserves to hear my regrets in person. I don't love her,
Beth. I can't marry her.

My dearest wife, every night, I dream of you, of us.
When I milk the cows, I remember naming the calves.
I remember Martin Dryer bringing the bull and how you
talked about the wonder of it all. Do you remember that
night? I do. We...

Dani read something so intimate she blushed.

A man can't marry one woman when he loves another.
Will I ever find peace without you? If it weren't for our
daughters, I'd ride west to escape the memories. I'd ford
rivers with the hope of drowning. I'd scale mountains
and hope to fall. But I can't do that. Our daughters
need a home. I'll give it to them, but it will be a home
without a mother. That's the best I can do.

Forgive me, Beth. I know you'd want me to marry again, but I can't. It wouldn't be fair to that poor, lonely girl who expects to be my wife. As soon as I break the engagement, I'll send her back to her family.

Dani stared at the page. Patrick hadn't loved her. Even worse, he'd lied to Dani and himself. Anger shot through her veins, cauterizing the cuts of grief. Being called a "poor, lonely girl" was the last straw. Still shaking, she forced herself to finish reading the letter.

I'm sure of my decision, Beth. My only worry is for the girls. If something happens to me, they'll need a guardian. Right now, Beau's named in my will. I haven't seen him since Lucy died. We both know he went crazy, but he's a blood relative. That counts for something. Not that it matters…I expect the Lord to torture me with a long life, watching as I miss you more with every passing day.

Your husband for eternity,

Dani stared at Patrick's signature in horror. His final words voided the letter in her trunk. She had no right to adopt his daughters. He'd wanted her to leave.

Numb with shock, she stared out the window. Where was God now? He'd taken Patrick from her, first through his death and then through his lies. He'd taken her pride, her hope and even the right to call Patrick's daughters her own.

Dani searched for a way to keep the girls and found a solution that made her cheeks redden with shame. If she burned the letters in the stove, no one would ever know about Patrick's change of heart. Beau had already agreed to the adoption. What difference did the letters make now? She looked at the sheets of newsprint scattered on the bed. One by one, she put them in a pile. She had to light the stove for breakfast. One stick of wood and the letters would be gone.

She *had* to keep the girls. They needed her as much as she needed them. Burning the letters was wrong, but showing them to Beau meant risking everything. He'd changed his mind about the adoption because of her abilities, but he also lived by a code of honor. Patrick's final request would matter to him. With her stomach churning, she put on her day dress and shoes. She glanced in the mirror but didn't braid her hair. Instead she tied it back with a ribbon, then stared hard at her own face.

Not once had she willfully done something as dishonest as destroying the letters. Beau deserved to know the truth, but showing him Patrick's final words meant casting herself fully on God's and Beau's good graces. She thought of his hand on her back and how strong he'd felt. She'd sensed kindness in his touch, but she'd also seen his face when he'd found her in his room. Beau didn't compromise. He saw black-and-white. Dani saw shades of gray.

"Now we see through a glass darkly."

The scripture came from her memory. She felt trapped in a mist, confused by circumstances and unsure of God's mercy. She couldn't bear to think about losing the girls. What if Beau shipped them off to Harriet Lange? Closing her eyes, she imagined a hawkish old woman ordering Emma to bring her tea. She saw Esther crying and Ellie unhappy in starched ruffles. Dani could spare them that misery, but it meant compromising her integrity. If she burned the letters, she'd be turning her back on God, Beau and everything she believed.

Are you there, Lord?

Silence.

Confused and trembling, she carried the letters into the

kitchen. The mantel clock chimed four times. Soon Beau
would come to the house for breakfast. She opened the stove's
firebox and peered inside. With the rush of air, the embers
flared. If she added the letters, they'd be gone in seconds.
Orange light burned through the gray ash. In that flare of heat
and light, Dani saw her own soul.

She'd been looking at the ash of her circumstances. The
charred ruins of her engagement and Patrick's deception. But
below the surface—through that glass darkly—a simple truth
burned as bright as the embers. God hadn't left her to cope
alone. She knew right from wrong, the difference between
truth and a lie. Someday she'd see the Lord face-to-face and
she'd know why she'd come to this place. Until then, she had
her faith to see her through.

With the letters safe on the table, Dani lifted newspaper
from the kindling box, crumpled it into a ball and added it to
the coals. As it caught fire, she closed the stove door. When
Beau came for breakfast, she'd show him the letters. Weak
in the knees, she sat at the table where the sheets lay in a pile,
a monument to lies and lost dreams. Bowing her head, she
wept so hard her shoulders quaked. She tasted the salt of her
own tears and felt them stinging her cheeks.

"I'm scared, Lord Jesus," she said out loud. "Without the
girls, I have nothing."

Nothing but me.

The voice was in her head, but the hand on her shoulder
belonged to a flesh-and-blood man.

"Dani?"

She looked up and saw Beau. With her thoughts in a
jumble, she blurted the truth. "He didn't love me."

"Who didn't?"

"Patrick."

Beau's eyes narrowed. "What brought this on?"

She nudged the letters with her fingertip. "I found those." She sniffed, then wiped her eyes with her sleeve.

Keeping one hand on her shoulder, Beau reached into his pocket and pulled out a ladies handkerchief. "Use this."

Dani opened the square and saw roses. The hankie, she realized, had belonged to Lucy. With more tears welling, she looked into Beau's eyes and saw a glow akin to the embers in the stove. Beneath the ash, he was very much alive. Judging by his expression, he wasn't happy.

He dropped into the chair next to hers. "What's in the letters?"

"The last one says it all."

He picked up the letter, read every word, then looked into her eyes. "I'm sorry."

Her heart pounded with dread. "I found them a few hours ago. I was upset, so I looked through Patrick's things. I wanted to feel…"

She hung her head to hide her eyes. Had she wanted to feel close to Patrick or separate from Beau? Right now, she felt the opposite. She'd never cry for Patrick again, but she felt closer to Beau than she'd ever felt to another human being. Lucy's handkerchief was more personal than a touch. Gripping the linen, she waited for him to decide her future.

With their gazes locked, he crumpled Patrick's letter into a ball. "If you don't burn this trash, I will."

Dani's mouth gaped. "Really?"

"My brother was a fool." Beau's voice shook with anger. "I'm sorry to speak ill of the dead, but he was a two-faced mama's boy who whined about everything. You're better off without him."

She clutched the hankie. "I can keep the girls?"

"Of course."

He picked up the letters, walked to the stove and shoved

them in the firebox. The newsprint caught with a whoosh. He latched the door and faced Dani. "If Patrick were alive, I'd haul him behind the woodshed. Of all the foolish drivel…"

She couldn't find her tongue.

Beau gave her a firm look. "Don't you dare doubt yourself."

"But I do." She hung her head.

"You shouldn't." He crossed back to the table. "You're a beautiful woman, Dani. If it weren't for Clay Johnson, I'd—" He sealed his lips.

She looked up. "You're being kind."

"No, I'm not."

"I know pity when I hear it." She faked a smile. "Thank you for trying, Beau. But I need to face the facts."

He looked baffled. "What facts?"

"I've been engaged three times now. I'm just not fit for marriage."

"That's flat-out stupid." His tone, warm like milk, softened the words but not the look in his eyes. "You're so full of goodness it shames me."

"Thank you for the compliment, but I have to be realistic." She shrugged. "There's something wrong with me. I've never felt what I thought I'd feel."

His gaze lingered on her face, studying her, reading her thoughts in the flush of her cheeks until his eyes glinted with understanding. "You mean the 'wanting' part."

Her cheeks flamed even brighter. "I don't know."

Beau stopped breathing. So did she. Ever so gently, he tipped up her chin with his fingers, then oh-so-tenderly, he kissed her on the lips.

Her knees went weak. Her first kiss…and Beau didn't even know it. He raised his head and looked at her with that glow in his eyes. Dani felt both naive and amazed. A kiss…the start of what God allowed between a man and wife. "And the two shall become one flesh." One life, one hope. A couple joined in body, mind and soul. Dani wanted that joy, and she wanted it with Beau. With her eyes wide, she watched his expression change from kindly to confident.

The man looked downright pleased with himself. "You're an amazing woman, Dani. Don't ever doubt it."

With a look that bordered on proud, he went out the back door, leaving her confused but sure of one thing. Not all men were as fickle as Patrick. And not all men smelled like bad onions. Dani may have been engaged to three men, but this was first time she'd truly been in love.

Beau wasn't the least bit sorry he'd kissed Dani. Patrick had shattered her confidence. With that brush of their lips, Beau had given it back to her. He'd go back later for breakfast and pretend nothing had happened. It had been a kiss, one so chaste it bordered on brotherly…except for the way it made him feel. Alive. Strong. Privy to secrets she didn't understand.

As he crossed the yard to the barn, he fought the urge to whoop like a fool. He'd given Dani something to think about, that was for sure. He hadn't felt this good in years, maybe never. Lucy would have been glad he'd given Dani the handkerchief. Beau had put it in his pocket as a reminder, but he was in no danger of forgetting Clay Johnson.

Last night, when he'd seen the light in his room, he'd imagined Johnson harming Dani. He'd half expected to find her tied up with the outlaw's pistol pressed to her temple. When he'd drawn his gun, he'd been ready for anything but what he'd found. Dani looking at the treasures he'd neglected to put away…. He'd seen tenderness in her eyes and a caring that linked the past and present. If he stayed in Castle Rock, he could take her for buggy rides and moonlight walks. If their hearts met—and he was certain they would—they'd be free to marry.

As he walked into the barn, Beau raked his hand through his hair. What was wrong with him? He'd made a vow to kill Clay Johnson. Until the outlaw met his eternal destiny, Beau couldn't rest.

He went to Daff, reached down and checked her udder. The hot spot still felt normal. He'd noticed the change earlier. Seeing the glow from the kitchen window, he'd gone inside to share the good news with Dani and found her weeping. He'd never forget the hurt in her eyes. Irritated, Beau stood straight, scratched Daff and headed for his room. With each step, he thought of Patrick's insulting words. Beau had meant what he'd said about taking his brother to the woodshed. Hurting or not, a man had to take responsibility. Beau understood about missing Beth. He knew about mistakes, too. What he didn't understand was not loving Dani.

The wanting… He felt it now. Not in the way of bodily lust but in his soul, the place in his heart that wanted to protect Dani from all harm and provide for her. As he walked into his room, he thought of the saddlebags stowed under the cot. He lit the lamp and saw the scratchy bedroll where he'd sleep alone. At the sight of his gun belt on the chair, he almost asked the Almighty to help him catch Clay Johnson. Once the outlaw paid for Lucy's death, Beau would be free. He could stay in Castle Rock and court Dani. He'd be Uncle Beau, not a bounty hunter cursed to work alone.

His jaw tensed. He thought of Josh preaching to the men at the Wednesday Ruckus. *Don't pretty it up, men. Speak your heart. God can handle a cuss word or two. Even more if that's all you can manage.*

"God—" Beau clamped his jaw shut.

The room seemed to press in on him, so he stepped back into the barn and blew out a breath. The thoughts in his mind were ugly but honest. Beau felt sure the Lord understood every cursed word. He was just as sure the Almighty didn't care. Beau tipped his face up to the rafters. He heard hymns bouncing and closed his eyes, then he murmured what might have been a prayer.

"Let me kill him, Lord."

"Vengeance is Mine…"

Beau muttered a foul word. He wanted to love and laugh and make Dani his wife. One bullet and Johnson would be dead. Justice would be served and Beau would be free. With his eyes shut tight and his hands knotted, he listened for God's voice.

Daff mooed.

A horse snorted.

But the rafters stayed silent. Heaving a sigh, Beau went back to his room. God might have heard his prayers, but He hadn't answered them.

"Now's the time, boss," Andy said to Clay. "I heard about it in town. Morgan's living on a dairy farm with three kids and a pretty blonde. I say *we* go after *him*."

The three men were sitting around a fire. Two days had passed since they'd raided the Rocking J. They'd ridden deep into a canyon with so many twists Clay wondered if he could find his way out. Last night they'd camped in a cave. Rain had washed away their tracks, so they'd decided to rest a day while Clay picked a horse. Goose had picked the spot well. The gorge narrowed, limiting the number of ways a posse could approach. If the law—or Beau Morgan—came after them, they'd have the edge.

Clay stubbed out his cigar. "Why are you worried about Morgan? He's my problem."

Goose shrugged. "He's trouble for all of us."

Andy played with his knife. "Right now, he's a sitting duck."

Clay didn't trust the kid's judgment. Before raiding the Rocking J, he'd sent Andy to town to listen for talk at the Silver River. The kid had spent two nights and come back late Monday. "How do you know about Morgan and the farm?"

"I went to church."

"You *what?*"

Andy grinned. "That fool pastor shook my hand and invited me back."

"That was flat-out stupid." Clay tossed the stub into the fire. "We wore masks at the Rocking J, but you could still be recognized. The Baylors are church folk."

Andy's expression turned wicked. "Don't worry, boss. I pulled it off."

"Who does the minister think you are?" Goose asked.

With a blink, Andy's face turned from leering to boyish. "I'm a lost soul looking for work and Jesus. I tell you, church is the best place for talk. Women gab, and the young ones look at a fella like he's special."

Clay knew Reverend Blue. Several months before Randall's gang started raiding ranches near Denver, the minister had ridden into their camp and asked for coffee. He'd said grace over their supper of beans and entertained them with a story about a man-eating fish. A kid named Chet had accepted Jesus that night. A week later, he'd left the gang.

Clay didn't know what had become of Chet, but he knew where *he* stood with God. He'd killed a woman. That crime put him beyond forgiveness. When the time came, Clay expected to meet up with his brother in Hell. Sometimes the thought made him nervous. Other times he didn't care. Lately he'd felt so bad about Lucy Morgan that he couldn't stop thinking about a person's final moments.

Goose stretched his legs. "Maybe Andy's right."

Clay didn't like Goose, but the man had good instincts. "Why do you say that?"

"If the woman's going to church, you can bet Morgan's sleeping alone in the barn. We could hit the ranch late at night and string him up before anyone knew what happened. You'd be rid of him."

Andy howled like a dog. "I've got first call on the blonde."

Goose threw hot coffee at him. "Settle down. We're doing this for Clay."

Clay stared into the fire. When he'd told Goose and Andy about killing Morgan's wife, he'd talked tough, as if he'd sniped her to pay for Zeke and had no regrets. They'd believed him, but it wasn't true. Her death had been a mistake, one that filled him with profound regret. Sometimes he thought about what Joshua Blue had said about that giant fish. A man named Jonah had lived in its belly for three days. He'd come out alive and told the story. The Reverend said a man named Jesus had done the same thing. He'd died on the cross and risen from the grave. The Reverend said men could make that death their own. He'd told Clay he could die to his sins and be reborn. He didn't have to be a murderer and a thief. He could be washed in the blood of the Lamb and be made brand-new.

Clay had thought about that talk for five years. He was still thinking about it. Sometimes he felt so bad about Lucy Morgan he wanted to die. If he prayed Reverend Blue's prayer, what would happen? He was afraid to find out. Guilt made a man do foolish things, and Clay had enough guilt to build a castle.

"What'll it be, boss?" Goose asked.

Clay's mind turned to Beau Morgan holding his dying wife. He couldn't stand the thought of putting another woman, let alone three little girls, in harm's way, but he'd had all he could take of the chase. He wanted it to end, but on his terms. Face-to-face. Man-to-man. But then what? Clay didn't know exactly. He just knew he had business with Beau Morgan.

"We're staying put," Clay said. "This time I want Morgan to come to me."

"But boss—" Andy whined.

"Shut up," Clay ordered.

The kid winked at him. "Can I at least go back to church?"

"Sure, just don't do anything stupid." Clay wished he could go himself. He liked the story about the whale.

Chapter Eleven

Supper was over and Dani had put the girls to bed. Needing to think, she lifted her shawl off a hook and went out to the porch. With the moon shining bright, she sat in the rocker closest to the side railing. Pushing with her feet, she wondered if she'd ever feel like her old self.

Two days had passed since Beau had kissed her. Everything about the man was rough, but his lips had been rose-petal soft. When he'd come to breakfast, he'd acted as if nothing had happened. He hadn't mentioned the letters and neither had she, though after he'd finished breakfast, Dani had fetched the letters she'd written to Patrick and burned those, too.

With the picnic on Sunday, she had a decision to make. She'd told Pastor Josh she wouldn't be bringing a basket for the auction, but Beau's kiss had given her second thoughts. The caress had been brotherly, but she'd seen a glint in his eyes that went beyond kindness. Considering how her own feelings had exploded into raw hope, she wanted to know what Beau felt for her. She felt certain he'd come to the picnic if only to keep an eye on her and girls. If he bought her basket, they'd be eating together. It would mean the kiss had meant as much to him as it had to her.

Rocking gently, she closed her eyes and pictured Beau sitting with her on a blanket under a tree, sharing a meal and trading sweet looks. The answer to her deepest prayers glimmered just out of reach. She knew how he felt about Clay Johnson, but she believed in a big God, one Who'd overcome hate with love through the gift of His son. Beau and God weren't on speaking terms, but Dani had hope.

Closing her eyes, she asked the Lord to heal Beau's heart. The words tumbled through her mind, mixing with her dreams until she heard Beau's boots scuff the dirt. She opened her eyes and saw him awash in moonlight, standing with one foot braced on the bottom step and his hand on the post supporting the overhang.

"A penny for your thoughts?" he asked.

She managed a smile. "They're worth more than a penny."

"Tell me."

Not in a million years. She hunted for another subject. "The girls are excited about the picnic."

Beau grunted.

Dani thought the sound was charming, a sure sign she'd lost her heart. She smiled at him "What does *that* mean?"

"I'm not fond of church picnics."

"Why not?"

Frowning, Beau climbed up the steps and sat next to her. Her rocker squeaked and thumped. His stayed still. "Is Adie doing a box lunch auction?"

"Yes, she is."

"That's how I met Lucy."

Dani thought of the hankie in her pocket. Was it Beau's love for Lucy that made him carry it, or was it a reminder of his hate for Clay Johnson? Dani understood grief. Time brought healing. Someday Beau would love again and she wanted to be that woman. Hate was different. It ate a man alive, feeding on his soul until there was nothing left. The only cure was forgiveness, a pardon that came from compassion.

Dani wasn't about to preach forgiveness to Beau. She didn't have that right, but she knew about love. So did Beau. Hoping to see the man who'd sung in the church choir, she turned the conversation to the past. "Did you buy Lucy's basket?"

A smile lifted the corners of his mouth. "No, but I arrested the man who did."

"What did he do?"

"I knew this so-called gentleman carried a whiskey flask, so I kept an eye on him. Sure enough, he got drunk and caused a stir."

"And you stepped in."

"I sure did."

Dani hummed softly. "I bet Lucy fell for you that very minute."

"Nope." He grinned. "It took six months of courting, mostly because she was enjoying herself."

Dani envied Lucy with every fiber, yet she wasn't jealous. They'd have been good friends. "She was blessed to have you."

"I was the blessed one."

She studied the square cut of his jaw, the arrow of his nose pointing west. He looked at peace in a distant way. "You liked being married," she said matter-of-factly.

"Very much."

"My parents were happy. So's my brother." She gave a light laugh. "Maybe there's hope for me after all."

Beau gave her a sideways glance. "There's hope, all right."

With you? If it weren't for Clay Johnson, would you stay?
She couldn't ask the question without revealing her heart, but
she could do a little fishing. "I think I'll make a basket for
the auction."

Beau's eyes narrowed. "What for?"

"For one thing, it's a fund-raiser for the Baylor family."

He said nothing.

"For another, it might be fun." Dani paused, then jiggled
the bait. "Maybe I'll meet someone."

With a bend of his knee, Beau put the rocking chair in
motion. "Like who?"

"Whoever buys my basket."

"That could be anyone."

"It's just a picnic," she replied. "But that's how things get
started, isn't it? A sunny day, sitting in the shade…"

Their chairs thumped in perfect time until Beau's creaked
to a stop. "If that's what you want, bring fried chicken."

She'd made a batch two days ago. "You liked it?"

"It's the best I've tasted."

Dani took his interest in the menu as a good sign. Blushing
with pleasure, she smiled. "What about raspberry pie? Should
I bring that, too?"

"Sure." He drummed his fingers on the armrest. "There are
some good men in town."

He sounded matter-of-fact, as if he were discussing cattle.
Dani's heart sank until she realized Beau had put his rocker
back in motion. Again, the rhythm matched hers. He was
fighting his feelings. She was sure of it.

He stopped the rocker with a thud. "Sometimes I wish for
things, Dani. But it can't be."

Her throat tightened. "The past hurts, I know. But the
future—"

"Is out of my hands."

But it wasn't. He had a choice. Dani wanted to fight for him, but the set of his jaw brooked no argument. His eyes, though, glimmered with a longing for love, a family, peaceful nights and a full belly. He also wanted to avenge Lucy. He'd made his choice, but that didn't mean he couldn't change his mind. Dani didn't know everything about Beau, but she knew he liked fried chicken.

She went back to rocking. "I'm definitely bringing a basket for the auction."

"Good idea."

"It's going to have that chicken you like, fresh apples, slaw and sweet tea."

Beau raised his chin. "Don't forget raspberry pie."

"I won't."

Dani kept rocking. Slowly, Beau matched the pace of his chair to hers, giving her hope that he'd bid on her basket. The conversation drifted to the cows, names for the new calves, the girls, the silo and the weather. Not once did their chairs lose their matching rhythms. She hoped it was a sign of things to come.

"There's a problem with the adoption."

Beau was seated across from Trevor Scott in the attorney's office. The meeting hadn't been planned. Twenty minutes ago, when Beau had dropped Dani and the girls at church, Adie had slipped a piece of stationery into his palm. The note had been from the attorney and had read, "Urgent. Come to my office during the morning service."

Beau had the note in his pocket now. "What happened?"

"Harriet Lange wants all three girls and she's prepared to fight for them."

"That's ridiculous."

"Don't be too quick to judge, Mr. Morgan." Scott leaned back in his chair. "I received a letter from her attorney."

"What does it say?"

"Miss Lange is appalled at the thought of Miss Baxter adopting the girls. To quote her attorney, she believes 'blood is thicker than water.'"

Beau had to grit his teeth. "Dani loves those girls."

"I believe you, but that doesn't change the facts. Unfortunately, my second letter stirred up a hornet's nest."

"In what way?"

"Miss Lange has enlisted the aid of other family members. They've pledged financial support for all three girls with Miss Lange acting as legal guardian."

Beau frowned. He'd made a promise to Dani and intended to keep it. "I won't agree to it."

"You may not have a choice."

"Why not?"

"Miss Lange is questioning your character."

Since hearing Emma's story about being slapped, Beau had regretted contacting Harriet Lange. He had his faults, but so did she. "What's she saying?"

"That you're a drinker."

"That's a flat-out lie."

"Is it?" Scott asked. "The family hired a Pinkerton's detective. He saw you in the Silver River Saloon."

"Did he tell Miss Lange I ordered *coffee?*"

"Apparently not."

"She knows you're a former lawman, but the detective was quick to note your more recent profession. Bounty hunting—"

"That's not the whole story." Beau didn't track killers for the money. He did it for the sake of justice.

"But you've lived that life."

"I'm after one man in particular," Beau said. "It's like fishing. A few others took the bait and got caught."

"That may be true, Mr. Morgan. But from what I understand, your profession has made you a wealthy man."

Beau didn't feel wealthy. Losing his wife had made him the poorest man on earth. "It depends what you call rich."

Scott laced his fingers over his chest. "Nonetheless, the money is evidence of your lifestyle."

"It's evidence of hard work."

The attorney eyed him thoughtfully. "Why do you go to the Silver River?"

"For coffee."

"You need to be straight with me, Mr. Morgan."

Beau didn't want to talk, but Scott needed the whole truth to do his job. "I go for information. The man I'm chasing is Clay Johnson. Rumor has it he raided the Rocking J."

Scott's features hardened. "Are you a target, Mr. Morgan?"

"Possibly."

"Are the girls in danger?"

Beau didn't know what Clay would do next, only what he'd done in the past. No one knew what tomorrow held. Beau looked Scott in the eye. "They're in as much danger as Patrick was riding home in a storm."

The attorney's gaze hardened. "You're telling me you're being pursued by a killer and you have children in your care."

"It's not like that."

"Maybe," Scott said. "But that's what the Lange family sees. Even the *appearance* of danger will work against you. I suggest you stop visiting the saloon."

Irritated, Beau walked to the window. He didn't want to give up his trips to the Silver River. They were his link to Clay, but Scott had a point. "I'll think about it."

"Good."

Beau drummed his fingers on the sill. Time wasn't on his side. "How long will it be?"

"A few weeks. Judge Hall is overworked these days. If there's no protest, he'll sign the documents and I'll file them in the Douglas County Hall of Records."

"Any way to speed things up?"

"I don't think so."

"Then get it rolling."

He looked at the pendulum clock on the wall. Church had ended ten minutes ago. He blinked and imagined Dani milling with the crowd, surrounded by single men looking for a wife. Beau had no intention of bidding on her basket, but he planned to watch every man who did. He knew exactly which basket she'd brought. She'd tied a bright blue ribbon on the handle and had asked him to carry it to the surrey. He'd put it in the back, but she'd moved it up front where the smell of chicken had wafted to his nose. It would be a small torture to watch her share that meal with another man, but Beau saw no alternative.

He lifted his hat off the hook, walked downstairs to the surrey and drove to the church where Josh was already auctioning boxes.

Dani scanned the crowd outside the church but didn't see Beau. Instead her gaze landed on the cowboy who'd sat behind her in church. Before the service, he'd introduced himself as Andy. Wearing a shy smile, he'd inquired about her picnic basket. Dani had no interest in sharing the meal with him, so she'd given him a vague answer. As the auction began, she searched the crowd for Beau but didn't see him. If Andy bought her basket, she'd have to be polite.

She glanced down the road to town, then shifted her gaze to the children playing "Mother May I?" She spotted the girls, giggling as Stephen, Josh and Adie's son, chased after Ellie. No matter who bought Dani's box, the girls would be sharing the meal. She looked back to the front of the church, where Adie had arranged the baskets on a table at the top of the steps. If Josh took the suppers in order, hers would be the seventh to go. Nervous and hopeful, Dani watched as Reverend Blue whistled for attention.

"Listen up, gentlemen. We have fourteen baskets today. Bid fast and bid high. The money's going to the Baylor family."

As the crowd clapped, Dani searched again for Beau.

"Howdy there, Miss Baxter."

Without turning, she recognized Andy's voice. Not only had they spoken before the service, he'd sung "What a Friend We Have in Jesus" as if he'd meant it, except he'd sung it loud like Mr. Rayburn in Wisconsin, whom everyone knew made trips to Madison for less than noble purposes. Dani didn't want to turn to Andy, but she saw no choice. Without smiling, she said, "Hello."

He winked at her. "Which basket is yours?"

"You'll have to guess." Dani looked straight ahead.

Andy leaned closer, crowding her to the point of discomfort as he made his voice low. "If you won't tell me which it is, I'll just look for the prettiest one."

Dani sidestepped. "I have children with me. I better check on them."

"I'll go with you."

"That's not necessary."

Andy's smile might have been friendly, but the glint in his eyes held a trace of anger. Dani wanted to call for help, but what could she say? He hadn't done anything except stand a little too close. She stayed where she was, in front of the steps where she could see Adie and the baskets. When Adie made eye contact, Dani waved. Ignoring Andy, she turned to check on the girls. Emma, seeing the auction had begun, rounded up Ellie and Esther and hurried in Dani's direction.

Andy grinned. "Cute kids."

"Yes." Dani willed Emma to go back to "Mother May I." She didn't want the girls near Andy, but she had no way to signal them to stay with their friends. They reached her side as Pastor Josh lifted the third basket. Andy tipped his hat to Emma, then smiled at the younger girls. "You three must be sisters."

"We are," Ellie said.

"How did you ladies meet Miss Baxter?"

No way did Dani want to share her business with this man. "It's a long story. One I won't bore you with Mr.—"

"Andy."

Dani ignored the familiarity. Turning, she scanned the crowd again for Beau. Pastor Josh handed the fourth basket to a gray-haired man who'd bought his wife's supper, probably for the thirtieth time in thirty years.

Andy stayed at Dani's side, making small talk with the girls about the town.

Pastor Josh held up another picnic supper, a large basket decorated with ribbons and red gingham. "What do I hear for an opening bid?"

"Six bits!" said a man in the back.

A few bids followed, but everyone knew Tim Landers would spend his last nickel for his fiancée's supper. When the bidding stopped, Dani looked down the road and saw Beau. Pastor Josh lifted the sixth basket. As he started the bidding, Beau walked from the surrey to the edge of the crowd where he spoke with Sheriff Dawes. A young man won the basket, picked up the supper and smiled boldly at a girl who'd struck Dani as shy.

Pastor Josh lifted Dani's basket next. "I smell fried chicken, gentleman. What do I hear for an opening bid?"

"That's ours!" Esther announced.

Dani wanted to put her hand over the child's mouth.

Andy raised his hand. "Two dollars."

Dani cringed. The other baskets had gone for a dollar and change. She sought Beau with her eyes, praying silently that he'd bid on her basket. Instead of signaling a bid, he crossed his arms over his chest. He hadn't looked at her once.

A man in a suit raised his arm. "Three dollars!"

Dani recognized the banker. He glanced at her and smiled.

Andy upped the bidding to three dollars and change. The banker raised it to five. A rancher in a paisley vest bid six.

"Seven!" Andy shouted.

The rancher smiled at her but tipped his hat in defeat. The banker raised his hand. "Ten!"

"Do I hear eleven?" Josh looked straight at Beau.

"Twelve!" The bid came from Andy.

Dani's heart shriveled. Beau hadn't bid at all.

"That's once," Pastor Josh said. "Twice."

"Twenty dollars." The voice belonged to Beau, and it rang with an authority that stunned the crowd into silence.

Looking at him from across the yard, Dani didn't know what to think. He'd just spent twenty dollars for her fried chicken, but he looked far from pleased.

Chapter Twelve

Beau strode to the front of the church, paid for Dani's basket and headed in her direction. His gaze snapped to the red-haired man at her side. During the auction, he'd spoken to Sheriff Dawes and learned the fellow was a stranger in town. Under any circumstances, Beau would have sidled up to the kid and asked questions. With Dani in the picture, he felt even more wary.

With the basket in hand, Beau approached Dani and the girls. The stranger locked eyes with him, then turned to Dani. "I'd say you're spoken for, Miss Baxter." He tipped his hat and walked away.

"Wait up!" Beau called.

Red kept going. Beau wanted to drop the basket and haul him to the sheriff's office for a little talk, but he had no evidence of wrongdoing, just a feeling in his gut and those weren't always right. Neither could he leave Dani and the girls. Red had raised Beau's hackles, but so had his talk with Trevor Scott. Beau didn't like being watched by a Pinkerton's detective. Heading to the church from Scott's office, he'd decided to bore the detective to tears by playing horseshoes and watching Dani from afar.

Now she was at his side, looking worried while they headed for the shade of a cottonwood. The girls ran ahead. Emma flapped the blanket, giggling as it settled into a crooked square. As the girls plopped down, Beau set the basket on a corner. Smiling nervously, Dani dished up his plate. He bit into the fried chicken, holding in a groan of pleasure as he chewed. The supper had been worth every penny, but he didn't compliment Dani. Instead he got down to business. "Who was that fellow?"

"Someone named Andy," she replied.

"Where's he from?"

"I don't know."

Emma wrinkled her nose. "He sat behind us in church."

The younger girls had been in Adie's Sunday school class and were more interested in dessert than talk. Beau wanted details from Dani, but she was wiping crumbs from Esther's face. With her shoulders angled and her chin dipped, she seemed almost shy.

Beau didn't understand. During the auction, he'd watched her from the corner of his eye and seen her agitation. He'd expected her to thank him for chasing away Andy. Instead she seemed anxious. Looking at her flushed cheeks, Beau worried that he'd made her angry.

He set his plate on the blanket. "Sorry I had to buy your basket. I know you're looking to meet people." He couldn't bring himself to say "men."

Dani's gaze snapped to his. "You're *sorry?*"

"I wrecked your plans, but that Andy fellow—I couldn't let him have supper with you."

"Why not?"

"I didn't like his looks."

She looked at him with a mix of hope and concern. "Was that all?"

He scowled. "What else would it be?"

Dani turned back to Esther. "I see."

The girls finished eating, then went to play with their friends. Dani stacked the dirty plates with a clatter and set them by the basket. Beau didn't know a lot about women, but he knew a snit when he saw one. He gentled his voice. "What's wrong?"

She slapped her own plate on to the pile. "I'm sorry you wasted your money."

"What?"

"The basket... You didn't want it."

Oh yes, I did. He couldn't answer truthfully without muddying the waters, so he shrugged. "It had to be done."

"No, it didn't."

In his better years, he'd have flirted with Dani until she smiled. Instead he set down his plate, leaving the pie unfinished. "Tell me about this Andy character."

"He's not your concern."

"Oh yes, he is," Beau said, grumbling. "He just cost me twenty dollars."

Dani's lips tightened. "You didn't *have* to buy the basket."

"What was I supposed to do? Let him eat with you?"

"Why not?"

Because you're mine... Because I want you for myself. Beau's thoughts stopped in the back of his throat, but his irritation leaked from his lips. "You're raising my nieces, that's why."

"Is that all?"

No, but it was enough. "You and the girls are in *my* care. Before a man comes courting, he's going to earn my approval."

Dani raised her chin. "You're leaving. What happens then?"

Beau couldn't say. Looking at Dani, all fierce and defiant, he felt a force he hadn't felt in a long time. He wanted to protect this woman and provide for her. What would it be like to make her his wife? They'd fight, that was certain. They'd make up, too. With kisses and forgiveness and the supple bending of their wills. All he had to do was set down his hate for Clay Johnson. He simply couldn't do it.

He picked up the glass of tea but didn't drink. He had to think of Dani, not himself. She deserved a husband. He couldn't be that man, but others today had shown interest. He drummed his fingers on the cup. "I'd be glad to see you married, but only to a good man."

She lowered her eyes. "Like who?"

"The rancher looked like a decent sort. So did the fellow in the suit. Anyone but that cowboy."

Dani grimaced. "To tell the truth, I didn't like him at all."

"Me, neither."

She looked at Beau with a sad smile. "Thank you for buying my basket. I appreciated it."

"It was nothing." Never mind that he wanted it to lead to everything. He drained the tea. It tasted sweet but splashed in his belly like acid. He had to stay focused on the business of finding Clay Johnson.

Beau lowered his glass. "What else happened with that Andy fellow?"

She described how he'd sat behind her in church and quizzed her about the basket. With each word, she looked more nervous.

Beau wanted to chase down Andy and slap him. "I don't want to upset you, Dani. But you have be careful."

"I know."

"Andy could be running with Johnson. They could be scouting out the next ranch to raid."

"Or looking for you."

"Yes."

He plucked a blade of grass and rolled it in his fingers. He wanted to crush Johnson with the same ease.

"Hey, Morgan!"

He turned and saw Wallace hurrying in their direction. When the barkeep reached the blanket, Beau made a hurried introduction, then motioned for the man to sit. "What's up?"

Wallace stayed on his feet. "Do you remember about Johnson coming in for whiskey?"

"Of course."

"He had two men with him that night. One of them just came back."

Beau had already stood. "What did he look like?"

"Young with red hair."

Just as he suspected, Andy had been up to no good. Beau thought of the surrey he'd driven to town and groaned. He couldn't go after the kid without a good horse, nor did he want to approach Clay without his long guns. The pistol on his hip was fine for a Sunday picnic but not the battle he felt coming. Andy had been the spotter. Clay Johnson was ready to strike.

Beau sensed Dani's gaze and turned. "You'll have to stay with Josh and Adie."

Her eyes clouded. "The cows—"

He'd never felt so tied up in his life. He wanted to go after Clay, but he couldn't leave Dani and his nieces unprotected on the farm. "I'll think of something."

Wallace interrupted. "We need to find Dawes."

Beau scanned the picnickers. By a tree he saw a crowd of children, his nieces among them, skipping rope. He spotted the sheriff eating with his wife and son. With Wallace in his wake, Beau strode through the crowd.

Dawes saw Beau and stood. "What's up, sheriff?"

Beau respected the use of his old title. What Dawes lacked in talent, he made up for in decency. "That red-haired kid, did you see him?"

"I sure did."

"Wallace saw him with Clay Johnson."

The barkeep described Andy's visit to the saloon. The kid had knocked on the back door, bought six bottles of whiskey and left. "That was twenty minutes ago. You can still catch him."

Beau's legs itched for a fast ride, but Andy had caught him unprepared. No horse. No guns. Nothing but fury and the knowledge that Dani had become a target.

The sheriff motioned to his son. "Come here, Howie."

Beau hadn't met the boy, but he knew Howie from the girls' stories. Emma, he guessed, had a crush on the sixteen-year-old. Beau looked him up and down. He had height, some muscle and seemed responsible.

Howie joined his father. "What happened?"

"Get Teddy and Ace. Tell them we have a lead on Johnson."

Howie's eyes glinted. "I want to go."

"Sorry, son."

"But—"

"You're too young."

Beau felt for the kid. He also saw an answer to his problem. He stuck out his hand, greeting Howie like a man. "I'm Beau Morgan."

Howie shook. "You're Emma's uncle."

"I'm riding out with your pa. Miss Baxter and my nieces are staying in town. Can I trust you to see to things at the farm?"

Howie looked at this father. "I'd rather go with you."

When Dawes gripped his son's shoulder, Beau's mind tripped down a dangerous road. What would it be like to have a son with Dani's eyes?

The sheriff spoke in a low tone. "We need your help, son."

Beau understood young men. Howie wanted respect, and Beau knew how to show it. "I'll pay you." He named an amount that matched the importance of the job.

Howie stood tall. "I'll do it."

"Here's the plan." Beau laid out the details. He'd borrow a horse from Dawes and ride hard to the farm. He'd get the tools of his trade—his own horse, guns, ammo, irons and a rope—and join the sheriff and his men. Howie would take the surrey to the farm and stay. Dani and the girls would go home with Josh and Adie. Beau had to speak to the Blues, but he felt certain they'd help.

The Reverend must have seen the men talking, because he walked up to them. "What happened?"

Beau told him about Andy.

Josh's face hardened. "I saw him bird-dogging Dani. If you hadn't bought that basket, Adie and I would have joined them for supper."

When a man didn't trust God, he needed friends. Beau had Josh. "I need a favor."

"Anything."

"Can Dani and the girls stay at the parsonage?"

"Sure. Stephen'll enjoy the company. What about your stock?"

Howie spoke up. "I'm headed out there now."

Dawes looked at his son with pride. "Stay alert."

"I will, Pa."

"It's settled," Dawes said. "We'll meet at the office."

As the sheriff left, Josh clapped Beau on the back. "Go with God, my friend."

Beau's mouth hardened. "He's welcome to ride along, but I doubt He's interested."

Josh didn't say a word. He simply looked at Beau with

the same eyes that had wept with him for Lucy, then he left to find Adie.

Beau strode back to the blanket where Dani was neatening up. At the sight of him, she pushed to her feet. She'd worn pink today. Until now, he hadn't noticed. Beau stopped three feet away. He could still smell the chicken. "I'm riding out with Dawes."

"Of course."

He hated himself for the quaver in her voice. He wanted to keep her safe, not cause her worry. He wanted other things, too. Things he couldn't have until Clay Johnson paid for Lucy's murder. To keep from touching her, he crossed his arms. "I spoke to Josh. You and the girls are staying with them."

Her brows snapped together. "What about the milking?"

"Howie's handling it."

"I see."

Beau had expected a fight. Instead Dani's expression melted into womanly concern. His stomach knotted with thoughts he couldn't afford. Beau couldn't bring himself to pray to the God who'd let Lucy die, but he wanted to. In the distance he saw the cemetery with its stone markers. He heard children skipping rope and the muffled voices of men and the women who'd fed them. Wordless, he turned to go.

Dani grasped his arm. "I have something for you."

His eyes followed her hand to the pocket of her pink dress. She reached inside and withdrew Lucy's handkerchief. "This is yours."

"Keep it."

"But—"

"I want you to have it."

Neither of them had spoken of their feelings, but he could see Dani's heart welling in her eyes. She cared about him…maybe she even loved him. Beau expected to come back in one piece, but bullets, like lightning, struck without warning. He couldn't leave without showing Dani how he felt, so he kissed her cheek.

She tipped up her face, putting them just inches apart. "Be careful."

"I will."

With his throat tight, he left to borrow a horse from Sheriff Dawes. The sooner Clay Johnson dangled from a rope, the sooner Beau could come home.

Dani and the girls sat huddled on the divan in the parsonage. Stephen had built a fort on the floor out of books and had lined up soldiers for a war. Adie was still in the kitchen, but Pastor Josh had started a story. He'd picked Noah's ark, a fitting choice with rain pounding the roof and thunder rumbling down the mountains.

Any child would have been frightened, but for these girls, Emma in particular, the storm evoked memories of Patrick's horse racing into the yard. Lightning flashed again, filling the room with a blue light. As the girls grabbed for each other, thunder shook the house. Dani whispered a prayer for Beau.

She'd learned from Josh that he'd left with Sheriff Dawes and two deputies. No one had seen Andy leave town, but Sparrow Canyon, a maze of gorges running north and south at the base of the Rockies, offered good grass and places to hide. Knowing Johnson, Beau had felt confident he'd be in those canyons and had led the men in that direction.

Dani prayed he was right. Her cheek still tingled from the brush of his lips. He'd bought the picnic basket to protect her from Andy, but the kiss had been a confession. He cared about her. The hankie, folded in her pocket, told her just how deep his feelings ran.

Adie came out of the kitchen with a lantern. "That's quite a storm."

Emma trembled. "I wish God would stop the thunder."

"Me, too," Ellie said. "Uncle Beau's out there."

No one said a word.

Dani's mind raced through possibilities. Patrick had died on a night like this one. Lightning could strike. A flash flood could rip away the sides of a canyon and carry a man and his horse to their doom. In His wrath, God had flooded the earth and cleansed it of iniquity. In His mercy He'd promised to never do it again. He'd given Noah a rainbow and a dove. Dani prayed Beau would find that peace.

Pastor Josh bowed his head. "Let's pray."

Stephen copied his father. Dani and the girls held hands. Adie sat next to her husband and reached for his hand.

"Lord Jesus, we come to You in faith." Josh spoke in a normal tone, but Dani felt it like thunder. His words soared on the wings of Noah's dove, rising higher and growing stronger.

"Beau Morgan, our friend and uncle, needs Your grace. His heart is weary, Lord. We ask You to sustain him in this troubled time. We pray he'll be guided by Your wisdom and protected by angels. We pray for the healing of his heart, Lord. Beau lost a wife and he wants revenge. You lost a son and offered mercy to the whole human race. We praise You for that gift. We thank You for the promise of Heaven, a place where there's no pain and no wrongdoing, where justice is complete and love abounds. May Beau have that assurance. Amen."

Six voices echoed Pastor Josh, making a choir of sorts. The thunder hadn't lessened nor had the lightning dimmed, but Dani felt calmer.

Esther, who hadn't sucked her thumb in spite of the storm, looked up at her. "My pa's in Heaven, isn't he?"

"That's right."

"I'll see him again."

"You sure will," Josh said.

Adie joined in. "And your mother, too."

Someday Dani would see her own parents again. Beau, she believed, would greet Lucy. And Patrick…he'd gone home to be with Beth, the woman he'd loved to the point of misery on earth. Christ had torn the veil between time and eternity. She knew Beau had that faith. She prayed he'd find the peace to go with it, and that he'd find it soon.

Thunder rolled again, more distant now.

Josh cleared his throat. "Let's finish Noah's Ark."

Stephen chimed in. "I like the animals. Did Noah bring horses?"

"Sure," Josh answered. "He brought two of everything—bears, horses, all the pretty birds we see."

By the time the Reverend finished the tale, the animals had names and personalities and the storm had passed. The girls, even Emma, were giggling about the messy ark. When the dove came back with the olive branch, Adie sent Stephen upstairs to bed, then offered to tuck the girls into bed in the guest room. Josh went with his son, leaving Dani alone.

She lifted her shawl off the hook by the door and went out to the porch. The rain had washed the air clean and left a million stars. Hugging herself, she looked up and wondered if Beau saw the same beauty.

The door creaked behind her. Adie came to stand at her side. "You love him, don't you?"

She meant Beau. Dani knew her feelings, but she feared Adie's opinion. She didn't want to appear fickle. "It's not that simple."

"Why not?"

"Things just don't make sense."

Adie's voice dipped. "I know you loved Patrick, but that doesn't mean you can't love again."

Dani almost laughed. "It's not Patrick."

"Then what?"

Clutching her shawl, she told Adie about Patrick's letters to Beth and his intention to send her home. In the middle of the story, she sat in the chair she'd used her first day in Castle Rock. That day she'd been afraid of Beau. Now she feared for him. If he didn't come back—she couldn't stand the thought.

Adie sat next to her. "Does Beau know about the letters?"

"Yes." Dani started to rock. "He burned them. I was crying. He gave me a handkerchief, then he…" *Kissed me.* She couldn't say the words. "He was so kind, so strong. I felt…I don't know what I felt."

"Safe?"

Dani nodded.

"Cared for?"

"And more." For that moment, they'd had one heart.

Adie hummed softly. "I know about the 'more.'"

"I like it."

"Me, too." Adie smiled. "Does Beau know how you feel?"

"I haven't told him."

"So you're waiting for him to speak first."

"Mostly I'm afraid."

The moon had turned the yard into streaks of silver and black velvet. Dani saw beauty yet knew a deeper truth. If she stepped off the porch, she'd be up to her ankles in mud. Her feelings for Beau glistened like the water, but she didn't know what lay below the surface. If she told him how she felt, would they walk on the water or sink in the mud? She pulled the shawl closer. "I care for Beau, but he won't rest until he catches Clay Johnson."

"How do you know?"

"He told me."

Adie rocked gently. "Maybe they'll catch him tonight."

"I hope so." But would it be enough? Dani flashed on the pistols she'd seen in Beau's room. "He's hated Johnson for so long, I wonder if he can stop."

"A man can change."

"If he wants to."

"God has a way of making that happen."

Dani stared at the puddles. They were growing smaller by the minute. "Maybe, but right now Beau's out in the storm."

"It's what men do. They fight for the people they love."

"You mean Lucy."

"No, I mean you." Adie's voice turned light. "I saw Beau's face when he bid on your basket. He'd have paid double for it."

Dani smiled. "He likes fried chicken."

"He likes *you* even more." Adie sat straighter in her chair. "There's just one thing for you decide."

"What's that?"

"Do you love him enough to fight for him?"

Her chest ached. "I do. But how?"

"Put arms on the love of God. Show him what he's missing. For some reason, the Lord dropped Beau into the middle of a good life. He brought you to the same place at the same time. I have to believe there's a reason."

"I can see it."

"It's a matter of courage," Adie said. "Can you trust God to finish what He started?"

Dani looked across the yard where the last puddle reflected the moon and stars. Someday she'd come face-to-face with her Lord and the past weeks would make sense. Until then, she had a choice. Believe God for the best or protect herself from the worst. Dani's heart swelled with longing. She wanted everything God had for her future. She wanted Beau and would fight for him with her best weapons.

A good meal.

Children at the table.

Listening when he talked. Staying silent when he didn't.

Warm to her toes, she smiled at Adie. "Of course, I'll fight. I love him."

"He's a blessed man."

Dani looked at the distant hills. She needed Adie's wisdom. "What should I do?"

The pastor's wife got a look in her eyes that made Dani think of Adam, Eve and the apple. "There's a dance next Saturday. It's to honor the church's third anniversary."

"I like to dance."

"So does Beau."

Dani's mind drifted to the dresses hanging in her wardrobe. She'd brought something special for her wedding, an ivory gown that had belonged to her mother. She wanted to wear it for Beau, but not yet. The rest of her gowns held memories of Wisconsin. "I wish I had a new dress."

Adie grinned. "We'll go shopping tomorrow."

Dani felt embarrassed. "I don't have much money."

"I'll raid the cookie jar."

"But—"

"No 'buts'!" Adie said. "I know just the dress. It's blue like your eyes. It'll be worth every cent to see Beau's face at the dance."

Dani imagined fiddles and guitars and whirling in Beau's arms. Worrying about a man was a trial, but courting promised a world of wonder. Shivering, she looked at the stars and prayed Beau would feel the same way.

Chapter Thirteen

Two days had passed since Beau had left Dani at the picnic. Every minute had been a torture. He missed her. He missed the girls and even the blasted cows. To add to his irritation, Dawes and his two deputies had as much grit as goose feathers. Beau bristled at their whining, but they had reason to be disgruntled.

A storm had destroyed whatever tracks Andy had left. A packhorse had gone lame, forcing them to visit a local ranch. Dawes had accepted the offer to spend the night, so they'd lost time. To add to Beau's misery, the youngest of the two deputies, a kid named Teddy, whined like a buzz saw. He'd gotten stung by a hornet and was still fussing. The other deputy called himself Ace and claimed to be "a real wild card." Dressed in a bowler and purple vest, Ace talked about poker and not much else.

Beau didn't give a hoot about cards and bee stings. He wanted to end his fight with Clay Johnson and he wanted to do it now. He blinked and saw Dani in her pink dress. She'd looked so pretty, so fresh and young and full of hope. His mind flashed to Ellie being a tomboy in the barn. Esther had stopped sucking her thumb and he didn't want her to start up again. Emma, for all her anger, maybe because of it, was the closest thing he had to a daughter.

Daughters.

Sons.

A wife…Beau had paid twenty dollars for Dani's basket. He'd have paid a hundred for it, but he couldn't give her what she most wanted…the next fifty years, every day of his life. He had to end his business with Johnson before he could think of Dani as more than a friend. If he'd been a praying man, Beau would have begged the Almighty to bring Johnson to justice, both on earth and for eternity, but the words stuck in his throat. Two fruitless days on the trail had rubbed him raw. Looking up at the sky, he blamed God for the rain, the injured horse, bees, poker and everything else that had gone wrong.

Even Dawes had been a thorn. The lawman had gotten confused and led them five miles into a box canyon, forcing Beau to hold in a snort. No outlaw would shelter in a canyon with one opening. Never mind the good grazing and fresh water. The spot didn't suit Johnson and Beau knew it.

But Sparrow Canyon did… Talking over jerky and beans last night, Beau had surmised from Dawes that Sparrow Canyon had three openings. The ravine lay within a day's ride of Castle Rock. A gorge ran west and led into the Rockies, and an easy trail stretched to the south. Sparrow Creek, the stream where Beau had caught fish with Dani and the girls, marked the way.

They were miles past that peaceful point, but Beau kept the memories of that day tucked in his heart. He hadn't stopped hating Johnson, but somewhere in the past few weeks, he'd started caring about Dani and his nieces. Josh had once told Beau that darkness and light couldn't fill a room at the same time. The light, he'd said, would always win. Beau hoped that was true.

"How much farther?" Teddy's whine cut into Beau's thoughts.

Dawes answered over his shoulder. "Just around the next bend."

They couldn't arrive soon enough for Beau. Aware of the pistol on his hip and the long gun in the scabbard, he urged his horse forward and followed Dawes out of a ravine. What he saw made the hairs on his neck prickle. The canyon had lush grass, a stream and good cover. Beau inspected the rocky slopes and spotted a cave. From a distance, it looked black, narrow and deep.

"That's the spot," he said to Dawes. "That's where Johnson would hole up."

The four of them stopped short of the cave. Taking charge, Beau turned to Ace and Teddy. "You two cover me from the trees." He looked at Dawes. "Go north and watch from the other side."

Beau motioned for the men to take position, dismounted, then walked along the creek where willows shielded him from view. As he neared the cave, he looked for tracks but saw none. He listened for horses but heard only a rustle in the trees. With his weapon drawn, he stared at the opening in the rocks. His gut told him Johnson had fled, but he fired one shot to be sure. Bats burst out of the cave, a sure sign no one was inside. Even so, he approached with caution. When he reached the side, he turned the corner with his gun drawn.

The empty cave stared back at him. Lowering his Colt, Beau took in tin cans, empty whiskey bottles and something he recognized…the tiny stub of a cigar. No one but Clay smoked them that low. More than a few wanted men had used the cave for shelter. Beau felt certain Johnson had been one of them.

He shouted for Dawes, Teddy and Ace, then squatted next

to a fire pit and took a pinch of ash. It couldn't have been colder. He let it go and watched it vanish into thin air.

Dawes walked into the cave. "Looks like we missed them."

Beau said nothing. If they hadn't dawdled at the ranch and gone down a box canyon, they might have found Clay.

The sheriff crossed his arms. "What do you want to do, Morgan?"

"Forge ahead."

Teddy and Ace walked up together. Teddy pouted like a little girl. "Johnson's gone. I say we go home."

"Me, too." Ace slouched against the opening. "There's a game at the Silver River tomorrow. If we hurry, I can make it."

Beau clenched his jaw. "We're not done."

Teddy frowned. "My bee sting hurts."

Beau pushed to his feet, faced Teddy and squared his shoulders. "Look, kid. I'm sorry about your *bee sting,* but you need to toughen up." He directed his gaze to Ace. "So do you."

Dawes frowned. "Now, Morgan—"

"I'm plenty tough," Ace said to Beau. "If anyone needs to wise up, it's you. Any *fool* can see Johnson's gone."

Teddy stood taller. "We're going home."

"Hold up," Dawes said. "I'll make that decision."

"Johnson made it for us." Ace waved his arm. "Look around. He's gone."

The sheriff rubbed his moustache, then turned to Beau with a pitiable lack of leadership. Beau understood lawmen like Dawes. He was a peacemaker at heart. He valued justice but didn't hunger for it. Beau wouldn't find peace until justice had been served, but he had to face facts. Being quick to compromise, Dawes would take a vote. Beau would lose three to one. He didn't like the lawman's methods, but he respected the badge.

He also had an ache in his gut that hurt as much as Teddy's bee sting. He missed Dani. She'd be worried about him. So would his nieces. Riding on alone, without a goodbye and finalizing the adoption, should have tempted him, but he couldn't stand the thought of leaving Dani in the lurch. Beau cursed God for His cruelty and Dawes for his incompetence. If they'd come to Sparrow Canyon first, they might have caught Johnson.

He kicked the ashes. "Let's go home."

He followed Dawes and his deputies out of the cave, but paused to stare up the canyon. It meandered for miles, an outlaw's paradise with jagged turns and places to hide. The meadow rippled with thick grass for stolen horses and the stream flowed fast with melted snow. Best of all, the trail veered south and west, giving a man on the run two routes of escape.

Beau couldn't shake the feeling that Clay was just a mile or two away, up the canyon and watching them, snickering at their lack of will. Beau itched to keep going, but he had a responsibility to Dani and his nieces. Johnson would have to wait. So would his feelings for Dani. Of the two delays, he didn't know which annoyed him more.

Clay lay on his back, staring at the night sky. A week had passed since they'd raided the Rocking J. The horses, grazing in the moonlight, whickered to each other like old friends. Goose and Andy had shuffled a deck of cards and were gambling for swigs of whiskey. Clay had expected Morgan to find them by now. Instead the lawman had come within a stone's throw and turned around.

Clay knew Morgan had come into Sparrow Canyon because of yesterday's ride. He'd gone after a stray mare, seen tracks near the cave and had gone inside. Someone had kicked the fire pit in a fit of temper. Clay felt sure it was Morgan. The man usually rode alone, but Clay had counted three more sets of boot prints. He didn't think for an instant Morgan had turned back by choice. Clay suspected he'd been with the local sheriff, a man known to be weak.

Looking at the stars, Clay called himself a fool for staying near Castle Rock. With Morgan stuck on a farm with a woman and three girls, Clay could have lost him, maybe for good. He'd had his fill of Goose and Andy, too. If they'd gone south, he could have given them a cut, said goodbye and gone east. He could have been free.

So why hadn't he done it?

Clay didn't know. He'd been irked by Andy's chicken sounds, but more than pride kept him in this canyon. Was it regret? Guilt? He wanted to think he was beyond such feelings—that he was beyond feeling anything at all—but his gut had been churning ever since he'd put down Ricochet. He couldn't stop thinking about death, Heaven and Reverend Blue's stories about Jesus.

"For God so loved the world, He gave His only begotten son…"

Clay snorted through his nose. No one—except Beau Morgan for the wrong reasons—cared whether he lived or died. The shedding of blood for sin? Someone dying in his place so he could be free? Clay knew nonsense when he heard it, yet somehow he felt a yearning for such goodness. He wanted to believe in Jesus, but he was afraid to pray the prayer Reverend Blue had said with Chet. Clay didn't know what would happen, but he doubted it would be good. Not even God could forgive a man like Clay.

"You awake, boss?"

Clay glanced across the fire and saw Goose staring through the flames. He grunted. "I am now."

"I've been thinking."

"About what?"

"Morgan," Goose said. "He should have found us by now. I say we smoke him out."

Clay couldn't sleep, so he decided to listen. "Got any ideas?"

"I say we hit another ranch. We send Andy down the canyon with the horses. You and I set up an ambush. When Morgan comes through, he's dead."

Clay saw the logic, but the plan left a bad taste. Killing Morgan in cold blood would solve one problem, but what about Clay's guilty conscience? He wanted to sleep at night, not lie awake feeling like pond scum. He already felt so bad that sometimes he wanted to die. Killing Morgan in cold blood wouldn't make the pain go away.

"I don't like it," he said to Goose.

"Why not?"

Clay wasn't about to bare his soul to Goose, so he looked for another excuse. "What about Dawes?"

"He's weak. He'll give up."

"I still don't like it."

Goose's face went hard. "There's another possibility."

"What's that?"

"We bring the fight to Morgan."

Clay wished he hadn't opened his eyes. The thought of putting children in harm's way made him ill. "I won't do that."

"Why not?"

"Because I won't."

"It would be easy," Goose said. "I'll go to the Silver River. Someone'll tell me where the farm is. We pay a midnight call and just like that—" he snapped his fingers "—Morgan's hanging from a tree."

For three little girls to find...for the woman to cut down and bury. Even worse, what would happen if the woman ran to Morgan's rescue? They'd have to hurt her. Clay muttered a curse. "It's too risky."

Andy rolled over. "I say we visit the farm."

"No."

"The woman's pretty. She smells good, too."

"Shut up," Clay growled.

Andy dropped flat and sighed.

Goose stared hard through the fire. "You're acting like a whipped dog."

Clay's pride flared, but he said nothing.

Andy clucked like a hen. He'd been drinking and was sloppy drunk. Clay hated sloppy drunks. His father had been one. He'd either laughed himself silly or beat his wife and sons. Clay's own father had broken his nose twice. Every time he looked in the mirror, he saw the crookedness and hated it. He pushed to his feet, walked past the fire and kicked Andy in the gut.

The kid curled into a ball. "What was that for?"

"For being you."

Clay was sick to death of these two clowns. Going east sounded better than ever. He had a cousin in St. Louis. He hadn't seen the fellow in years, but last he'd heard, he ran a dry goods store. The two of them had been boyhood pals, kicking each other in church while the minister droned.

Goose broke into his thoughts. "What'll it be, boss?"

Clay was still in the St. Louis dry goods store, thinking about his cousin and the Bible stories he'd heard as a boy. He'd had enough of running. Enough of the guilt. But Morgan would never stop.

Goose gave him a stare that challenged more than Clay's pride. It gave him a choice. Fight like a man or put up with

Andy's chicken sounds. The only feeling in Clay's life stronger than guilt was a yearning for peace. He couldn't explain that feeling to Goose or Andy. They were young men intent on leaving their mark. Clay had seen more than forty years of life, and the last few had been tiresome to say the least. He'd had enough. One way or another, he wouldn't leave this canyon until he settled the score with Morgan.

But settle it how? With a confession? *I'm sorry… I didn't mean to shoot her.* Or with bloodshed and a quick trip to Heaven or Hell? Looking at the sky, Clay didn't think Beau Morgan would care that he was sorry. He doubted God would, either. Clay thought hard about his choice. Another raid would satisfy his men and add to their bankroll, but it would also draw out the law. He didn't want to deal with Dawes and a posse. He just wanted to settle things with Morgan. That meant sending the man a message.

Clay looked at Goose. "Andy can't go to town, but you can."

"What do you have in mind?"

Clay went back to his bedroll, dropped to a crouch and slipped a single bullet from his gun belt. He handed it to Goose. "Leave this at the Silver River. Tell the barkeep to give it to Morgan."

Goose palmed the casing. "How will he know it's from you?"

"It's the same caliber that killed his wife."

Goose laughed.

Clay felt sick.

Andy rolled over in his bedroll. "Let me take it. There's a social on Saturday. I want to go."

Andy, Clay decided, was an idiot. "You're the one they followed down this canyon."

"For no reason." Andy pouted. "I was nice to that girl."

"You're staying put." Clay turned to Goose. "Leave the bullet with the barkeep at the Silver River but skip the dance."

Goose pinched the brass casing, turning it to catch the light of the fire. The bullet glowed orange, reminding Clay of a setting sun. Weary, he slid into his bedroll, put his head on the ground and closed his eyes. Unless Morgan had lost his instincts, it wouldn't be long before he came all the way down the canyon.

Chapter Fourteen

Back in Denver, Beau had enjoyed church socials. He'd liked flirting with pretty women and he didn't mind dancing. Once Lucy had come into his life, dancing had been more than fun. They'd found the rhythms unique to them. Beau wanted to find that rhythm with Dani, but nothing had changed since he'd ridden out of Sparrow Canyon. When he'd reached Castle Rock, he'd stopped at Scott's office and told the man to push hard for the adoption. As soon as the papers were signed, Beau intended to go after Johnson. One way or another, the chase would end.

After seeing the attorney, he'd ridden to the parsonage. He'd greeted Dani with a tip of his hat, not the embrace he'd wanted, but the girls had all hugged him. Now, standing in the Castle Rock schoolhouse, dressed up for the dance and holding a cup of punch, he could still feel their skinny arms around his middle.

For the third time in ten minutes, Beau looked at his pocket watch. He wanted to visit the Silver River for news, but he couldn't leave Dani. He didn't know where she'd gotten the dress, a royal blue gown that matched her eyes, but it fit her to perfection. Riding next to her in the surrey, he'd stared at the dirt road to keep from noticing her dainty shoes and the way she'd tapped her toes to an imaginary waltz.

She'd volunteered at the punch bowl, a place where every man in town would have a reason to talk to her. Dani didn't know it, but Beau was standing five feet behind her, keeping a watchful eye.

A few bars into the opening polka, the first man dared to approach her. Beau recognized the rancher from the picnic. While riding with Dawes, he'd quizzed the sheriff about every man in Castle Rock. The rancher, a recent widower, had a little boy. He never missed church, paid his hands well, didn't gamble or drink and was the first to show up when a neighbor needed help.

His only fault was bad taste in vests, but Beau counted that reason enough to dislike him. As the man approached Dani, Beau crossed his arms and stared. Unaware he was being watched, the man turned on the charm. Dani gave him a cup of punch. As he lifted it to his lips, Beau lowered his chin. The motion caught the rancher's attention. So did Beau's hardest stare. The poor fellow nearly choked. With a stiff nod, he set down the cup, walked away and asked another woman to dance.

Good, Beau thought. Dani didn't need a goody-two-shoes rancher for a husband. She needed a man who understood her. Beau watched as she squared her shoulders. The blue silk puffed at her shoulders, then narrowed to fit her arms. He thought of her hands. She was wearing white gloves, dainty things trimmed in lace with pearl buttons at the wrist. Beau thought the gloves were nice but unnecessary. He liked Dani's hands just fine.

Another man approached. Beau didn't know him from Adam and didn't care to. The fool hadn't bothered to shine his shoes. He took a cup of punch, saw Beau and left without a word. Dani followed him with her eyes. When he asked another woman to dance, she sagged a bit but not for long.

Looking at her back, he imagined the smile pasted to her face and felt bad. Then again, if a man couldn't meet Beau's stare, he didn't deserve to dance with the prettiest woman in the room. Dani didn't need a weakling for a husband. She needed a man who knew how to fight and love. A man who could be tender with children and cows but fierce with everything else. A man like… He clenched his jaw.

Five more men wandered to the refreshment table. All five looked at Dani, saw Beau and turned a pasty white. They each asked other women to dance, leaving Dani alone at the punch bowl with her shoulders as stiff as those of a stone angel. Beau's gaze drifted to the dance floor where he saw Josh and Adie gazing into each other's eyes. They'd been married for years, but they danced like newlyweds. As the couple turned with the music, Josh spotted Beau. He said something to Adie. They stopped dancing and walked toward Beau.

To hide the fact he'd been watching Dani, Beau went to greet them. "Nice social," he said as they met at the punch bowl.

Josh grinned. "It would be nicer if you were dancing."

Adie leaned close to Dani and pretended to whisper in her ear. "I hear Beau's light on his feet."

Dani's cheeks turned pink. They both knew Josh and Adie were playing matchmaker. The effort irked Beau to no end. He didn't need any prodding to ask Dani to dance. He'd been fighting the urge all night.

Still blushing, Dani gave Adie a cup of punch. "You must be thirsty after all that dancing."

She sounded wistful. Beau felt bad about chasing away her dance partners, but no one had measured up.

Josh and Adie traded a look. Without a glance at Beau, Josh offered his hand to Dani. "May I have this dance?"

Dani turned pinker. "I don't think—"

"Go on," Adie insisted.

Josh swept Dani into the crowd. Adie said something friendly, but Beau didn't hear the words. His eyes were glued to Dani, who looked happy for the first time all night. The fiddler played a fancy scale. The guitarist joined in, followed by the bellow of the accordion playing the first bars of a polka.

Dancers crowded the floor, but Beau had eyes only for Dani in her blue dress, whirling with Josh, who'd said something that made her smile. Four bars into the song, Beau spotted three men closing in on Josh, intending to cut in. Not caring that Adie was in midsentence, he strode onto the dance floor, beating out the other men, including the rancher who'd been ahead of him.

He tapped Josh on the shoulder. "I'm cutting in."

No small talk. No smiles. Just an order to hand Dani over and do it now.

Josh had the bad manners to chuckle. "Of course," he said, making a slight bow to Dani.

The next thing Beau knew, they were spinning and whirling and he'd never felt so sure of the rightness of having this woman in his life. Nor had he felt such conflict. He wanted to make Dani his wife, but first he had to finish with Johnson. One dance, Beau told himself. Just for now, he'd enjoy the smile he'd put on her face. He'd let the scent of her hair drift into his nose. He'd look at the gold waves and imagine them free from pins and ribbons, cascading down her shoulders. Just for now, he'd let himself feel the blessing of two hearts beating as one.

When the song ended, Dani looked into his eyes. Short of breath and flushed, she smiled. "That was a surprise."

Without the shelter of the music, Beau felt the bleakness of the future. He had to leave. Now. Before the band struck up a waltz or reel. It didn't matter what the musicians played. He had to resist.

Beau hooked his arm around her waist and aimed for the door. "It's time to go home."

"What?"

"It's late."

"But we haven't cut the cake."

"Forget the cake. I want to leave."

She gave him a look that tore him to shreds. He didn't know if she was angry, hurt or both. Before he could decide, the musicians played the opening chords of "Camp Town Races." The music tripped him like a rope.

Dance with her… Just one more.

He saw the interest in her eyes, a curiosity that reminded him of her innocence and her tender heart. She wanted a husband. She wanted a family of her own and to be loved for herself. Beau wanted to give her those things.

But he couldn't. Not now.

"Beau?" Her eyes clouded. "Are you all right?"

He sobered instantly. He couldn't let Dani see his feelings. He'd already crossed the line by kissing her in the kitchen and again at the picnic. Brotherly caresses, he told himself. Except her feelings, he suspected, were growing as fast as his. He couldn't risk hurting her. He had to be her friend, nothing more.

Beau schooled his features. "Sorry," he said in a level voice. "If you want cake, we'll stay."

She touched his arm. His bicep bunched, a reflex he couldn't stop.

Dani looked into his eyes. "I'd like to dance some more."

"I can't."

Her voice dropped to a murmur. "Because of Lucy?"

Beau fought the urge to lie. If he claimed to be grief stricken, Dani would let him off the hook. If he told the truth—that he loved her and it hurt too much to hold her—she'd fight for him. He didn't think he could resist, so he thinned his lips to a line. "It's got nothing to do with Lucy."

"Then why?"

He didn't want to hurt her, but he had to make her leave. "Mind your own business."

Dani blinked in disbelief. "I don't deserve that."

She was right, but Beau couldn't apologize. They'd be dancing to a waltz and finding that rhythm he wanted. He couldn't let that happen, at least not yet, so he said nothing.

Dani's mouth tightened. "Excuse me. I'm going to help with the cake." She brushed by him.

Instead of going to the refreshment table, she raced out the door. Beau held in a curse. He couldn't let her walk alone in the dark, so he followed her, pausing on the steps to let his eyes adjust to the night. As his vision cleared, he scanned the landscape. To the west he saw a stand of pines, pale grass and nothing else. He looked east and saw an empty meadow. He hadn't seen anyone suspicious tonight, but that didn't mean a thing. Back in Denver, he hadn't seen Clay Johnson on the roof. With his heart pounding, he shouted Dani's name.

Holding her skirt and fighting tears, Dani hurried away from the schoolhouse. She feared Adie had seen her spat with Beau and would come after her, so she ran for the cover of a group of pines. When she reached the farthest tree, she circled away from the schoolhouse and slumped against the rough bark. She could hear the music coming from the open windows, but the shadows made her invisible.

That's how she'd felt at the punch bowl. Not a single man

had asked her to dance. The rejection had reminded her of embarrassing times in Wisconsin. After she'd broken the engagement to Virgil, she'd become a wallflower. A pariah. Unloved and unwanted by anyone. She hadn't been bothered when the rancher left her alone. She wanted only Beau, but after the third man walked away looking pinched, she'd faced a hard truth. She didn't measure up.

Dani didn't understand. She tried to be kind. She had a good mind and pitched in wherever she could. The blue dress fit perfectly and flattered her figure. She'd seen Beau's eyes when he'd helped her into the surrey and silently thanked Adie for being a tad bit bold. Riding to town, she'd imagined dancing with Beau but not the way it had happened. He'd cut in on Pastor Josh because he'd been worried about someone like Andy, not because he wanted to move with her to the music.

He cared about her, but he cared more about killing Clay Johnson. That was the sad, hard truth.

"Dani!"

His voice roared over the music. She felt bad for hiding but didn't want to be found sniffling like a child. She reached in her pocket for a handkerchief, felt Lucy's embroidery and burst into tears.

"Dani!"

He sounded close to panic. Hurt or not, Dani couldn't let him suffer. Hoping the darkness would hide her puffy eyes, she raised her voice. "I'm over here."

Beau walked through the pines, stirring the needles as he peered into the shadows until he found her against the tree. "Why are you out here?"

"I'll go back in a minute." Her voice quivered.

"What's wrong?"

"Nothing."

"Then why did you leave?"

"I needed air. That's all."

She could smell the starch of his shirt, the bay rum he'd splashed on his jaw. Even blind in the dark, she felt Beau's nearness. So much remained unsaid. Unfinished business. Unspoken promises. With the moon turning the meadow a pale green, Dani flashed on Patrick's failure to share his true feelings. He'd left her with a mountain of doubt. She wouldn't do the same to Beau. He deserved to know how she felt.

Before she could find her tongue, he aimed his chin at the schoolhouse. "I'll walk you back."

"Not yet."

"It's not safe out here."

I love you. The words were strangling her, but Beau's eyes stopped her from saying them. Bitterness glinted in his dilated pupils. She could hear the tension in his voice. She'd felt it in his hands when they'd danced. She longed to spill her heart, but not with Beau on the verge of a rant. She turned on her heel and fled.

He grasped her arm. "Dani—"

She sidestepped to avoid him, then left the shelter of the pines. A full moon lit the meadow, turning the grass into shimmering blades. The next thing she knew, Beau had his hand on her shoulder. Without a word, he spun her around. Their gazes collided in the dim light that revealed her tear-stained cheeks.

"You've been crying," he said. "Tell me why."

"No."

"I didn't mean to hurt your feelings."

She didn't know what to do. She couldn't tell Beau that she loved him, but neither did she want to turn away. She settled for the easiest truth. "Tonight reminded me of the dances in Wisconsin."

"Why?"

She gave a rueful smile. "After the fiasco with Virgil, no one ever asked me to dance."

Beau hesitated. "Josh asked you tonight."

"He's a minister!" Dani couldn't believe her ears. "It was like dancing with my father."

"I cut in, didn't I?"

She huffed. "*That* was like dancing with my brother." It hadn't been, but that's how she saw it now.

His eyes stayed locked on hers. "Is that how you felt?"

"No." Her voice squeaked. "But no one else asked. Josh danced with me out of pity. You did it out of worry."

"You're wrong."

She could at least be honest. "I know what I saw."

"I know what you *didn't* see." He was still holding her arm, lightly, but she felt the warmth of his grip. "I was standing right behind you. If a man didn't measure up, I gave him the evil eye."

"You *what?*"

"I chased the men off—all of them."

"You don't have that right!" Not even her brother had been so high-handed. "Why did you do it?"

"I care about you."

Her breath hitched. "You mean as a friend."

"I mean—" He sealed his lips, then slipped his arms around her middle and held her gently against his chest. His lips brushed her hair, her temple. When she tilted her face up to his, he kissed her lips. The caress held all the restraint he'd shown in the kitchen, but this time his arms were around her. She felt…wanted.

Beau raised his face from hers, then tucked her head under his chin where she heard the pounding of his heart.

"You're beautiful, Dani. Any man—"

"I don't want any man." The truth had to be told. "I want you, Beau. I love you."

"Don't."

He'd spoken firmly but hadn't let her go. Dani took it as a confession. "Why not?"

"I can't love you back. At least not yet."

He kissed the top of her head, then released her. Warmth filled Dani from top to bottom. Beau hadn't denied his feelings for her. He'd gone to war with them. It was a battle he had to win for himself, but Dani intended to fight at his side. She looked into his eyes. "It's because of Clay Johnson, isn't it?"

"Yes."

"There are other ways to find him," she said. "You could hire a detective."

He shook his head.

"What about the law? Sheriff Dawes—"

"Isn't much of a lawman."

Dani's heart sank. "The U.S. marshals?"

"They don't care like I do." Beau turned his back on her. "I don't expect you to understand. What I feel goes beyond reason. Bringing Johnson to justice is something I have to do."

"For Lucy," she said.

Beau shook his head. "She'd call me a fool."

"Then why keep going?"

"If I give up now, I've wasted five years."

"You could waste five more."

"I know that, but I can't rest until Johnson's dead."

Dani felt as if she'd stumbled into a grave waiting for a body. The hole was deep and dark with slick slides. She didn't know how to climb out. Beau hadn't said he loved her, but his kiss had given her hope. She braided that hope with love and faith, then prayed silently that God would be merciful to this man who'd lost so much.

"What are you going to do?" she asked.

"Same thing as before. As soon as the adoption's final, I'm leaving. You'll have a farm and three little girls."

Dani's heart squeezed with loneliness. "You were right, you know."

"About what?"

"I want more. I want a husband."

He turned around but didn't come closer. "I care for you, Dani. I won't say how much because there's no point. I'm leaving."

"But you'll come back."

Beau shook his head. "It could be months, even years. I won't ask you to wait for me. There are some good men here. Find one who'll love you and the girls."

Beau meant well, but she'd had it with his domineering ways. "Isn't that for me to decide?"

"No."

Dani's temper flared. "It's not for *you* to decide, either."

"All right," he said. "We'll toss a coin. Heads you marry the rancher. Tails you waste the next five years of your life waiting for a man who's so filled with hate he's not worth knowing. Is that what you want?"

"You're not filled with hate. You love the girls." *Do you love me, too?* She didn't need to voice the question. Beau could see it in her eyes. In his, she saw the answer but knew he wouldn't say it.

He angled his chin at the schoolhouse. "Go dance with the rancher."

She refused to budge. "Do you know what I think?"

"What?"

"You're tired of the chase but too stubborn to admit it."

"You bet I'm tired." His voice shook with fury. "I want this fight to be over, but it's not. That *almighty* God of yours let a killer get away."

"I could be angry, too." She'd lost Patrick, yet that suffering had brought her into Beau's world and given her a new life. "We don't always understand why things happen the way they do, but we can still trust God to know our needs."

"That's rubbish."

"It's true." She set down her pride. "The letters from Patrick, do you know what I realized?"

"What?"

"He's been reunited with Beth. He's happy now."

Beau sneered. "Tell that to the girls."

"They've suffered," Dani admitted. "But it's just for now. They'll see their parents in Heaven. I can't explain the in-between times, but I know that love matters."

Beau crossed his arms. "You don't know squat."

"I know you're living in the past." Dani could scarcely believe her boldness, but Beau needed to hear what she had to say. "Lucy would be ashamed of you. She'd want you to live a good life."

Beau stared at her with burning eyes. Dani ached to reach for his hand but resisted. She loved him and wanted to help him, but only God could soften his heart. Until he made peace with the past, the future glimmered beyond their reach. They were trapped in the present between hate and love. Dani didn't like the tension between them. Believing love would win, she held out her gloved hand. "I'm sorry we argued."

Beau looked at her fingers, cotton-white in the dark, then took her hand and squeezed. "I am, too. Let's go inside."

"I'd like that."

She didn't expect to dance again, but she could stand at

Beau's side. At least that's what she hoped until they reached the front of the schoolhouse where he stopped in the yard. "Go on," he said. "I have an errand to run."

"Where are you going?"

"The Silver River."

"Oh." If he left, the rancher and others would ask her to dance. She didn't want to dance with anyone but Beau. She squeezed his hand. "Could we go home instead?"

"I have to see Wallace."

Before she could tempt him with cake, the doors to the schoolhouse opened and the crowd spilled into the yard. Ellie spotted Beau and ran up to him. "The fireworks are starting! Let's get a good spot." The child gripped her uncle's hand and tugged.

Dani looked at Beau. His expression changed from a mulelike stubbornness to the way T.C. looked with a ball of string.

"Sounds like fun," he said to the child. He turned to Dani, who'd been joined by Emma and Esther. "We'll stay for the fireworks."

With the girls clutching their hands, they walked to the field behind the schoolhouse, the one where they'd kissed in the pines. Someone launched a rocket that exploded into a giant star. It lit up the sky then faded to nothing. Beau reached for Dani's hand and squeezed. The show lasted for ten minutes, with each burst of light soaring into the dark and filling the night with hope. The girls clapped and cheered. Even Beau had an air of joy as the manmade stars filled the sky with sulfur and smoke.

When it was over, Esther yawned.

Dani looked at Beau. "Do you still want to go to the Silver River?"

He glanced at Esther, then ruffled her hair. "The girls are tired. We'll head home."

Dani smiled her approval.

For tonight, Beau had put love ahead of hate. He made a good uncle. He'd be an even better father. She didn't know what tomorrow held, but God did. Silently she prayed for a future with Beau, one full of stars and sleepy children.

Chapter Fifteen

When Beau saw Trevor Scott driving his buggy into the yard, he knew the man had bad news. Tomorrow at twelve noon, he and Dani were supposed to sign the adoption papers in the presence of a judge. Something must have gone wrong to pull the attorney away from his desk. Dressed in a suit and a bowler hat, he'd come on a formal call.

Beau had been questioning the choice he'd made, to chase Clay rather than stay in Castle Rock, with every waking breath. Aside from his feelings for Dani, he'd lost more of his heart to the girls. He wanted to be a part of their everyday lives, not a favorite uncle who showed up once a year with presents. They needed a man who'd be a father to them. Someone who'd teach them things and chase away boys when the time came.

Once the judge signed the papers, Beau would be free to leave. Howie had agreed to work for the rest of the summer, and Josh had offered to help Dani with any hiring she had to do. The alfalfa had sprouted, and Beau had finished the silo. Two days from now, he expected to be riding into the heart of Sparrow Canyon.

"Hello, Morgan," Scott called. "I'm glad you're here."

"What happened?"

"I'd like to speak in private. Is there a place—"

"This way."

Beau led the attorney to the side of the barn where he sat when he couldn't sleep. Dani wouldn't see them. Earlier she'd lugged the washtub into the backyard and asked for his dirty clothes. Confident he and Scott would be alone, Beau indicated the only chair. "Have a seat."

Scott stayed on his feet. "I received a letter from Harriet Lange's attorney. She's fighting for custody. Judge Hall put a hold on the adoption."

Beau couldn't believe his ears. "On what grounds?"

"She claims you're unfit to be guardian."

"That's ridiculous."

Beau didn't drink, rarely cussed and treated women with the utmost respect. In Denver he'd upheld his badge with an integrity that still made him proud. Harriet Lange had slapped Emma for touching a teacup. The woman had a fight on her hands and it wasn't with a little girl. Beau tucked away his temper and focused on Scott. "What's she saying?"

"The things I mentioned before."

"The Silver River?"

Scott nodded.

"I haven't been since we spoke." But he'd wanted to go. Badly. Not visiting Wallace after the dance had left Beau twisting in the wind. Late at night, he imagined Johnson watching, waiting for him. Only his concern for Dani had kept him from making a late-night ride.

"There's more," Scott said. "Miss Lange doesn't believe Miss Baxter will provide a secure home for the children."

Beau fought to stay calm. "That's ridiculous."

"Is it?" Scott asked. "Miss Baxter is young and single. What will happen to the girls if she marries?"

"Dani loves them. That won't change."

"But surely you can see the concern."

Beau had shared it. He still did but for different reasons. He wanted to marry her himself. "Like I said, Dani's loyal."

"That may be true," Scott said. "But what matters is the judge's perception. As things stand, Miss Lange and Miss Baxter are both single women. Miss Lange is a blood relative, has a small but stable income and family members who'll provide moral and financial support. Miss Baxter is young, unemployed—"

Beau frowned. "She runs this place."

"Again, Mr. Morgan. I'm talking about *perceptions.*"

The attorney spoke as if he were in court, planting seeds that would grow into thoughts. Beau had used that trick, too. "What are you getting at?"

"If you and Miss Baxter were to marry—"

"*Marry?*"

The attorney held up one hand. "Hear me out, Mr. Morgan."

Beau didn't know whether to cover his ears or hang on to every word the man said. Marry Dani? But what about Clay Johnson? Beau had spent too many years to give up now.

Scott laced his hands behind his back. "As I was saying, if you and Miss Baxter were to marry, Miss Lange's case would be significantly weakened. The girls would have a mother *and* a father." The attorney looked Beau in the eye. "What happens after the legalities is no one's business but yours. An annulment—"

"I know what you're saying." Beau had taken vows. He knew what made a marriage real. "When do we have to decide?"

"The sooner, the better."

"I'll let you know."

The attorney tipped his hat and walked back to the buggy, leaving Beau alone behind the barn. His mind spun with the possibilities. If he and Dani took vows, the adoption would be settled. He'd be free to leave, but Dani wouldn't be free at all. She'd be tied to him until he came back or she had the marriage annulled. They wouldn't consummate the union. He wouldn't even kiss her again.

Once he found Johnson, he'd come home. He'd be free to make the marriage everything Dani dreamed it would be. Cozy talks and morning coffee. Children of their own… Beau stopped himself from going down that road. If he thought too long about loving Dani, he'd go to her and drop to one knee. He'd ask her to marry him for real, then regret it every time he saw the color pink. Tonight he'd tell Dani about Scott's suggestion. If she agreed, he'd make arrangements for the ceremony. A judge would marry them without questions, but Beau wanted Josh to do it. This would be a marriage in name only until he caught Clay, but the vows mattered to him.

Before he spoke to Dani, he wanted to clear the plan with Josh. He headed for the barn to saddle his horse. T.C., well fed from milk and hunting mice, lay asleep in a pile of straw. Beau envied the cat to the point of sinfulness. The feline had a soft bed, food in his belly and four females who scratched his ears. Beau liked living on the farm. He had a reason to get up in the morning and went to bed satisfied with a day's work. What more could a man ask? Nothing…except peace of mind.

He saddled his horse, led it into the yard, then went to find Dani. He didn't like leaving her alone on the farm, but more than a week had passed since he'd ridden with Dawes. He felt certain Johnson had either left to sell the stolen horses or holed up somewhere to plan another raid. Even so, Beau wouldn't be gone long. He'd have a word with Josh, visit Wallace and be home by supper.

He found Dani behind the house, scrubbing the collar of his shirt with a vengeance. The dirt didn't stand a chance. Neither did Beau's heart. With wisps of hair sticking to her neck and her cheeks flushed, she couldn't have been prettier. Beau surveyed the yard and saw Emma hanging a pinafore on the clothesline. In the garden he saw Esther digging in the dirt and Ellie pouring out a bucket of rinse water.

The girl had a sly look in her eyes. Before he could speak, she touched her finger to her lips, signaling him to stay quiet. Being fond of mischief himself, Beau winked at her.

Tiptoeing, Ellie snuck up behind Emma and splashed the dregs of the bucket on her older sister.

Emma cried out in shock.

Ellie dropped the bucket and took cover behind Beau. Showing no fear—a fact that warmed him—Emma grabbed a second bucket, the one at Dani's feet, and charged at them. Ellie had been armed with a cup or so of water. Emma had two gallons and wanted revenge. She got it by dousing Ellie. Beau got caught in the crossfire.

Dripping wet, he laughed. "You're going to regret that, young lady!"

Emma grinned. "Now you don't need a bath!"

"No, but Esther does." Beau indicated the little girl in the garden. "I think she's eating bugs."

Groaning, Ellie and Emma went to fetch their sister. Beau turned to Dani. Her eyes were focused square on his chest. Her expression made his heart pound.

Looking down, she went back to scrubbing the shirt. "You're as wet as I am."

"Almost."

Blotches of water had turned the white apron to a dull gray. Beau looked in the tub where he saw more of his clothes. Dani worked hard. She deserved the best life he could provide. That meant securing the adoption and settling his score with Johnson.

He rested his hand on the edge of the tub. "I have to go to town."

She stopped scrubbing. "Why?"

He didn't want to mention Scott's visit. "I have to see Josh."

She raised her eyes. "Is something wrong?"

"Not a thing," he said. "Do you need anything from town?"

She smiled. "Butterscotch?"

Dani liked sweets. He'd buy a pound of the candy, maybe two. He felt generous these days, as if he couldn't give her enough. He'd be leaving in a few days. That called for gifts for the girls, something special for Dani. They deserved more, but trinkets were the best he could do. After promising to be home for supper, Beau went back to his room to change his shirt, climbed on his horse and rode to the parsonage.

As he neared the house, he saw Josh in front of the church with a brush and a can of paint. Half of the front wall looked new. The other was weathered and worn from the sun.

Beau dismounted and called a greeting.

Josh looked over his shoulder. "Perfect timing. Grab a brush."

"I can't stay."

"So what's up?" Josh kept painting.

Beau felt like a louse for not helping, but the thought of whitewashing the church left a sour taste. In Denver, he'd pounded nails and hauled lumber. God might have noticed his efforts, but he hadn't cared enough to save Lucy.

"Come on down," Beau called.

"You come up."

Josh could be stubborn. If Beau had to shout, so be it. "Something's come up with the adoption." He told the minister about Miss Lange's concerns about Dani. "I'm sure you can see the problem."

Beau hoped Josh would put the pieces together and bring up marriage. Instead the minister dragged the brush up and down. To Beau, each stroke felt like a mile. He wanted to arrange the wedding and be on his way. Josh acted as if he had all the time in world. "How can I help?"

Beau tried to sound matter-of-fact. "We need a marriage certificate."

Josh stopped the brush at the highest mark, then brought it down with a long swipe. He put it in the bucket, then faced Beau. "That's an odd way to ask me to marry you and Dani."

"It's a marriage in name only."

"I see."

"This is the surest way to give Dani and the girls a real home." Beau heard his pleading tone. He'd begged just once in his life—for God to save Lucy. The answer had been no and he'd never done it again.

Josh ambled across the porch and sat on the top step. "Has Dani agreed?"

"I haven't told her yet."

"I see." Josh's eyes drilled into him.

Beau widened his stance. "Will you help us or not?"

"I have a question for you."

"Go ahead."

"How does a fake marriage give Dani a real home?"

Beau should have seen the fight coming. Josh took marriage seriously, but he'd also been unpredictable. He made some couples wait a year for his blessing. For others he spoke the vows the same day. Beau didn't need Josh's help. He and Dani could go to the courthouse, but he wanted the minister to understand. For Dani's sake, he wanted Josh's approval.

Beau wished he'd picked up the paintbrush. "It's a legal arrangement, nothing more."

"What'll you tell the girls?"

"Nothing."

"What's Dani supposed to say when men come calling?"

"She'll say no." Beau didn't like the thought of other men at all. "We have feelings for each other. I'd stay if I could."

"You can."

"You don't understand."

"I think I do," Josh replied. "You love Dani and the girls. You want to provide for them. Is that right?"

"Yes."

"You also want to see Clay Johnson hang."

Beau nodded.

"You've figured out how to have it all. You tie up the woman you love in an empty marriage, get revenge against Clay, then come home and expect her to be happy about it."

Beau felt sucker punched. He hadn't considered Dani's feelings at all. "If she wants an annulment, I'll give it to her."

"And that will fix things?" Josh looked incredulous.

"It's all I can do."

"It's flat-out stupid."

Beau didn't want to hear a rant, but he'd knocked on the door and Josh had swung it wide. The minister came down the steps, hooked his thumbs in his trousers and got in Beau's face.

"This plan is so selfish I can't believe *you* conjured it up! If you marry Dani in name only, you'll break her heart. Both today and every night she goes to bed alone. You *know* what marriage means. Dani doesn't, not yet. I'm not going to ruin her hopes with a big, fat lie."

"It's not a lie," Beau said. "It's an answer."

"A bad one."

Josh started to pace. "I'm not naive, Beau. People marry for all sorts of reasons. Not everyone's head over heels in love. Sometimes marriage is born out of need and the love comes later. But what's got to be at the foundation—always— is truth."

"I *am* being truthful."

Josh's expression turned mild. "I don't think you are."

"What do you mean?"

"Do you really want to leave?"

"It's necessary."

"Says who?"

Right and wrong seemed plain to Josh. Beau saw gray mist. It didn't matter, though. He lifted the reins from the post. "My mind's made up."

"So change it. Raise your nieces and make Dani your wife. Give her all the things she needs."

Beau thought of the butterscotch he planned to buy. She deserved far more. A husband. A partner. A man who'd sit next to her in church. The smell of whitewash filled his nose to the point of sickness. The church looked brand-new. He wanted that freshness for himself, but paint only covered the marks of time. It didn't remove them. Beau turned to his horse.

Josh gripped his arm. "Stay. Marry Dani, but do it right."

"I can't."

"You won't."

How could Josh say such a thing? He'd buried Lucy. Beau swung onto his horse. "Thanks for nothing."

Josh kept talking. "Clay stole Lucy from you. Don't give him Dani, too."

Beau tasted bile. "I want *justice*."

"Then let God have His way," Josh insisted. "He's far smarter than you."

"He had His chance. It's up to me."

"Is that so?"

Beau frowned. "What are you getting at?"

"You've been chasing Clay Johnson for five years and he's still on the loose. Clay's not that smart. Either you're a lousy lawman or God's keeping him a step ahead of you."

Beau often had the same thought. In five years, he'd caught twenty-two men. Why not Clay? Sometimes he imagined God baiting a hook and jerking it away. The thought made him furious.

He glared at Josh. "If you won't do the ceremony, I'll get a judge."

"Suit yourself." The minister went up the stairs and picked up the brush. "I'll be around if you need me."

Beau clicked to his horse. He still had candy to buy, but he felt pulled to the Silver River. Maybe Wallace had news… Maybe Johnson was close enough to kill. Tasting bile, Beau rode to the wrong side of town. As he neared the saloon, he looked for Harriet Lange's detective. He had no intention of avoiding the man. He wanted to fight and the man who'd been spying on him was a worthy target.

Seeing no one, Beau dismounted and went into the Silver River. He smelled chili and thought of the graybeard with the bad teeth. Beau didn't want to become that man, but he could see the signs. Without Dani and the girls, he had nothing.

Wallace came out of the back room. "It's been a while. Where've you been?"

"Around."

"Coffee?"

Beau nodded, then watched as Wallace poured. The barkeep set the mug in front of Beau, then took something from a drawer. He rested his closed fist on the counter, then opened his fingers to reveal a bullet. "Someone left this for you."

Beau saw the caliber. Lucy's pink dress flashed before his eyes. Only Clay Johnson would leave a bullet for the rifle that had killed Beau's wife. He pinched the casing until his thumb ached. "Who left it?"

"Some fellow with dark hair. I've never seen him before. He said to give it to you, that was all."

"Did you tell Dawes?"

"First thing, but he didn't act concerned. He said bounty hunters brought trouble on themselves."

Beau couldn't believe his ears. "What about the raid at the Rocking J?"

"He thinks the thieves are long gone. He said the bullet was your personal business."

"Fool," Beau muttered.

Wallace wiped a glass. "Do you know who left it?"

"No, but I know what it means." Johnson had sent him a summons. "When did he leave it?"

"Last Saturday."

The night of the social… If Beau had come to the Silver River instead of watching fireworks, he'd have seen the man for himself. With his palm warming the casing, he made a decision. Tonight he'd offer Dani a marriage in name only. Tomorrow they'd take vows in front of a judge. He'd be out of Castle Rock by noon. With a little luck, he'd be home in a week. The other possibility, that he'd be doomed to wander for five more years, made him ill. Either way, Dani and the girls would be secure.

Smoke stung his eyes. He loved Dani, but he hated Clay Johnson even more. The truth shamed him, but as Josh had said, it couldn't be denied.

Beau put the bullet in his pocket, paid for the coffee and walked out of the saloon. At the store he bought three pounds of butterscotch, dolls for the girls and the one thing he'd sworn not to buy. A ring for Dani. He picked a silver band with a pretty blue stone that matched her eyes. Someday he'd put a gold band on her finger. For now, silver and blue would have to do.

Dani worried every minute of Beau's absence. The instant he mentioned Pastor Josh, she'd sensed trouble. When he walked into the house with enough butterscotch for a year and toys for the girls, her worry hardened into fear. Supper didn't ease her heart. She'd expected him to be quiet as usual. Instead he was charming to them all. With the girls giggling and Dani enjoying his praise, the meal couldn't have been more normal.

The girls washed the dishes and went upstairs, leaving Dani alone on the porch. She could see a light in Beau's room and was tempted to knock on his door. Before she could decide, he strode across the yard. He'd shaved, something he usually did in the morning. He'd also put on his best shirt.

"It's a nice night," he said. "Let's take a walk."

"Sure."

As she came down the steps, Dani considered Beau's behavior. He'd gone to town to see Josh. He'd come back with candy, gifts and a secret. Her heart beat with the rhythm of a waltz. Her mind raced to reasons a man spoke in private to a minister.

With the moon lighting the way, Beau hooked his arm around her waist and guided her down the path to the stream behind the pasture. Full of snowmelt, it tumbled over rocks and made deep pools. When they reached the bank, Dani crouched and dipped her hand in the water. Her fingers tingled.

Beau cleared his throat. "I brought you here so we could speak in private."

Dani blushed. "It's a lovely night."

He looked nervous. It charmed her until his eyes glinted with irritation. "I have bad news about the adoption."

The tingle from the stream turned to a burn. Dani pushed to her feet. What a fool she'd been to expect talk of love. Putting aside thoughts of rings and her ivory dress, she faced Beau. "What happened?"

She listened as he described Trevor Scott's visit. With every word, her anger grew. She didn't care about Miss Lange's opinion of *her,* but Beau deserved respect, even kindness. For the sake of his nieces, he'd stayed in Castle Rock. He'd done it for her, too. How much longer would he stay? Afraid to ask, Dani looked upstream and said a silent prayer.

Please, Lord. Show me what's right. Protect the girls and show Beau You love him. You know my heart. You know what's best. Amen.

Beau stepped to her side. "That's the bad news. There's good news, too."

"There is?"

"Scott had a suggestion."

Dani turned her head. Her eyes landed on Beau's shoulder. She saw strength. It made her brave. "What is it?"

He kept his eyes on the stream. "If we got married—"

"Married?"

"In name only, of course."

"I see."

Dani blinked and saw her wedding gown. Earlier she'd imagined it touching her skin. She'd felt a ring on her finger, but Beau hadn't offered that kind of marriage. "I don't know what to say."

"It sounds crazy, but Scott has a point."

Dani huddled in her shawl.

Beau crossed his arms. "If we got married, the adoption would be secure. Harriet Lange couldn't even sneeze at us."

Dani liked the sound of "us," but he didn't mean it the way she did. "What about you?"

"I'm leaving."

"For how long?"

"As long as it takes to find Johnson."

Dani wished she hadn't asked. She turned to the stream and dipped her hand into it. The cold jarred her senses but failed to numb her feelings.

Beau stepped up behind her. "Once the adoption's settled, you can get an annulment."

Not once in her dreams had she even thought that word. She understood the principle. An unconsummated marriage wasn't a marriage at all, but what about her feelings? If he thought she could stop loving him, he'd lost his mind. Dani bit her lip to hold in an angry remark. Lecturing Beau—even telling him she loved him—wouldn't make a whit of difference.

He touched her arm. "I have to say something else."

"Not now."

He leaned closer. "I care for you, Dani. Johnson's close. If things go as I hope, I'll be back in days, not months."

But what then? Would killing Clay bring Beau peace? He thought so, but Dani had her doubts. Beau had been fighting God as much as he'd been battling Clay. Dani loved him, but she feared for the future. She also feared losing the girls.

Sighing, she faced Beau. "When do I have to decide?"

"The sooner, the better."

"So you can leave."

He nodded.

"That's why you went to see Josh," she said. "To arrange the ceremony."

Beau frowned. "He won't do it."

Dani respected the pastor for his choice. She felt the same inclination, but she had to consider the girls. Before she made a decision, she wanted to hear Josh's opinion for herself. She looked at Beau. "I'll give you my answer on Sunday."

He looked peeved. "That's three days."

"I need time. Surely—"

"Fine. Sunday it is."

With her heart breaking, Dani led the way back to the house. Of all the marriage proposals she'd received, this one was by the far the saddest.

Chapter Sixteen

Beau drove Dani and the girls to church on Sunday. He'd been on his best behavior after visiting Scott, but he had no intention of stepping inside the building. He had nothing more to say to Josh, and he doubted Adie would take his side. Dani alone controlled the future.

Beau stopped in front of the church, helped Dani down from the seat, then watched as his nieces went to Miss Adie's Sunday school in the parsonage. Dani walked up the steps without looking back. If she had, she'd have seen Mr. Paisley Vest with his son, a young boy who needed a haircut. The kid saw the girls, spoke to his father and scampered off to be with Miss Adie. Beau wondered if she still used puppets to teach Sunday school. He'd helped her once. He'd been a bear named Jed and had hammed it up.

Stifling that memory, he sat in the surrey, waiting for stragglers to pass before he lifted the reins. The last couple went inside the building, but no one closed the door. When the pianist struck the opening chords of "Blessed Assurance," Beau sat paralyzed. The hymn carried him beyond the moment, beyond his hate. When the music ended, a man read a Psalm filled with utter anguish. Beau understood every word. When it ended, the pianist struck a ponderous chord. Beau recognized "A Mighty Fortress is Our God." He'd always liked that hymn. He found himself mouthing the words until the last note.

In the sudden silence, he heard Josh's deep voice.

"Who is among you that feareth the Lord, that obeyeth the voice of His servant, that walketh in darkness, and hath no light?"

Beau felt a chill. He'd feared God his entire life. He'd obeyed the Lord's commands, yet here he was…walking in darkness with no light.

Josh kept going.

"Let him trust in the name of the Lord and stay upon his God."

Beau held in a curse. He'd trusted God and where had it gotten him? In the weeks after Lucy's murder, he'd prayed every day. He'd waited for God to bring justice and received nothing. Beau wanted to leave, but Josh's voice had the same quality as the familiar hymns. It struck chords that rang true. Instead of lifting the reins, Beau stared at the open door.

"Behold, all ye that kindle a fire, that compass yourselves about with sparks."

How many fires had Beau kindled on the open trail? At least a thousand, maybe more. Alone, he'd stared into the blaze, imagining the moment he'd find Clay Johnson. Those flames had encircled his soul.

Josh deepened his voice.

"Walk in the light of your fire, and in the sparks that ye have kindled. This shall ye have of Mine hand; ye shall lie down in torment."

Rage poured through Beau's veins. He'd walked by the light of his own fire for five years, but only because God hadn't given him so much as a matchstick to light the way. At night, when Beau had lain devastated on the hard ground, God hadn't done a thing to help him. The stars had winked in the cold sky, reminding him that somewhere Clay Johnson was seeing the sky and Lucy wasn't.

Beau stared at the church. The white boards glistened in the sun, forcing him to squint. Who needed a God that would whitewash a murder? Not Beau. Before Josh could utter another word, Beau picked up the reins. As soon as he married Dani, he'd be riding out. He needed supplies, so he headed for town.

Dani had come to church needing a special touch. For three days, she'd agonized over Beau's proposal. She could justify a marriage in name only in her mind, but she couldn't settle it with her heart. She didn't know what to do, and Heaven had remained silent. God, she believed, was listening. He just wasn't talking.

He seemed to be talking now, though. The instant the organist played "A Mighty Fortress," Dani felt like a child at her father's knee. Her own father had been a man of few words, but he'd loved that hymn. After the music, Pastor Josh opened his Bible and read from Isaiah. His impassioned tone reminded her of the nights her father had read out loud to his family. He finished the verses, closed the Bible and looked right at Dani. "Some of us have hard decisions to make today. We know what we want. We know what other people want. But what does God want?"

Dani sat straighter. Josh had described her situation exactly. She didn't want to be selfish or naive. She wanted to make the right decision no matter the personal cost. As Josh told stories about people in the Bible and the choices they'd made, she hung on to every word. When men trusted God, they triumphed. When they acted on their own, as Moses had when he'd struck the rock, they paid a price. She didn't want to make that mistake.

Pastor Josh locked eyes with her. "How do we know God's will?"

Dani thought of the obvious answers. Prayer. Reading the Bible. But what did a woman do when her choice would put others at risk? A marriage in name only struck Dani as wrong, but it would protect the girls. Saying no to Beau would protect her integrity, but the girls could end up in Minnesota.

The Reverend held her gaze. "God hasn't spoken through a prophet like Isaiah in a lot of years, but he speaks to each of us every day. Sometimes he whispers in our ears. Sometimes he gives words to a friend. I've found when people say God's not talking, most of the time—not all—they're not listening. Why is that? The Creator of the Universe loves us. He sent His son to lead the way to eternity, yet we hold on to our ideas, our plans, as if we know everything. Why do we put faith in ourselves when the Lord knows far more than we do?"

He gave the congregation a minute to think.

"The answer's simple. We're afraid of the dark. We stop trusting God and start our own fires. They give off light but just for a while. They give us heat but only in a tiny circle. Those fires die out, leaving us colder than ever. Sometimes our fires do the opposite. They burn out of control and destroy our lives. Either way, we end up back in the dark."

Josh paced some more. "So what do we do? How do we manage when the night stretches beyond our understanding and we're as scared as children? The answer's both easy and hard. We wait for the Lord to light the way. We walk by faith, not sight. That's what this story is about."

The words settled into Dani's soul. If she married Beau, she'd be doing it out of fear, not faith. Her body tensed with dread. She couldn't marry him, not even for the sake of the girls. God, she had to believe, had a better plan than a deceitful marriage. Her stomach was doing flips, but she had peace about her decision. Tonight she'd tell Beau she couldn't marry him. She didn't think he'd leave without finalizing the adoption, but she couldn't be sure. Refusing his offer could cost her everything, but so could taking it. She wanted a real marriage, not a compromise.

With that thought, the light of her own fire went out completely, plunging her into the dark. She couldn't speak to Beau until the girls were asleep, which meant she had all afternoon to imagine a lonely train ride back to Wisconsin. As the organist played the closing hymn, Dani prayed for strength.

Tired of pacing by the stream, Beau glanced up at the moon. After church, Dani had whispered that she'd reached a decision and would speak to him after the girls went to bed. Ever since, he'd been tense and way. He almost wished he'd gone inside the church to hear Josh preach. Back in Denver the man's sermons had been like a match to tinder. Beau's faith had caught fire, but Lucy's death had doused those flames.

Beau didn't know what the Reverend had said today, but Dani had come out with her chin held high. She'd looked ready to fight, but with whom? Beau or Harriet Lange?

He didn't know, but he'd find out soon. Twenty minutes ago, she'd asked him to meet her at the stream. He'd been grateful to walk alone. Every minute he spent with her made him doubt his decision to leave. To stay focused, he kept the bullet in his pocket. He had it now. He also had Dani's ring. If she said yes, he'd give it to her tonight.

Beau sensed movement, turned and saw Dani walking along the fence. The sight of her stole his breath. She had on a pale blue dress, one he'd never seen before. It matched her eyes. She'd taken time with her hair, too. Instead of a coiled braid, she'd pinned it up in a smooth knot. Had she dressed up for the occasion? He hoped so but chastised himself. They were conducting business, not a courtship.

"Hi there," he called.

"Hi."

"Nice night," he said, sounding casual.

Dani didn't seem to hear him. She stopped two feet away and raised her chin. "I've reached a decision. While I appreciate your offer, I can't agree to a marriage in name only."

Beau had been in a lot of fights but never one with so many players. Dani had Josh on her side, Adie, the girls and Lucy, too. In a bizarre twist of irony, Beau's only ally was Clay Johnson. That fact should have told him something, but he turned a deaf ear to the small voice of his conscience. He couldn't leave until the judge finalized the adoption. He had to make Dani change her mind.

"Why not?" he asked.

She stood ramrod straight. "It would be dishonest."

"It's necessary. Think of the girls."

"I am."

His blood started to burn. "What about Harriet Lange? She's already causing trouble."

"It doesn't matter."

"Of course, it matters!" Beau thought she'd lost her mind.

Dani laced her fingers at her waist. "I have to believe that God has a plan. He knows what's best."

"He doesn't give a hoot!" The only man Beau trusted these days was himself. He didn't want to antagonize Dani, so he tried to sound mild. "I know this is hard for you, but a marriage in name only is the easiest way to settle the adoption."

"Maybe, but it's not the best way."

"Dani—"

"I can't, Beau." Her voice shook. "It would be wrong in so many ways."

"Name one."

"We'd be telling three girls that marriage is nothing but a business arrangement."

"They don't have to know."

"So we'd be lying."

She had a point, but so did he. "This arrangement is no one's business but ours."

"I'd be lying to myself and to the girls." Her voice dropped to a murmur. "I can't do it."

He shook his head in disgust. "Josh must have preached a barn burner of a sermon."

"He made me see the truth."

"What truth?"

"God has a plan for us, and it doesn't include a fake marriage. If we do it *His* way, not ours, He'll see us through."

Beau's jaw tightened. "Like He saw Lucy through?"

"I'm so sorry—"

"*Sorry* doesn't cut butter."

If she told him to set down his hate, he'd walk away. He half hoped she would. He'd have a reason to storm off. Instead she looked at him with heartfelt sympathy, then held

out her hand. Beau stared at her fingers. Long and strong, they
reminded him of the twigs a bird used to build a nest. She
deserved a nest of her own. He wanted to build that home and
share it with her, but he couldn't. If he took her hand tonight,
he'd never leave.

Dani crossed the two steps between them and cupped his
face in her palms. "There's another reason I can't say yes."

"Don't say it."

"I love you, Beau. You know that."

"Dani—"

"I want everything God has for us."

Beau knew what it meant to love a woman, to carry her
burdens and share her dreams. He'd have died in Lucy's
place. He felt the same way about Dani. He also knew how
it felt to be loved. A woman's smile made a man stand tall.
It made him stronger and better in ways no man understood.
Beau felt that love now. It was time to be a better man—
Dani's man—but he couldn't do it without denying his own
need for justice.

He jerked away from her touch. "Maybe you're right."

Her eyes filled with hope. He hated himself for what he
was about to say, but it couldn't be helped. "You need a
husband, a man who won't leave. I'm not that man."

"You could be."

He clenched his teeth. He loved this woman, but he
couldn't tell her how he felt. Leaving would be hard enough
without an empty promise.

She stepped closer. "I want you to be that man."

Beau breathed in the scent of her hair. If he reached for
her, she'd be in his arms. He'd kiss her and tell her he loved
her…then where would they be? He had to finish his business
with Clay. He reached into his pocket, pinched the bullet and
raised it for her to see. "Johnson left this for me."

Her eyes filled with revulsion, then fear. "He wants to kill you."

"The feeling's mutual."

"Stay," Dani pleaded. "We can have a good life. We can—" She bit her tongue, then turned her back and gave a dry laugh. "I've never begged in my life. I'm embarrassed."

Beau touched her shoulder. "Don't be. I'm honored." He wanted to turn her around but settled for looking at every hair on her head. "I have to go, Dani. With a little luck, I'll be back soon and free to say what's in my heart."

Her shoulders quivered. "When are you going?"

"The instant the adoption's final."

"But Harriet Lange—"

"I'll visit Scott tomorrow. Maybe he can speed things up."

"I see."

"No, you don't." He sounded as hoarse as a mule skinner. "I'd stay if I could. I'd do a lot of things."

"I'm sorry," she replied. "I wish I could make things easy for you."

"I feel the same for you."

Either one of them could have ended the standoff, but at what cost? If Dani sacrificed her integrity, she'd stop being the honest woman he loved. Beau could let Clay live, but he'd still be consumed by bitterness. He couldn't change his own heart. He didn't have that ability.

No, but God did. Beau heard the voice in his head. He knew God's ways. He also had Clay Johnson's bullet in his pocket. It promised finality, the only kind Beau trusted. He saw the choice as plain as day. He could put his faith in God or in a brass casing filled with gunpowder. Of the two, gunpowder was more reliable.

"Let's go home," he said to Dani's back.

She squared her shoulders, then gave him a sad smile. "You can always change your mind."

"So can you."

He followed her to the house, walking in the dark because God had hidden the moon.

Chapter Seventeen

"When will we know about the adoption?"

Emma had asked the question, but all three girls looked up at Dani from across the kitchen table. They were making cottage cheese the way Dani had made it a thousand times, the way her mother had taught her. Yesterday she had clabbered the milk. Today she and the girls were squeezing the whey and adding salt to taste. She'd serve it with tonight's supper.

Emma looked at Dani expectantly. The question deserved an answer, but Dani didn't have one. She kept her voice mild. "Mr. Scott's working on papers for the judge."

The girls didn't know anything about Harriet Lange or Beau's marriage proposal. Earlier she and Beau had explained that Mr. Scott had to write up a contract to make the adoption permanent, and that a judge had to approve it. They didn't mention Harriet Lange's threats to fight in court.

Emma squeezed the cheesecloth. Whey dripped into a bowl. "It's taking a long time."

"Too long," Ellie added.

"I think so, too," Dani said. "But it can't be helped."

Had she just lied? Last night she'd refused Beau's offer. They could have been married today if she'd compromised. Dani didn't doubt her decision, but she feared the consequences. Last night, lying in the dark, she imagined Harriet Lange slapping Emma.

"Dani?" Esther sounded older. She hadn't sucked her thumb in days.

"What is it, sweetie?"

"I'm scared the judge will say no."

"Me, too," she answered. "We have to trust the Lord to know what's best."

The girls had grown up with prayers and Bible stories. They knew Jesus for themselves. With time, their faith would grow. Dani hoped to help them down that path. No matter what happened, she wouldn't waver or doubt. Life, she decided, was like the curds she'd spread in a pan. Yesterday they'd been raw milk, but heat and time had turned them into something even better. She was trusting God for the same miracle in her life.

Did I make the right choice, Lord?

She thought of her favorite Psalm and the sparrows that had a nest for themselves. She wanted a nest of her own, a home with children and Beau for a husband. Last night she'd helped him with the milking. Over and over, she'd hummed "Amazing Grace." When they'd finished, Beau had muttered something about grace being wasted on Clay Johnson and had left the barn.

Dani finished covering the tray of curds and set it aside. A knock on the front door startled all four of them. Praying Trevor Scott had come with good news, she wiped her hands on her apron. "I'll get it," she said to the girls.

As she stepped into the front room, she craned her neck to see through the window into the yard. She saw a horse and buggy with a driver, a well-dressed man she didn't recognize. She thought of calling for Beau, but he and Howie were repairing the fence on the far side of the meadow. Dani opened the door and saw an old woman in a gray traveling suit. She stood five feet tall and had pretty white hair. Dani was a regular at church now and had been invited to join a sewing circle. The woman at her door, with her round face and dainty nose, seemed familiar. Perhaps she'd come with another invitation.

Dani smiled. "May I help you?"

"I believe you can," she said sweetly. "Is this the Morgan farm?"

"Yes, it is."

"I'm Harriet Lange."

Dani had expected the girls' aunt to be a crone. This woman had laugh wrinkles and twinkling eyes. Slightly plump, she had the pillowy softness of a grandmother. Dani felt sick inside. What right did she have to deny this woman her nieces? None, but appearances could be deceiving. Dani glanced at the woman's hands and saw fancy gloves. Did the silk cover fingers capable of a tender touch or a hand that would hurt a child?

"I've taken you by surprise," the woman said gently. "May I come in?"

"Of course." Dani wished she had on a better dress. She opened the door and motioned for Miss Lange to step into the front room. "We were just making cottage cheese. If you'd give me a minute—"

"Of course." The woman scanned the room.

"Please, sit down." Dani motioned to the divan, but Miss Lange walked to the hutch displaying Beth's collection of teacups. The girls, especially Emma, treasured the reminders of their mother.

The older woman picked up a cup with a silver rim. "I gave this to Beth when she married Patrick."

Dani didn't know what to say. "It's lovely."

"So was my niece."

She'd clipped her words. Dani heard a hint of bitterness and wished she knew more about Beth's side of the family.

Miss Lange set the cup back in place. "I'd like to see my nieces."

"I'll get them." Dani hurried to the kitchen where the girls stood by the door, frozen like scared rabbits.

"Your Aunt Harriet is here." She focused on Emma. "Go get Uncle Beau."

Emma ran out the door. With Ellie and Esther hovering at her side, Dani filled the teakettle, smoothed her hair and looked out the window to the spot where Patrick and Beth lay side by side. She no longer loved him, but she wondered what he and Beth would want for their children. Beau had a piece of paper on his side, but Miss Lange seemed genuinely concerned. She'd taken a long train trip, one that had to be expensive and tiring. Dani's own happiness hinged on the adoption, but she couldn't think about herself. Only the girls mattered now.

Aware that Esther had put her thumb in her mouth, Dani said a silent prayer. *You know what's best, Lord. Your will be done.*

She poured two cups of tea, set them on a tray with milk, sugar and a plate of cookies. She picked it up and turned to the girls. "I'll be with you."

Ellie shook her head. "I want to wait for Emma."

"Me, too," said Esther.

Dani saw no reason to force them. She carried the tray into the front room and set it on the table. Miss Lange smiled her thanks, sipped, then looked carefully at the sugar bowl. "That belonged to my mother."

So much history... If Dani kept the girls, the details of their family heritage would be lost. Was adopting them wrong after all? Had God stopped her from marrying Beau because these children belonged in Minnesota, surrounded by their mother's family?

Miss Lange peered through the doorway. "I heard you speaking to my nieces. Where are they?"

"Waiting for Emma."

"Posh!" said Miss Lange. "Girls, come out here this instant. I want to see you."

Dani bristled. She used a gentler tone when she called the cows. Hoping to reassure two frightened children, she made her voice friendly. "It's okay. Come and sit with us."

They walked into the front room side by side. Ellie's pinafore had a blotch of whey from squeezing the curds, but at least she had on a dress instead of coveralls. Esther, wide-eyed and frightened, saw her aunt and jammed her thumb in her mouth.

Miss Lange huffed. "Child, take your *thumb* out of your *mouth* right now. For goodness' sake, you'll give yourself buckteeth!"

Esther whimpered. Ellie put her arm around her sister's shoulder. Holding tight, she looked to Dani for help.

"Miss Lange—"

"That child needs discipline," she said. "If you smack her hand, she'll stop that bad habit. Mark my words, Miss Baxter. Spare the rod and spoil the child."

Beneath Miss Lange's silk gloves, Dani felt sure she'd see gnarled fingers that would slap a child at will. She wanted to throw the woman out of the house, but losing her temper wouldn't help the children. Dani shot Ellie a look that promised she'd fight, then faced Miss Lange. "The girls have had a difficult time."

"That's no excuse for sloppy behavior." Miss Lange sounded almost cheerful. She focused again on her nieces. "Our little thumb-sucker must be Esther. You must be Eleanor."

"I'm Ellie."

"That's a silly name," Miss Lange said. "Eleanor suits you."

It didn't suit the tomboy Dani knew.

Miss Lange looked the child up and down. "Your pinafore has a stain. Perhaps you'd like to go upstairs and change?"

Ellie's eyes glinted. "Yes, ma'am. I would."

"You're excused."

Esther, clinging to her sister's hand, turned to follow Ellie upstairs. Miss Lange huffed. "Esther, you're a big girl now. Let go of your sister's hand."

Esther did as she'd been told, but her lower lip trembled. As Ellie turned to argue, Dani caught her eye and motioned for her to go upstairs alone. She hurried to Esther, hugged her and told her she could sit with the grown-ups and have a cookie.

"Really?" Esther asked.

"You sure can."

No way would Dani allow Miss Lange to pick on a frightened five-year-old. She led Esther to the divan and gave her the treat. Dani didn't believe in bribing children for good behavior, but Esther needed a distraction. When they sat, Esther climbed on Dani's lap. The child's weight numbed her legs, but she let her cuddle.

Harriet Lange arched her brows. They looked like gray worms. "Miss Baxter, you're spoiling these girls."

"I disagree."

The woman harrumphed. "Of course, you do. You're a child yourself."

"I'm twenty-two."

"You're barely older than Emma."

Dani had heard enough. "Why are you here, Miss Lange?"

"To take custody. You have no claim to these children. As for Mr. Morgan, he's not fit to raise them."

"You don't know him," Dani countered. "You don't know *me,* either."

"I know that children need a firm hand."

Ellie's footsteps pounded down the stairs. She walked into the front room wearing coveralls and boots.

Miss Lange gasped. Before Dani realized what she intended to do, the woman marched up to Ellie and raised her hand. "Why you disrespectful—"

"Stop!" Dani plopped Esther on the divan and ran to Ellie, who had already jumped back.

Miss Lange stayed still.

Gripping Ellie's shoulders, Dani glared at the older woman. "You can't have these children, Miss Lange. You're not fit to raise them."

The old lady turned and arched one brow at Dani. "And *you* are?"

"Yes."

"You're no more qualified than I am, Miss Baxter. You're a single woman. So am I. I have the wisdom that comes with age. What do *you* have?"

Dani had what mattered most. She had a heart full of love and the faith to believe God would see them through this hard time. She flashed on the girls seated at the supper table, smiling and feeling safe. She saw herself at one end, loving them as her daughters. She also saw an empty chair at the head of the table, Beau's place if he chose to fill it. Dani would do anything—give up her dreams, live with that empty chair—to protect the girls from Harriet Lange. Her heart ached with the sacrifice she was about to make, but it had to be done.

She raised her chin. "I can give the girls a real home. Mr. Morgan and I are getting married."

Ellie gasped. "Really?"

"Yes." Dani smoothed the child's hair. She and Beau would be married in the eyes of the law and Harriet Lange. Someday, if he made peace with himself and Clay Johnson, they'd be married in the eyes of God.

Miss Lange narrowed her eyes. "When is the wedding?"

"As soon as we can arrange it."

"This is rather sudden, isn't it?"

Dani said nothing.

The woman's eyes glimmered with suspicion. "Is this marriage legitimate, Miss Baxter? Or is it a scheme to hold on to the life you expected from Patrick?"

Dani's cheeks flushed red. She couldn't lie, but neither would she hand this woman a weapon to be used against her. She sealed her lips.

"I see," said Miss Lange.

The back door opened and slammed shut. Dani looked down the hallway where she saw Beau pacing like a man on fire. His gaze shifted from Harriet Lange to Ellie and finally to Dani. "What's going on?"

"I told Miss Lange about our engagement."

Beau put the pieces together in an instant. He'd already seen the buggy and the Pinkerton's agent. Miss Lange, it seemed, had come to make threats and Dani had protected the girls with the only weapon she had. She'd sacrificed herself, her dreams and her hope for a real marriage. Her goodness shamed him. Spoiling for a fight, he looked at Harriet Lange. She seemed mild enough in her gray frock, but he didn't like the set of her mouth. The lawman in him sensed trouble.

"Good afternoon, Miss Lange. I'm Beau Morgan."

"I know who you are, sir."

"Why are you here?"

"To take my nieces, of course."

"I have custody."

Her cheeks turned pinker. "May I remind you, Mr. Morgan. Your attorney approached *me.* He made it clear that you wished to return to your *business* as soon as possible. He offered me money—a goodly sum—if I'd take all three girls."

Beau regretted that offer more than he could say. He also wished Emma, Ellie and Esther had never heard it. The three of them had clustered on the divan and were hanging on to every word. They needed to know he'd keep them safe, so he looked at them one by one, then said, "That offer was a mistake. It's off the table." He turned back to Miss Lange. "I'm keeping custody."

"Forgive me, Mr. Morgan, if I'm not convinced of your sincerity. Your engagement to Miss Baxter seems rather fortuitous."

The woman smiled like a grandma but hissed like a snake. Beau crossed his arms. "Our plans are none of your business."

Her expression turned smug. "I'll ask you the same question I asked Miss Baxter. When are you getting married?"

"Soon." Beau didn't know what Dani had said. If he contradicted her, Miss Lange would use the confusion against them.

"In church?"

Beau answered by crossing his arms. "It's none of your concern."

"I'll be blunt, Mr. Morgan. I don't believe for a minute that you intend to provide a home for my nieces. My detective tells me you've been a bounty hunter for five years, and that you make a good living. I suspect Miss Baxter has charmed you into giving her what she wants."

The irony left Beau speechless. Instead of making Dani's dreams come true, he'd denied her what she desired most— a family, a husband, a home.

Miss Lange's expression turned smug. "When it's settled, you'll go back to bounty hunting. Is that correct?"

How could the truth be so right and wrong at the same time? Beau couldn't deny the facts, but he had the power to change them. He could stay in Castle Rock. He could marry Dani. The thought burned like fire, but so did his hate for Clay Johnson. He had to send Lucy's killer to eternity and he had to do it now. Not in a month or a year, but by Sunday so he could take Dani to church. To protect the girls, he had to marry her. To protect Dani, the marriage had to be real. That meant bringing Clay to justice and coming home for good.

Beau's next words were for Harriet Lange, but his eyes stayed on Dani. "If Miss Baxter will have me, we'll get married this Sunday."

"In church?" Dani asked.

Beau nodded.

Questions burned in her eyes. He had to explain his plan, which meant getting rid of Harriet Lange. He turned to the gray-haired witch. "Are you satisfied?"

"I suppose."

"Miss Lange?" Dani had spoken.

"Yes?"

"I love your nieces. I'll take good care of them."

To Beau's surprise, the old lady looked at the girls with misty eyes. If they hadn't exchanged words, he'd have thought she was kind. She even smiled at Dani. "Just remember what I said. 'Spare the rod and spoil the child.'"

Not in Beau's book. Judging by Dani's expression, something ugly had happened. Emma's mouth tightened and Ellie's eyes burned with venom. Esther whimpered, then jerked her thumb out of her mouth. The sooner this woman left the house, the better off they'd be.

"That settles it," he said.

Miss Lange smiled as if nothing had happened. "Of course I'll be attending the wedding."

Beau wanted to tell her to stay away, but he couldn't stop her from attending church.

Dani squared her shoulders. "Of course."

Miss Lange looked at the girls with something close to tenderness. "I know I seem harsh, but I want what's best for you." She eyed Esther, who was still cowering, then looked Ellie up and down. She sighed at the sight of Emma, then faced Beau. "If there's no wedding, you'll hear from me."

"I'd expect so."

Eager to be rid of her, Beau opened the door. She went to the buggy, where the detective helped her onto the seat, then lifted the reins. Not once did the old woman look back. That told Beau everything he needed to know about Harriet Lange. She had the discipline of a general. She'd keep her word about attending the wedding.

He closed the door and turned to Dani. Before he could speak, his nieces ran to him and hugged his waist. Beau dropped to a crouch so he could reach Esther. Her skinny arms twisted around his neck and he picked her up. He tousled Ellie's hair and kissed the top of Emma's head. He'd slain a dragon for them. Now he had to slay one for Dani and himself.

He set Esther down. "I need to speak with Dani. How about checking on T.C.?"

As obedient as lambs, the girls went outside. Dani looked weak in the knees, but she stayed on her feet. "What just happened?"

"Let's sit down."

He guided her to the divan. On the table he saw a cold pot of tea, the only evidence Harriet Lange had turned their world upside down. Beau dropped down next to Dani, then touched her back. "Are you all right?"

"I don't know."

His throat felt like gravel. "I meant what I said about Sunday."

"But how? Josh won't marry us."

"He will if my heart's right." Beau hurried his words. "Clay's waiting, Dani. I can feel it. I'm going to hunt him down and be done with it."

"Oh, Beau."

"No matter what, I'll be back by Sunday."

When she closed her eyes, he imagined her thinking a prayer and dreaded what she'd say next. When she raised her face, he saw the woman who'd told him no at the stream.

"What if you don't come back?" she asked.

"I will. I promise."

Patrick had once said the same thing and they both knew it. She stood and walked to the window. "I want to believe you, Beau. But how can I? Anything could happen."

He stayed silent.

Dani stared through the glass at the rutted yard. "We have to consider the girls."

"I am."

"Then stay." She turned to him. "You weren't here when Harriet Lange made Esther cry. She almost slapped Ellie. How can you leave, knowing she'd take them away?"

Her voice cracked. Beau wanted to throw the blasted teacups against the wall.

"Stay," she said gently. "Let the authorities worry about Johnson."

"I can't."

Her eyes burned with defiance. "I'm not sure I want to marry you."

"Why not?"

"Because you hate Clay Johnson more than you love me."

Beau pushed to his feet. He loved Dani. He'd just asked her to marry him, but he'd done a poor a job of it. He'd been so choked with hate for Clay that he hadn't told her that he loved her. He wanted to say the words now, but he knew they'd sound hollow.

His throat hurt. "You and Clay… It's apples and oranges."

"It's still a choice."

She went to the door and opened it wide. "Go on, Beau. Leave. Do what you have to do."

"All right," he said. "Get your things."

"What do you mean?"

"I'm taking you and the girls to town. You can stay with Josh and Adie."

"Absolutely not!"

"It's not a choice."

"Oh yes, it is! I'm staying right here."

Beau raked his hand through his hair. "I can't leave you and girls unprotected. Clay could be watching right now."

She raised her chin. "If you're that worried, stay."

"Six days," he insisted. "That's all I'm asking. Even if I don't find Johnson, I'll be back."

"Then what?" she demanded.

"We'll cross that bridge when we get to it."

Dani had a gleam in her eyes, the one he remembered from the day of the milking contest. It filled his mind with harmonies and the rhythm they'd found at the dance. He couldn't stop himself from loving her, nor could he hold back a need as profound as air.

Protect this woman, Lord. Be with her. I'm a low-down cur bent on revenge. She deserves a man with a clean heart. Keep her safe, Lord. Give her joy.

With that silent prayer, Beau crossed a line. He wasn't willing to listen to God, but he hoped God would listen to him. He wanted to quit hating Clay Johnson but didn't know how. Dani had become an obstacle, one he had to shatter.

"Get packed," he said with a growl.

Before she could argue, he stormed out of the house. He had to get ready for Johnson, so he strode into his room, where he kept his guns, ammunition, ropes and irons. He lugged his things into the barn, saddled his horse and tied down the tools of his trade. In the past, he'd have touched Lucy's handkerchief and recalled her goodness. He couldn't do that today. Dani had the hankie. In its place Beau carried the bullet from the Silver River. He touched the casing but found no comfort, only warm metal and a reminder of the ring he'd bought for Dani. He'd grown accustomed to carrying something that linked him to what he knew to be good, so he went back to his room, fetched the ring and put it in his pocket. Lucy's hankie had reminded him of what he'd lost. The ring stood for what he hoped to gain.

He had six days to hunt down Clay Johnson. On the seventh, Beau would be in church with Dani. God willing, he'd find peace at last.

Chapter Eighteen

Dani called the girls inside, told them Beau had to take a short trip and explained they'd all be staying with Pastor Josh and Adie. They went upstairs to pack a few clothes, leaving Dani to finish the cottage cheese. She packed it in a crock to take to the parsonage, made sandwiches for Howie who'd be tending the cows alone, then put a change of clothing for herself in the satchel she'd carried on the train.

Her decision to stay with Josh and Adie had nothing to do with Beau's order. Dani needed to sort her thoughts, and Adie would listen all night if that's what it took to understand why Beau couldn't set down his hate for Clay Johnson. If Dani understood, maybe she could forgive him for leaving. As things were now, she felt wounded and alone. Earlier, she'd put Lucy's hankie in her memory box. She took it out, pressed it in her Bible and added both things to the satchel. She carried it to the front porch where she saw Beau's horse. A looped rope hung from the saddle, a leather scabbard held a rifle and the saddle-bags bulged with provisions. Beau came out of the barn, leading the horse and surrey. Dressed in his duster and the faded clothes he'd worn the day they'd met, he looked like Cain.

As he lifted Esther into the surrey, Dani strode across the yard. Saying nothing, he helped her on to the seat. She took the reins, watching as he swung his tall body into the saddle, pulled his hat low and clicked to his horse. He might have been clicking to her, too, but Dani paid no attention. She had to see Adie and Josh.

When they arrived at the parsonage, Adie, as always, opened her home to them. Josh saw Beau and led him to the stable for a private talk. Ten minutes later, with Dani watching from the window, the men came out of the building. Josh headed to the parsonage. Beau rode west without a goodbye.

She hated parting company with unkind words between them, but she had nothing more to say. She'd begged Beau once and wouldn't do it again. He knew the stakes, yet he'd chosen to go his own way. Dani stood at the window, watching him grow smaller with every stride of his horse. When he turned to a speck against the mountain, she let the curtain flutter back into place.

Pastor Josh opened the door. "How are you?"

"Angry. Afraid."

"Let's sit outside."

Dani followed him out the door and took the chair facing the church, the same one she'd used her first day in Castle Rock. She'd been grieving, confused and doubtful of God's plan in her life. Now she felt sure of the Almighty's hand but feared for everyone she loved.

Josh walked past her to the railing and crossed his arms. "Beau's an arrogant fool, but I understand why he's going after Clay."

"You do?"

"If someone harmed Adie, I'd be hard-pressed to practice what I preach."

Dani wanted an ally. "But we have to forgive."

"True." Josh sat next to her. "But we're not made that way. We need God's mercy. It's knowing we're forgiven that gives us the grace to forgive others."

"Beau will never forgive Clay Johnson."

"Maybe, but God already has."

Dani understood the cross. Christ had died to set men free. Ever since, human beings had battled between their sinful desires and the goodness of God. As the soul prospered, the flesh died. Until a man surrendered, he lived with constant conflict. A lump pushed into her throat. "Beau's at war with himself, isn't he?"

"And with God."

She thought of Josh's sermon about a man walking by the light of his own fire. He'd described Beau that day. She didn't want to be that kind of woman. "I have to stay strong."

"You will." Josh sounded confident.

"It's a matter of faith."

"And knowing God loves Beau even more than you do."

Dani almost smiled. "Loving him can be a trial, that's for sure."

Josh looked pleased. "Most men are. Beau's stubborn and willful, just the way God made him. The Lord knows how we feel."

"Beau wants justice."

"So does the Lord."

"It's hard." Dani's voice quavered.

"We have a hard God," Josh replied. "He loved us enough to sacrifice His own son. I don't know what Beau's going to face in that canyon, but I know with certainty he's not riding alone."

The minister's faith gave Dani comfort, but she had to face the facts. Beau had gone to war. Soldiers died.

Dani's stomach clenched. "I feel so helpless."

"We're not. We can pray."

Before they could bow their heads, Adie opened the front door. "Josh? We need you. The girls are frightened."

Dani pushed to her feet. "Where are they?"

"In the front room," Adie replied. "I'm hoping Josh will tell us a story."

"Sure," he answered.

Dani followed Adie into the house, with Josh ushering both women through the door. She saw the girls on the divan. Stephen had gone to a friend's house, but Adie had set up his checkerboard. It sat untouched on the table. As Dani settled next to Emma, Josh and Adie took their usual chairs. They traded a look that made Dani ache.

"Adie thinks we need a story," Josh said to the girls. "What'll it be?"

Ellie spoke up. "The one Dani told us."

"About Daniel and the lions," Emma explained.

"Good choice," Josh said. "Who knows how it starts?"

"I do," Ellie said. "The king put Daniel in a cave."

"Was he alone?"

"There were lions," Esther said. "*Hungry* ones."

"They roared," said Ellie.

"That's right." Josh sounded serious. "Was Daniel afraid?"

The girls said nothing. Dani took the lead. "I know he was, because I'm scared right now."

"Me, too." Emma's voice trembled. "What if Uncle Beau doesn't come back?"

Josh looked at the girls one at a time, then focused on Emma. "Your uncle isn't in a cave with a real lion, but he's locked up with something just as big."

"What?" Ellie asked.

Josh looked to Dani for help. The girls had heard about their Aunt Lucy, but they didn't know she'd been murdered.

How did an adult explain hate to a child? Dani didn't know, but she understood love. She wanted the girls to understand that part of Beau. "Do you remember about your Uncle Beau being married?"

The girls nodded.

"Your Aunt Lucy died because of bad man in Denver." Dani skipped the details. "The bad man got away. Your Uncle Beau wants to put him in jail."

Esther looked puzzled. "Is he in a cave with the bad man?"

"Sort of," Dani answered. "He can't stop being angry. That feeling roars all the time, just like a real lion."

Josh chimed in. "Who knows what happened to Daniel?"

"I do," said Emma. "God put the lions to sleep."

"He kept Daniel safe," Josh said. "I'm praying the bad things around your uncle go to sleep just like the lions."

"Me, too," Dani said.

Josh looked at Adie. "Feed our guests, but I won't be having supper tonight."

"Why not?" Ellie asked.

"We can pray in all different ways," he said. "We can talk to God out loud or think in our heads. Tonight I'm praying with my whole body. Every time my belly growls, I'll be saying a prayer for your uncle."

Dani looked at Adie. "I won't be eating, either."

"That's three of us," Adie said. "We'll spend the evening on our knees."

"Four," Emma said. "I can pray, too."

"Five," said Ellie.

"Seven!" cried Esther.

Emma frowned at her. "You mean six."

"No, I mean seven. I'm counting Jesus."

Dani's eyes misted. How could God not honor the faith of a child?

* * *

Beau rode down the same trail he'd traveled with Dawes, only farther. Pressing his roan, he went past the cave where he'd seen the ash and straight down the throat of Sparrow Canyon.

He'd been riding for three days now, almost four. If he turned around this instant, he'd get back Saturday afternoon. He'd have time to clean up and have a word with Dani before they took the vows Beau now feared he wouldn't be able to keep. He loved her. He'd be faithful to her in body and mind, but his soul would still be hunting Clay.

Clay… When had Beau started thinking of the outlaw by his given name? He tried to pinpoint the moment but couldn't. Neither could he decide whether to go forward or turn around. He had a few more hours of daylight. The ride back, all downhill, would be quicker than the ride up the canyon, but he had to consider the weather. The afternoon had turned sultry. The still air promised a storm, anything from a drizzle to a downpour.

Beau looked carefully at the sides of the ravine. The trail cut deep into the mountain about ten feet above the streambed. Boulders secured the base. Even if the stream flooded, a distinct possibility if it stormed, Beau felt certain he'd be secure. Looking ahead he saw a bend around a ridge. He knew from Dawes that Sparrow Canyon opened up beyond that spot. A meadow would offer grass and fresh water, the perfect place for Johnson to linger. One more mile… Beau couldn't turn back now. He nudged the roan up the trail.

A hundred yards later, he heard thunder. Clouds boiled over the mountains and turned the sky gray. A drop of rain hit his hat. Another landed on his gloved hand. Ten feet below him, Sparrow Creek rushed past the boulders like an animal on the run.

Common sense told Beau to go home, but he ignored the nudge. He had to see around the next bend.

Lightning flashed across the sky. Thunder rolled through Beau like an erratic heartbeat. One minute it pounded; the next it stopped with a hint of death. Rain fell in buckets. He flashed on Emma dousing him in the garden, but he kept going. Below him, Sparrow Creek had picked up speed. A new roar filled Beau's ears. Unlike the thunder, it came from the earth itself. Suddenly skittish, his horse backpedaled. Beau looked up the ravine and saw a wall of water, six feet high and rolling over itself, rushing down Sparrow Canyon.

He had considered the possibility of a flash flood, but he'd expected two or three feet at the most. He'd never seen anything as high and deep and wide as the water coming straight at him. He believed the trail would hold, but his horse didn't have the same hope. The animal balked. At the same instant, a boulder the size of a melon tumbled down the mountain. It caught the roan's back leg and knocked the animal half off the trail. To give the horse a chance, Beau rolled out of the saddle. He smacked facedown in the mud and lost his wind. The roan's churning legs cut away at the mountain. Beau started to slide. The horse found purchase and heaved itself to safety, but Beau couldn't get a toehold in the mud. He slid a foot, then another. Water filled his boots. The current sucked at his knees.

He lost his gloves and clawed with his bare hands. When he found a stringy root, he gripped it. No thicker than a pencil, it bore his weight. He found a second root, thicker this time, and pulled his legs out of the water. A boulder tumbled past his head. He looked up, saw another ready to fall and slithered on his belly until he reached a stable part of the trail.

With his sides heaving, Beau pictured red apples, little girls with pink cheeks and Dani in a white dress. He heard milk hissing into a bucket and imagined her rose-petal lips. Rocking with the rhythm of their one dance, he called himself a fool. He had business to do with God and he knew it, but movement up the canyon caught his eye.

Peering into the rain, fading now, Beau saw a man on a gray horse. He hadn't seen Clay Johnson in five years, but he knew the slope of his shoulders. When the outlaw went for his rifle, Beau cursed the weapon that had killed Lucy.

Johnson raised the Winchester to his shoulder.

Beau went for his Colt.

Clay squinted down the barrel.

Beau took aim and pulled the trigger.

Nothing happened. No recoil. No smoke. Only the empty click of a misfire. Beau cursed himself for a fool. Mud and rain had dampened the gunpowder.

Looking at Clay now, he expected to die. If the rifle shot didn't kill him, the ride to Castle Rock would. He'd grieve Dani and the girls. He'd die without telling her that he loved her. She'd go back to a lonely life in Wisconsin, and the girls would be doomed to tea parties with Harriet Lange. This moment, Beau realized, had been born of his own arrogance. Life and death—only God could make the call. Beau knew that now.

Have mercy on me, Lord.

He saw the next two seconds the way he'd seen Lucy die. Every detail came alive. Water dripped from Clay's hat and splashed on his glove. His oilskin poncho turned from black to silver and cast a bluish light on his hollow cheeks. His eyes, black and empty, couldn't have been more lifeless. Beau could have choked on the irony. He'd spent five years chasing a man who was already dead, at least on the inside.

He steeled himself for the bullet, but it didn't come. No blast. No smoke. Only the rush of the stream as Clay lowered the weapon. Wordless, the outlaw turned his horse and disappeared into the mist, leaving Beau to wonder what in the world had just happened.

A hundred yards up the canyon, Clay slid off his horse, dropped to his knees and threw up. When he'd seen Morgan crawling in the mud, he'd instinctively aimed his rifle. He'd told himself to fire, but his finger hadn't pulled the trigger. Not even when Morgan shot first had Clay been able to do the deed. Why not?

With mud soaking his knees, he thought about Goose and Andy driving him crazy with their taunts. Spring had filled the canyon with pink flowers, and Lucy Morgan had haunted his dreams every night. This morning when a horse went missing, Clay had ridden down the canyon alone to search for it. The gray had good instincts, but he'd missed Ricochet so much he'd cried. All morning, he'd wondered if horses went to Heaven.

Chilled to the bone, he hung his head. If Morgan's gun had fired, he'd have made the trip to eternity himself. He'd have been worm food. Dry bones. Maybe something worse… A man being eaten alive for all time in the belly of Reverend Blue's whale. But Clay hadn't died. Neither had he killed Beau Morgan. He'd done something right. How could that be?

Blinking, he thought of his mother reading him Bible stories. He could see her brown hair piled on her head. He smelled bread and candles and recalled one night in particular.

Jesus loves you, little boy. I do, too. But I have to leave.
Why, Mama? Where are you going?

She'd coughed until she was breathless. She'd done that a lot in those days. He recalled the handkerchief she kept tucked in her sleeve, a cotton square dotted with blood. A month after that talk about Jesus, she'd died of consumption. Recalling her stories now, Clay knew she'd gone to be with the Lord. Blinking, he recalled asking her a question.

Can I go with you?

Not now, but someday.

She'd prayed with him. He'd been a mere boy, but he'd understood that Jesus loved him. After his mother's death, for a time he'd gone to church with his cousin, but that had changed when Clay got his height and muscle. He'd been an angry young man and life's temptations had called to him. He'd put his boyhood prayer out of his mind, but then Ricochet died. Now he couldn't stop thinking about eternity.

"Help me, Lord."

As he bowed his head, he expected to feel the whack of his father's fist breaking his nose. Clay had done terrible things. He'd stolen. He'd maimed. He'd killed six men. Worst of all, he'd shot Lucy Morgan in the back. He didn't deserve to live, yet here he was…breathing in gray mist when Beau Morgan's bullet should have sent him to eternity.

Someone had spared his life and it hadn't been Beau Morgan. Startled, he opened his eyes. Where did a man look for God? In the sky with its promise of Heaven? In a meadow full of pink flowers? Clay didn't know, but he understood a simple truth. God had been in the canyon. For reasons Clay couldn't grasp, the Almighty had spared his life. He'd spared Morgan, too. The men had made a trade of sorts. An eye for an eye…a life for a life. As a boy, Clay had learned about another trade. Jesus had died for Clay's sins. But what about now? How did a man wash a woman's blood from his hands? The answer came in a whisper.

A man told the truth.

He paid a price.

If need be, he faced the gallows. Jesus had paid for Clay's sin for the sake of eternity, but Beau Morgan had a right to justice in the here and now. Clay had the power—the need—to give it to him. Feeling as if he'd set down a fifty-pound stone, he climbed on the gray. Rain had washed the dust from the canyon. Grass glistened as if covered with morning dew. Not even the smell of mud filled his nose as he neared camp, where Goose and Andy were splitting a pint of whiskey.

Goose saw him and frowned. "Where have you been?"

Clay ignored him. "I'm leaving."

"You're *what?*" Goose said.

"We're splitting up."

"Why?" Andy asked.

"I'm done."

Goose looked him up and down, taking in his muddy hands and the stains on his knees. "Did you fall and hit your head?"

"I'm sick of it," Clay said. "I've had enough."

Andy chimed in. "What about the horses? We agreed to a three-way split."

"I'll buy you two out."

Clay wasn't worried about going to jail for stealing horses. He figured he'd hang for Lucy Morgan's murder. Returning the horses was a matter of pride. It made him feel like a man.

Andy knocked back a slug of whiskey, then wiped his mouth on his sleeve. "How much?"

Clay named the amount of cash he had in his saddlebag.

"We'd get more in Durango," Goose said.

"You don't know what you'd get," Clay said mildly. "This is a sure thing."

Goose wrinkled his brow. "I don't get it. What are you going to do with the horses?"

"Give 'em back."

Andy knocked his head as if he had wax in his ears. "What'd you say?"

"I'm taking them back." Clay didn't want his partners to think he'd gone soft. A man had his pride. "I've got a plan. I just saw Morgan."

"Did you kill him?" Andy asked.

"I had a misfire." Not the gun. Clay's finger had failed. "If I were you, I'd head south. This fight is mine." So was the surrender.

Goose grunted. "I'm sick to death of this canyon."

"Me, too," said Andy.

Clay crouched by the fire and poured himself a cup of hot coffee. It tasted good. He hadn't enjoyed coffee in a long time. Feeling generous, he looked at his former partners. "I'm giving you two a chance for a clean start. Take it."

"What about you?" Goose asked.

Clay smiled. "I'm going to church."

Andy smirked. "You're going after Morgan."

"That's right."

Only Clay knew he'd be going unarmed. He knew from Andy that Morgan would bring the woman and the girls to church, but that he wouldn't stay. Clay planned to slip into a back pew, listen to Reverend Blue and even sing a hymn or two. When the service ended, he'd turn himself in for Lucy Morgan's murder. It didn't matter if he hanged or went to prison. He'd found peace.

Chapter Nineteen

Beau had been gone for six days when Dani heard a knock on the parsonage door. She opened it with a prayer on her lips. *Please, God… Let it be him.*

Instead of Beau's broad shoulders, she saw Howie Dawes with mussed hair and windburned cheeks. His horse stood behind him, glistening from a fast ride.

"What's wrong?" she asked.

"It's Daff. Her udder's hot."

"Come inside."

As she held the door, Adie came out of the kitchen. "What happened?"

"It's one of the cows." Dani explained Daff's history. "We could lose her. I have to go."

More than Daff's milk was at stake. Dani had spent hours with Adie, praying and trying not to worry about Beau. What if he didn't come back? She'd been with the Blues for six days. Tomorrow would be the seventh. Without Beau there would be no wedding. Without a wedding, she'd lose the girls. Dani would fight for them, but it would take a miracle for a judge to rule in her favor.

If she lost a cow now, she wouldn't stand a chance against Harriet Lange.

Dani hoped Adie would understand. "The girls and I need to go home."

Her brow creased. "What about Beau?"

"He knows where to find us." Dani turned to Howie. "Would you hitch up the surrey?"

"Sure."

As the boy walked to the stable, Adie touched Dani's arm. "Will we see you in church tomorrow?"

"I'll be in church, but I won't be getting married."

"Don't give up," Adie said.

"I already have."

She'd spent six days worrying about Beau and praying for him. She'd begged God to keep him safe and give him the peace he couldn't find on his own. She'd prayed for the girls, too. They needed protection, the kind she couldn't give alone. Beau had let them down, but Dani had her faith. The future belonged to God, not Beau Morgan.

"There's still time," Adie said. "If he—"

"It's too late."

Dani went to the backyard to fetch the girls. When she told them they were going home, no one said a word. They said goodbye to Stephen, then went to the guest room to gather their things. The girls understood the impact of Beau's absence as well as Dani. Harriet Lange loomed like a specter.

Dani had more than a few harsh words for the man who'd put them in this position. Even if he made it back in time for a wedding, she had doubts about the marriage. Beau had chosen Clay over her. His decision hung like a cloud, but so did Harriet Lange and her threats. With two bad choices— marrying Beau in spite of her resentment or saying no and fighting Harriet Lange—Dani thought of Josh's sermon about a man walking by the light of his own fire. Right now, she had no light at all.

As she guided the girls into the yard, Howie drove up in the surrey. "Are you ready, Miss Baxter?"

"Yes. Thank you."

He climbed down from the seat and took off his hat. "Would it be okay if I went to see my ma?"

At the sight of Howie's eager expression, Dani felt her heart crack with longing. She wanted children who'd call her mama and be eager to see her. "Of course. In fact, you can stay home until Monday."

"Thanks!" The boy climbed on his horse and rode off.

Adie hugged Dani. "Stay strong, honey. Beau's a mere man, but the Lord won't let you down."

The girls said goodbye to Adie and climbed into the surrey. Dani steered for home. The future loomed like a long night, but she wouldn't be facing it alone. Even in the dark, the Lord was at her side.

Beau stopped to rest his horse, but he didn't indulge in real sleep or eat more than jerky. At the spot where he'd gone fishing with the girls, he washed the mud from his face and arms. His clothes were caked with it, but he didn't bother to change. He had to get home to Dani. He had amends to make and he knew it.

What he *didn't* know concerned Clay Johnson. Why hadn't the man fired his rifle? Beau didn't know and the lack of understanding troubled him. Johnson had shown him the ultimate mercy. He'd spared Beau's life. Beau wouldn't have been so kind. All the way down the trail, he'd thought about the look in Johnson's eyes. If it hadn't been for his promise to Dani, he would have followed Clay into the canyon.

But for what purpose? Beau didn't know what to think.

Was he supposed to be grateful to Clay for sparing his life? He wouldn't have been there if Clay hadn't killed Lucy in the first place. It added up to one big tangle. Beau intended to marry Dani and stay with her, but a piece of his soul had ridden into the mist with Clay. He didn't feel at peace with God, either. The Almighty had saved his life twice, but Beau still hadn't hit his knees. Had justice been served? God had spared Clay, too. Beau wanted finality. Instead he had more loose ends than ever.

Riding into Castle Rock, he tasted his old bitterness. Johnson and his men were still wanted for raiding the Rocking J, so Beau rode to Dawes's office and went inside. Instead of the sheriff, he saw Ace at the desk with his feet up. The deputy saw Beau and smirked. "You're a mess."

Beau ignored the barb. "I found Johnson."

"Where?" Ace slammed his feet to the floor.

"Deep in Sparrow Canyon."

"Did you get him?"

Beau grunted. "My weapon misfired. He got away."

"Tough luck," said the deputy. "Though it might explain Baylor's horses."

"What about them?"

"They showed up at the ranch. All of them except a gray."

Beau knew the horse and who was on it, but he didn't know why Clay and his partners had turned the horses loose. He'd expected them to ride south. It didn't make sense. Beau didn't think Clay would come after him, but he couldn't be sure. That moment in the canyon had been crazy, even unreal. For three days, Beau had struggled to make sense of it. Maybe Clay had done the same thing. Maybe he'd changed his mind about killing Beau. Maybe he liked the chase and had let Beau live just to torture him.

"Where's Dawes?" he asked.

"Having supper." Ace stood and reached for his hat. "He needs to know what you saw. I'll take you to his house."

"You tell him." Beau headed for the door.

He had to get to Dani. He didn't expect Johnson to go after her, but neither could he rule it out. With the sun hovering above the hills, he urged the roan to the parsonage. Expecting to stay for supper, he led the horse into the stable where he saw Josh's rigs but not the surrey. Beau could think of only one reason for the surrey to be missing and he didn't like it. Dani had gone home. Leaving his horse saddled, he strode to the parsonage.

Josh stepped through the front door. Crossing his arms, he looked Beau up and down. "Did you crawl out of a grave or dig one?"

"Both."

"I take it Clay's dead."

Beau chuffed. "Not hardly. Where's Dani?"

"At the farm."

"I told her to wait here."

"One of the cows had a problem. She went to tend it."

Beau worried about Daff. As he turned to leave, Josh kicked a chair away from the wall. "Sit down."

The minister wasn't prone to foul moods, but he was in one now. Beau raised one brow. "Is that an order?"

"Only if you want to get married in *my* church."

"It's God's church."

"And he put me in charge."

Thanks to Harriet Lange's interference, Beau needed Josh's approval. He feared for Dani's safety, but the odds of Clay beating him to the farm were slim. Beau had ridden hard. The Rocking J lay on the opposite side of Castle Rock. Beau strode up the steps and sat. "Make it quick."

"What happened?" Josh stayed on his feet.

Beau told his friend about the flood, the mud and the misfire. "He could have killed me, but he didn't."

"What do you think stopped him?"

"I don't know."

Josh lowered his voice. "It was a long time ago, but I planted seeds in Clay's life. He knows about God's grace. Maybe those seeds finally sprouted."

Beau flashed on Clay lowering the gun. Josh's explanation made as much sense as Beau's belief that Clay had gone crazy. Either way, the outlaw had lost his mind. For good or for evil? It remained to be seen.

"You know the parable," Josh said. "Some seeds fall on good soil and grow. Others break through but die when the weather turns bad. Some don't grow at all. Frankly, Clay struck me as hard soil, but dirt changes with time and bad weather. So does a man."

Beau thought of the storm in the canyon. Rain had softened the earth to mud. Water had moved boulders and ripped away trees, changing the course of the stream and its very nature. The rain had blurred Clay, as well. Even with his gun in hand, he'd seemed as formless as his name.

Josh's voice dipped low. "Be careful, Beau. I hope Clay's changed, but we can't know for sure. Nothing's more dangerous than a man who sees the light and then turns his back."

Beau had made that choice when he'd left Dani. She'd offered the light of love. He'd chosen the darkness of his hate and had almost destroyed their future. He'd never make that mistake again. Before this night ended, he'd have that overdue talk with the Lord. In the meantime, he needed Josh's help.

"I know about turning my back on the light," Beau said. "I'm home to stay."

"That's good news."

"It'll be even better if you'll agree to marry Dani and me."

Josh looked at Beau with an expression befitting the seriousness of the question. "Do you love her?"

"I do."

"Will you raise your nieces as your own?"

"You bet I will."

"I have another question," Josh said. "A hard one."

"Ask it."

"Do you love them enough to forget Clay Johnson?"

Beau hadn't seen the question coming. "I won't lie, Josh. I'm not done with it. I don't understand what happened in that canyon, but I know one thing. Dani matters more than Clay."

"You need to tell her."

"I will," Beau answered. "Will you do the ceremony?"

"When?"

"Tomorrow."

Josh's eyes twinkled. "I'll do it, but I'm not the one you have to convince."

Beau pushed to his feet. "Say a prayer. I have some apologizing to do."

"It's good practice." Josh chuckled, but Beau barely heard it. He'd already gone down the stairs.

He didn't have to push his tired horse. When they reached the road to the farm, the roan went into a lope. As they passed the charred pine, Beau thought of his brother. This journey had begun with his passing, but it wouldn't end in sorrow. Silently he promised Patrick that he'd love Emma, Ellie and Esther like his own children. He didn't mention Dani. She was Beau's alone.

He rode into the yard and swung down from his horse. The front room and kitchen were dark. So was Dani's window. Beau looked up to the second floor where he saw a lamp burning in the girls' bedroom. He pictured Dani reading them a story. Someday she'd read to a child carrying his blood.

That is, if she'd have him.

Needing to care for his horse, Beau headed for the barn. As he gripped the reins, his gaze landed on a gold triangle stretching from the open door. A shadow—Dani's shadow—inched into the light. He took in the length of her body, her crossed arms, the tilt of her chin as she spotted his horse. She stopped at the threshold. "You're back."

Beau stopped, too. "I kept my promise."

"I see."

"If you'll have me, Josh will marry us tomorrow."

Dani didn't know what to say. Six days ago, Beau had left the farm as Cain, a man doomed to wander without God. He'd come back for the sake of the children, but had he come back for *her?* Even more important, had he come back with the piece of his soul he'd given to Clay Johnson? Looking at him in the moonlight, she couldn't tell. He'd pulled his hat low, hiding his eyes but not his ragged jaw. His duster, blotched with mud, looked as stiff as his spine.

She wiped her hands on her apron. "I'm still milking."

"I'll help."

"It's not necessary. Buttercup's the last one."

Beau's brow creased. "Josh said a cow was sick. Is it Daff?"

"She's fine." As soon as Dani had arrived at the farm, she'd checked the fussy cow and found nothing. Daff, she decided, had missed her family. Looking at Beau, she wondered if he felt the same way.

He pushed back his hat. "I'm glad Daff's okay."

His concern riled Dani beyond reason. If he thought he could waltz home and she'd fall at his feet, he had some more thinking to do. Dani went back in the barn, sat on the stool and went to work on Buttercup. She had her back to the door, but she heard the clop of hooves as Beau led his horse to its stall. He set the saddle on a rack with a thud, then brushed his horse and gave it a measure of oats.

Dani lifted the milk bucket and carried it to the can. While she poured, Beau took the cow to the pasture. She covered the milk cans, then went outside to wash the bucket. She finished the chore, turned and saw Beau in the doorway, blocking her from putting the pail away. She wasn't in the mood for his high-handed ways.

She marched up to the barn. When he didn't move, she planted her shoes across from his muddy boots. "I need to get by."

"No, you don't." He lifted the bucket from her hand, set it inside the door and snuffed out the lamp, plunging them into darkness. Beau touched her jaw. "I love you, Dani. Marry me."

He'd said he loved her, but he reeked of mud, maybe death. He'd left his duster in the barn, but she could still smell the rot. She jerked away. Before she let down her guard, she needed answers. "Did you find Clay?"

"He found me."

"What happened?"

"It's a long story. Right now, only one thing matters. I'm back. I spoke with Josh. He's willing to marry us."

The girls would be safe.

He'd said that he loved her.

Two stars glimmered in Dani's mind, shedding divine light but not enough to show her the way. Had Beau really changed? Had he made peace with God and himself? She smelled the mud and wondered. "I have to know what happened."

With a crescent moon shedding the dimmest light, he told her about the canyon, the flood and the misfire. Her blood chilled with the knowledge that he'd almost died, then warmed with gratitude for God's mercy. The Lord had been with Beau in Sparrow Canyon. Judging by his eyes, he knew it. Two more stars pierced the dark around Dani's heart, but she worried when his lips thinned to a line.

"I won't lie to you," he said. "I'd be glad to see Johnson hang. He spared my life, but I don't know why. I still hate him, Dani. I always will."

She wanted Beau's whole heart, not most of it. What would he do if he caught wind of Johnson in a month or a year? Could she trust him to stay? Promises could be broken as easily as they were made. She watched as he reached into his pocket, then opened his palm to reveal the bullet Clay had left for him. He closed his fingers again, hauled back and threw it as hard as he could into the night.

"That takes care of Clay," he said. "Now for us."

He reached into his pocket a second time. When he opened his fingers, she saw a silver ring with a blue stone. It made a perfect circle. Endless. Complete. She imagined him taking her work-roughened hand, seeing the calluses and the broken nails, the imperfections that came with being human. That's when she knew she'd say yes to Beau in spite of her fear that he'd go after Clay Johnson. She wasn't a perfect woman. She made mistakes every day. Beau would make them, too. Big or small. It didn't matter. Love, as complete as the circle, covered their failings.

He clasped her fingers. "I love you, Dani. No matter what happens, I'll never leave again."

Her heart pounded. "I love you, too."

"Will you marry me?"

"Yes, I will."

He slid the ring into place. Expecting a kiss, she tilted her face to his. Beau answered with a lazy smile. "I want a son. A boy with your blue eyes."

Dani's heart hummed. "I want that, too."

"And another girl." He grinned.

She grinned back.

He kissed her then, a tender brush that made her see stars. A thousand of them—each as bright as the sun—burned away the rest of the darkness, leaving her warm in Beau's embrace. Tomorrow, she decided, would be the happiest day of her life.

Chapter Twenty

Beau walked Dani to the house, kissed her again, then headed alone to the creek. He washed off every speck of mud from the canyon, put on clean clothes, shaved, then sat on a rock. He'd promised to do business with the Almighty and that time had come. With his head bowed, he confessed his arrogance, praised God for his mercy, then looked up and counted the stars. With each one, he thanked the Lord for a different blessing until he reached the one gift he couldn't understand.

Why had Clay spared his life?

Beau had no desire to go after the man, but neither did he have as much peace as he wanted. He'd hated Clay for five years. It would take more than five days to break the habit. Tonight, when he'd touched the bullet, the hate had burned as bright as ever. Even now, with Dani's kiss fresh on his lips, he could feel the old resentment.

A month ago, he'd have raised his fist at the heavens. Tonight he bowed his head. "I want peace, Lord. What do I have to do?"

Beau knew the answer in his gut. He had to forgive Clay Johnson.

"Not in a million years," he said out loud.

The silent nudge to his heart turned into pain, but he could only groan. The Lord was asking too much. Beau wouldn't go after Clay, but neither could he forgive the man for what he'd done. Beau knew he had a problem. His hate for Clay had the potential to stand between himself and Dani. It also made it hard for Beau to see past the stars to the God who'd made them. "I can't forgive him," he said out loud. "If You want me to forgive that scum, I need help."

Irked, Beau gathered his dirty clothes, the bar of soap and his shaving kit. He'd cleaned up as best as he could, but he still felt the grit of his trip. He'd said no when Dani asked him into the kitchen for supper, but he couldn't deny his need for sleep. Exhausted in every way, he headed back to the barn where he slept until the sun spilled through the window. As if he'd never left the farm, he awoke the next morning and milked the cows. It felt good to do chores and even better to walk into the kitchen where he saw Dani at the stove.

She smiled shyly.

Beau wanted to kiss her but didn't. They couldn't honor the tradition of the groom not seeing the bride before the wedding, but he wanted everything else to be perfect. Nothing else mattered, least of all his turmoil concerning Clay Johnson.

He eyed the bacon. "Smells good."

She blushed.

Before he could tease her, Emma walked into the room. She saw Beau and gasped. Ellie came up behind her, shrieked and ran to hug him. Esther charged at his knees. Beau looked at Dani and grinned.

She nodded, a silent signal to tell the girls their news. Just like Josh and Adie, he and his wife-to-be could trade thoughts without a word.

Beau sat down, putting him level with girls. "Dani and I have something to tell you."

All three straightened. Emma looked wary. Children who'd lost a parent learned to be cautious. Beau intended to erase that fear. "We're getting married today."

The younger girls squealed, but Emma stayed serious. "Are you staying for good?"

"I am."

She turned to Dani. "Is it true?"

"It better be." She smiled at him. "I stayed up half the night pressing my dress."

"Can I see it?" Ellie asked.

"Sure," Dani answered. "After breakfast."

As if this were an ordinary day, they sat at the table and ate. While the females chattered, Beau took in the blush of Dani's cheeks, the awe in Emma's eyes and the sight of Ellie and Esther eating oatmeal as if it tasted like ice cream. As a man who'd once lost everything, he knew the value of a single moment. He and Dani would remember this day forever. Every minute counted; every gesture meant more because of the vows they'd take. Nothing would spoil this day. Beau wouldn't allow it.

When they finished eating, the girls cleared the table. He went to his room where he shaved a second time, put on a suit and fancy tie, then hitched up the surrey and pulled it into the yard. Ellie, dressed for church with a red ribbon in her hair, waved to him. Emma and Esther came out the door, followed by Dani who had a satchel in hand. She'd done up her hair with white ribbons but hadn't put on her wedding dress. She had it in the bag and would change at the parsonage. He met her on the steps, took the satchel and stowed it in the back of the surrey.

The girls climbed in on their own, but Dani waited for him.

When he offered his hand, she took it and squeezed. "This is the best day of my life."

"Mine, too."

He helped her onto the seat, then took the reins. As they pulled out of the yard, Beau felt a mix of joy and tension. Five years had passed since he'd been inside a church. The last time had been in Denver and he'd walked out in the middle of a hymn. He wanted to erase that memory, so he winked at Dani and started to hum.

She heard the first notes of "Camp Town Races" and laughed.

The girls laughed, too.

That's how they arrived at the parsonage, a family sharing a moment they'd never forget. Beau halted the surrey at the foot of the steps. As his nieces climbed down, he took Dani's hand. A man didn't kiss his bride before the wedding, but his wife-to-be had a look that made him think about it. Feeling mischievous, he leaned a bit closer. Her eyes gleamed with a dare. Beau moved another inch. So did she.

Their lips were inches apart when Adie opened the parsonage door. "Beau Morgan! Don't you *dare* kiss the bride. At least not yet!"

Laughing, Dani drew back and hopped down from the seat. After fetching the satchel, she ran up the steps, stopped at the open door and blew him a kiss.

Adie hugged Dani, then approached Beau. "I'm glad to see her happy."

"Me, too."

"What about you, Beau?" she asked. "How are you feeling?"

"Good."

"Just good?"

He grinned. "More than good. I'm a happy man, Adie."

"Josh told me about Clay. It's a strange story."

Beau wished she hadn't mentioned it. Just hearing Clay's name stirred up old feelings. He had to put them aside, especially today. When Dani came down the aisle, she'd see love in his eyes. Nothing else.

He forced his jaw to unclench. "That story will have to wait."

"Of course." Adie stepped back. "Go find Josh. He wants a word before the ceremony."

Beau nodded, but he had no intention of speaking with his friend. If Josh mentioned Clay, Beau would be hard-pressed to keep his composure.

He clicked to the horses, then steered to the field where farmers would leave their rigs. He'd brought Dani early so she could dress, but he had a need of his own. It had been a long time since he'd been in God's house, and he wanted a moment alone. He tied the horse, then ambled to the front of the church where he saw the brass knobs shining in the sun.

A sudden dread turned Beau's feet to sand. He'd made his peace with God last night, but he had the terrible feeling his anger was about to erupt again. A month ago, Beau could have left in a snit. Today he *had* to go inside. He'd promised Dani a perfect day and he intended to give it to her. With his hat in hand, he walked into the church.

The building matched the one he'd known in Denver. Seven windows, the width of a man's shoulders and as tall, lined the two longest walls. Sunshine poured in through the glass, casting beams that met on the floor and made a row of diamonds. Two sets of pews waited to be filled and Josh's podium, the same one he'd used in Denver, displayed an elaborate etching of an eagle.

Peace settled around Beau like the blanket Dani had spread for their first picnic. It opened, fluttered down and landed in a perfect square. Beau blinked and tasted apples. He felt God's mercy in the cool air. Divine love abounded in the light. Beau had come home.

Thank you, Lord.

With the prayer on his lips, he raised his eyes to the front wall of the church. In Denver, he'd have seen a wooden cross. What he saw now turned the picnic blanket into a bloody pink dress. Stones of pink rhyolite, the finest he'd ever seen, formed a cross in the center of a gray wall. Someone had polished the rocks to a shine, bringing out veins of red and black.

Bitterness gripped him from the inside and squeezed. He didn't want these feelings. Not now. Not with Dani about to become his wife. He wanted to be rid of them forever, but he couldn't control his reaction. Hate lived in his blood. It pumped from the very core of his being. A horse couldn't change its color. Neither could Beau stop the hatred burning in his gut.

He wanted to walk out of the church and never come back.

He wanted to see Clay Johnson die.

He wanted God to end the pain. A stifled groan tore at Beau's throat. He wanted to fight. He wanted to weep. More than anything, he wanted to be free from his own stupid thoughts. "Help me," he whispered.

The stones stayed silent. Beau spun on his heel and walked out the door. He'd marry Dani in spite of the shiny pink cross, but his heart had gone dark. Struggling to stay calm, he paced to the far end of the porch, as far as he could get from the people arriving for the service. In spite of Beau's scowl, men called out to him and women smiled.

Trevor Scott walked the length of the porch to offer congratulations. Beau shook his hand but said nothing.

Sheriff Dawes said hello.

John Baylor tipped his hat. "Thanks, Morgan."

Harriet Lange saw him and offered a gracious dip of her

chin, a sign of surrender. After today, the girls would never have to worry about stupid teacups.

Beau was close to breathing normally when Josh came out of the church. "There you are."

Beau grunted.

Josh's smile died. "Are you as nervous as you look?"

"I'm fine."

"You don't look fine."

"I just need a minute."

Josh lowered his voice. "Memories?"

Beau shook his head.

"Second thoughts?"

"Not a one." His voice rasped. "It's Johnson. He's got me by the throat."

"No, he doesn't." Josh's expression turned as hard as flint. "You're the one who won't let go."

Beau scowled. "I don't need a lecture."

"I don't want to give one," Josh said. "Considering what Johnson did to you, I don't have that right. But there's someone who does."

"For God so loved the world, He gave His only begotten son... Forgive your enemies as I have forgiven you."

Beau's jaw tensed. "I don't want to hear it."

"You think forgiving Johnson's impossible, don't you?"

"It is."

"Not for God." Josh stepped closer. "Are you willing, Beau? That's all that counts. The Lord does the rest."

Before Beau could tell Josh to drop dead, Adie opened the parsonage door and waved.

"That's our signal," the minister said. "Your bride's waiting."

Nothing would stop Beau from making this day perfect for Dani. Not Clay Johnson and not a pink cross. He pushed by Josh. "Let's go."

With the minister in his wake, Beau walked down the aisle to the front row where he sat alone. The pianist struck the chords to a lively hymn. When the music ended, Josh stepped to the podium.

"Ladies and gentlemen, I have a surprise. Most of you have met Daniela Baxter. I'm pleased to announce that she and Beau Morgan are getting married this morning."

Applause broke out.

Josh signaled to him. "Come up here."

Beau stood and turned to the congregation. Josh signaled to the pianist, who played "Blessed Assurance," Dani's favorite hymn. Someone closed the door. Any minute it would open again and the wedding would begin. Dani would enter in a cloud of white. Thoughts of her calmed Beau's nerves. When the knob turned, his heart soared. Someone cracked open the door, but just a foot. Instead of Dani, he saw a man. And not just any man... Clay Johnson had come to church.

Expecting Dani, the congregation turned to look. No one paid attention as Clay slipped into the back pew. Dawes had never seen him. Wallace didn't attend church. John Baylor had seen three men in masks. He didn't know Clay Johnson from Adam, but Beau did. So did Josh. The minister gripped Beau's shoulder but didn't speak. The decision to confront Johnson now or stay silent belonged to Beau alone.

Instinctively, he sized up the situation. If Clay had something ugly in mind, the people in the pews were lambs waiting for slaughter. Beau had a two-shot pistol in his boot, but he hadn't worn his gun belt. Dawes carried a revolver, but the man had no instincts.

With Beau watching, Clay squeezed between a matron with a feathered hat and the blacksmith, a man twice his size. He had on a worn shirt and trousers. No hat to hide his face.

No coat to hide weapons. When the matron smiled, Clay smiled back as though he meant it. Beau didn't know why the outlaw had come to church, but he felt certain it wasn't for the wrong reasons. As long as he stayed in the pew, Beau could endure the confusion pulsing through him. This was Dani's day. Nothing else mattered.

Unaware of the drama, Adie opened the door wide. The pianist pounded the keys with a new vigor. Esther, holding a bouquet of roses, walked down the aisle with surprising dignity. Ellie followed and Emma came next. The three of them lined up opposite Beau. He didn't know where to look—at Clay or the door where Dani would appear.

The pianist struck the opening notes of a bridal march. The music soared to the rafters, bounced off the walls and filled Beau's head with memories of singing hymns in the barn. He had a new life…a good life. He loved Dani more than he could say. God had saved Beau's soul, but she'd saved him from his hate. No way would he give Clay Johnson this precious moment. Without a whit of hesitation, he focused on the spot where he'd see his bride for the first time.

Just as he imagined, Dani came through the door in a cloud of ivory and gold. A veil hid her eyes but not her smile. Her dress, a mix of lace and silk, made him think of snow melting in the sun. When she'd first arrived at the farm, he'd complained of too much purity and light. Now he cherished it. When Dani reached his side, he touched her elbow and smiled. Together they faced Josh.

When he saw the minister's scowl, Beau remembered Clay Johnson. "It's okay," he whispered. "Do the ceremony."

Dani didn't understand. Why would Beau tell Josh to go ahead with their vows? Had Harriet Lange threatened to protest the wedding? Dani glanced at Beau and saw nothing but confidence. It settled her nerves until she saw Josh peering over Beau's shoulder. She wanted to turn but couldn't. Every eye in the room was focused on her back.

The minister cleared his throat. "Dearly Beloved, we're gathered here today to witness the joining of Daniela Baxter and Beau Morgan in holy matrimony. Marriage is a sacred bond, one that unites a man and woman for the rest of their lives."

Josh sounded steadier, but he glanced again to the back corner of the church. His eyes hardened. She'd seen him use that look once before. Harold Day had been harsh with his wife and Josh had escorted him outside for a talk.

Was he looking at Harriet Lange? Who else would disrupt the wedding? Dani didn't know, but she'd go toe-to-toe with anyone who'd question her love for Beau. Apparently sensing her unrest, he gripped her elbow. Josh opened his Bible, looked from Dani to Beau, then focused on the congregation. "I know Beau and Dani well. They've overcome loss, heartache and challenges to their faith. It's a privilege to lead them in their vows."

Dani breathed a sigh of relief. In a moment she and Beau would be joined forever.

Josh looked first to Dani. "Face Beau and repeat after me. 'I,' then say your name."

Dani looked into Beau's eyes. "I, Daniela Sarah Baxter."

"Take you, Beaumont Christopher Morgan."

"Take you, Beaumont Christopher Morgan—"

"To be my wedded husband."

"To be my—"

Footsteps pounded up the stairs. Startled, Dani turned and saw a balding man in a white apron charge into the church. "I gotta talk to Beau!"

Beau looked mad enough to spit. "Not now, Wallace."

"But I saw Clay Johnson!"

"I *said*—"

"But he's here," said the barkeep. "I saw him ride into town."

Sheriff Dawes pushed to his feet. John Baylor followed. The room broke into a tumult. Johnson and his gang spelled danger for everyone but something even more sinister for Dani. Beau's greatest temptation lay within his grasp. Today he would choose between love and hate.

She looked up at his face, but his eyes were skimming the congregation. She started to lower her flowers, a surrender to the inevitable, but he clasped her fingers under the bouquet and kept it level. He raised his other hand to signal the crowd.

"Hold up!" he shouted.

The room went still.

"Sit down. All of you."

They sat…except for a ragged-looking man in the back pew. Needing to see clearly, Dani lifted her veil. She'd seen the stranger slip into the church just before her entrance. She hadn't given him a thought. Looking at him now, she put the pieces together. Clay Johnson had come to church.

The outlaw glanced at Dani. "I'm sorry, miss. I didn't mean to spoil your day."

Dani didn't need the wedding hoopla, but she feared desperately for Beau.

He still had his hand on hers. "What do you want, Johnson?"

"What happened in Denver…" His voice quavered. "I didn't mean to kill your wife. It wasn't exactly an accident. I was aiming for you, but that seemed fair at the time. When she fell, I…" His eyes rose to the pink cross, lingered on the stones, then focused on Josh. "I can't live with what I did. My mama was a God-fearing woman. She'd be ashamed of me."

Josh met his gaze. "You're not alone, Clay."

"I know, Reverend. You told me about the whale."

Dani didn't know anything about whales, but she saw a broken man. Was Beau's quest for justice finally over? With a prayer on her lips, she turned to read his expression. She saw wonder in his eyes, even awe.

He looked at Clay without rancor. "You came to turn yourself in, didn't you?"

"That's right."

"In the canyon," he said. "You could have killed me, but you didn't."

"I have a bullet coming. You don't."

Beau squeezed Dani's hand so hard she felt the tension in her wrists. "I'm no better than you, Clay." With a shine in his eyes, Beau faced Dani. "As sure as Clay took Lucy's life, I almost destroyed our future. I put the girls at risk, and I left you to suffer the consequences of my stupidity. I will *never* make that mistake again."

He'd make others and so would she, but today promised a new beginning.

Beau turned back to Clay. "I chased you for five years with more hate than a man should feel. I'd have done anything to see you dead. I wanted vengeance, but only God can make that call. Today you've given Lucy justice. I think it's time for mercy for us both."

Clay took a deep breath. "I expect to hang for what I did."

"We'll leave it up to a judge," Beau answered.

Dawes pushed to his feet. So did John Baylor. "You got my gray?" the rancher asked.

"Yes, sir."

"I want it back."

Clay looked proud. "It's out front."

Dawes maneuvered past the people in the pew. "You're

under arrest, Johnson. For Lucy Morgan's murder and raiding the Rocking J."

Clay stepped into the aisle. Dawes jerked the outlaw's hands behind his back and herded him out the door. Beau's chase had come to an end. Dani touched his arm. "Are you all right?"

His eyes twinkled. "I'll be better after I kiss the bride."

She smiled. "That sounds good to me."

Josh spoke in a low tone. "I can finish up or—"

"Finish up," they said in unison.

Josh signaled the congregation for quiet. "Ladies and gentlemen, we have a marriage to witness."

As the crowd settled, Dani and Beau laced their fingers together. She glanced at the girls, wide-eyed but unafraid, dressed in white with red ribbons in their yellow hair. Her gaze rose to the pink cross, then shifted to Beau's meadow-green eyes. The ring on her finger sparkled with silver and blue.

In that blending of all colors—the fullness of perfect light—Dani and Beau took the vows that made them man and wife. One flesh, one life, one hope. Forever and ever. Amen.

* * * * *

Dear Reader,

Halfway into writing this book, I came to a scary realization. I didn't know a thing about dairy cows and I had to learn. I'm very grateful to Patricia Schroedl, who kept me from making some embarrassing mistakes. I thought cows gave milk all year round. Nope! The mamas get a break before delivering their calves. Patricia gets credit for everything that's right in this story. If there are any mistakes, they're mine.

By the time I finished the book, I was in awe of the men and women who gave life to this country's dairy industry. I'll never pour a glass of milk again without being grateful for someone's hard work. It takes love, skill and discipline to make a dairy farm a success. Cows don't like to be kept waiting. They can be as cantankerous as Beau Morgan and as sweet as Dani.

Another thank-you goes to my brother. He's a genuine cowboy these days, riding the Colorado trails and helping to run a ranch. We both grew up listening to Marty Robbins singing "El Paso" and "Big Iron." While I've chosen to write about the West, John's living it. I'm proud of him!

Best wishes,

Victoria Bylin

QUESTIONS FOR DISCUSSION

1. Beau Morgan is determined to catch Clay Johnson, the outlaw who murdered his wife. Does he cross the line between seeking justice and seeking revenge? If so, when and how?

2. Dani comes to Castle Rock expecting to marry Patrick and adopt his daughters. Instead her world is turned upside down. How did she cope with Patrick's unexpected death? Why did she feel so strongly about adopting his daughters?

3. Emma, Ellie and Esther cope with their father's death in different ways. Which daughter most touched your heart? Why?

4. The color pink is significant throughout the book. What does it represent?

5. The milking contest is a test for Beau. What happens to crack his reserve with Dani and the girls?

6. How does Dani cope when she finds Patrick's letters to his deceased wife? Would she have been justified in burning them to protect his daughters? How would burning them have affected her future?

7. In spite of his reluctance to love again, Beau slowly loses his heart to Dani. Which events in the story are turning points for Beau? Describe how his feelings evolve.

8. When Beau proposes a marriage of convenience, Dani must choose between her desire for a loving marriage and a compromise that would allow her to keep Patrick's daughters. What tools does she use to make that choice? How does she find peace?

9. Reverend Joshua Blue preaches on Isaiah 50:10. What does this verse mean to you? What happens when Beau puts his faith in himself instead of God?

10. When Harriet Lange threatens to take the girls to Minnesota, Dani compromises her beliefs and agrees to a marriage of convenience. Is her decision noble or desperate? Is she acting in fear or faith?

11. Beau follows Clay Johnson into Sparrow Canyon in spite of a coming storm. It's an act of stubbornness, but he survives. How does the experience change his perceptions of God and Clay Johnson?

12. Beau's unrelenting pursuit of Clay Johnson comes at a personal cost. What does he sacrifice? What motivates him to finally give up the chase?

13. What motivates Clay Johnson to turn himself in? What role does prayer play in his decision?

14. Dani and Beau both endure personal tests. What is Dani's greatest challenge? What is Beau's most difficult choice? What motivates their decisions?

Love Inspired
HISTORICAL
INSPIRATIONAL HISTORICAL ROMANCE

An English gentleman by day, Matthew Covington becomes the mysterious crime-fighter Black Bandit at night—and nothing can tempt him to reveal his secret identity. Until he meets reporter Georgia Waterhouse, who shares his passion for justice. What will become of their growing love if he reveals the truth that lies behind the mask?

Look for

Masked by Moonlight

by

ALLIE PLEITER

*Available June 2008
wherever you buy books.*

**Steeple
Hill®**

Love Inspired.
HISTORICAL

INSPIRATIONAL HISTORICAL ROMANCE

Arizona, 1882: Saloon owner Jake Scully knows his rough frontier town is no place for delicate Lacey Stewart. Now, ten years later, Lacey is a grown woman who deserves a respectable man, not a jaded rogue like Jake. But Jake's "delicate lady" had a mind of her own....

Look for

THE REDEMPTION OF JAKE SCULLY

by *New York Times* bestselling author

ELAINE BARBIERI

Available June 2008
wherever you buy books.

Steeple
Hill®

REQUEST YOUR FREE BOOKS!

2 FREE INSPIRATIONAL NOVELS
PLUS 2
FREE
MYSTERY GIFTS

Love Inspired.
HISTORICAL
INSPIRATIONAL HISTORICAL ROMANCE

YES! Please send me 2 FREE Love Inspired® Historical novels and my 2 FREE mystery gifts (gifts are worth about $10). After receiving them, if I don't wish to receive any more books, I can return the shipping statement marked "cancel". If I don't cancel, I will receive 4 brand-new novels every other month and be billed just $4.24 per book in the U.S. or $4.74 per book in Canada, plus 25¢ shipping and handling per book and applicable taxes, if any*. That's a savings of over 20% off the cover price! I understand that accepting the 2 free books and gifts places me under no obligation to buy anything. I can always return a shipment and cancel at any time. Even if I never buy another book, the two free books and gifts are mine to keep forever. 102 IDN ERYA 302 IDN ERYM

Name _____ (PLEASE PRINT)

Address _____ Apt. #

City _____ State/Prov. _____ Zip/Postal Code

Signature (if under 18, a parent or guardian must sign)

Mail to Steeple Hill Reader Service:
IN U.S.A.: P.O. Box 1867, Buffalo, NY 14240-1867
IN CANADA: P.O. Box 609, Fort Erie, Ontario L2A 5X3

Not valid to current subscribers of Love Inspired Historical books.

Want to try two free books from another series?
Call 1-800-873-8635 or visit www.morefreebooks.com

* Terms and prices subject to change without notice. N.Y. residents add applicable sales tax. Canadian residents will be charged applicable provincial taxes and GST. This offer is limited to one order per household. All orders subject to approval. Credit or debit balances in a customer's account(s) may be offset by any other outstanding balance owed by or to the customer. Please allow 4 to 6 weeks for delivery. Offer available while quantities last.

Your Privacy: Steeple Hill Books is committed to protecting your privacy. Our Privacy Policy is available online at www.SteepleHill.com or upon request from the Reader Service. From time to time we make our lists of customers available to reputable third parties who may have a product or service of interest to you. If you would prefer we not share your name and address, please check here. ☐

LIH08

Love Inspired.
HISTORICAL

TITLES AVAILABLE NEXT MONTH

Don't miss these two stories in June

MASKED BY MOONLIGHT by Allie Pleiter
When night falls in San Francisco, Matthew Covington takes
on the role of a crime fighter known as the Black Bandit.
Nothing would tempt him to reveal his secret identity,
until he meets Georgia Waterhouse, whose pseudonymous
newspaper accounts have made his exploits famous. What
will become of their growing love if he reveals the truth that
lies behind the mask...?

THE REDEMPTION OF JAKE SCULLY by Elaine Barbieri
Jake Scully knows his rough frontier town is no place for a
delicate lady like Lacey Stewart. But Lacey has a mind of
her own. She refuses to let him keep his distance. And when
danger begins stalking her, Jake realizes the only safe place
for Lacey is by his side.

LIHCNM0508